Never Let Me Go

Boulder Beaumonts Book 2

Nika Rhone

P9P PARK NINE PUBLISHING

Content Note

This book contains references to serious physical injury and suicide. If you or anyone you know is having thoughts of suicide, please call or text the US National Suicide and Crisis Lifeline at 988 or call 1-800-273-TALK (8255) or go to SpeakingOfSuicide.com/resources for international numbers and other resources.

"It is not the mountain we conquer but ourselves."
~Sir Edmund Hillary

Chapter 1

It hurt like hell when an entire mountain crashed into you.

At least it felt like the whole mountain. In reality, it was only a few hundred pounds of fast-moving man, ripping her skis out from under her and plowing her face-first into the frigid snow.

Pain screamed up her body from the double impact, waking what had been a nagging ache to an agony of suffering. Snow clogged her nose, making it hard to breathe. The person who'd just taken her down lay across her legs for a few dazed moments before rolling off with a curse.

"Stupid bitch, you got in my line!"

Pushing up on her elbows, Rachel wiped the snow from her face before gingerly rolling over.

An arrow of pain shafted through her left hip and leg. Memories of pinwheeling helplessly down another mountainside pressed in on her, wanting to send her into a familiar state of panic.

She pushed them back.

No, damn it. Not today.

There hadn't been a flashback in over six months. No way in hell was she going to let one sneak in now and set back all the progress she'd made.

If the idiot snowboarder muttering curses at her hadn't done that already by screwing up her Frankensteined leg.

Rachel ignored his litany of complaints about stupid, slow-moving people always getting in his way. She'd been the one downhill. Since no one had eyes in the back of their head, that made it his responsibility to watch where he was going. Not that it mattered at the moment whose fault it was. First came damage assessment.

Then she could give him a piece of her mind about sharing the slopes responsibly.

"Hey, are you okay?"

Before she could reply to the concerned hail from the approaching skiers, Snowboard Guy rocked to his feet and took off in a plume of powder without bothering to see if she was hurt. Angrier at the blatant breech of common decency than the actual collision, she flipped off his retreating form.

"Jerk!"

Three dark shadows suddenly surrounded her, blocking out the sun, their skis making a quiet *shush* against the snow as they all came to expert stops within inches of one another. It was like being trapped in a forest of giant trees.

The closest to her asked again, "Are you okay?"

"I think so." Another twinge of pain as she finished rolling onto her butt had her biting back a wince. "Nothing's broken, anyway." This time.

Thank God for small favors.

"We saw that wanker playing chicken with other skiers on the way down," one of the other towering Sequoias said, a British accent in hard evidence. "We were going to report him to the first Ski Patrol we met, but he took you out first. Sorry, love."

"I'll report him when I get down, but I doubt it'll do any good."

Late afternoon, the lifts would be closing any minute now. Snowboard Guy would probably be in his car and long gone by the time she hit the bottom of the slope. Not that she could have picked him out of a crowd, anyway. It had all happened too fast.

"I'll just see if I can catch him, then, shall I?" With a nod to his friends, Yummy Accent Guy shot off down the slopes before she could tell him not to bother.

With an aggravated sigh, she did a quick check of her skis and bindings to make sure nothing had been broken or come loose. The last thing she could afford right now was having to replace any equipment. Luckily, it seemed the only thing the worse for wear from the collision was herself.

"Need a hand up?"

She looked up, blinking away ice crystals that still clung to her lashes. Backlit by the sun, she couldn't make out her Good Samaritan's features as she reached up and grabbed the offered hands to help lever her to her feet.

It burned that she needed the assist. Normally she would have rejected it, insisting on getting up on her own, no matter how much it hurt. Sheer stubbornness, her father called it. She preferred to think of it as sheer determination.

In truth, it was probably a bit of both.

"Thank you." Further words evaporated like snow in July as she got her first look at her rescuer's face.

Holy freaking hotness!

The eyes looking at her with such concern had to be the most gorgeous shade of chocolate brown she'd ever seen. Flecked with bits of amber, they were surrounded by thick brown lashes with a wicked curl at the ends that made them his most striking feature.

Which was saying a lot, considering the rest of him was no slouch, either.

Golden brown hair poked out from beneath the edges of his red knit cap, matching the heavy dusting of stubble on his cheeks and chiseled jawline. Even his cold-reddened skin couldn't detract from the overall impact of his good looks.

The man was far too attractive for her peace of mind. But that didn't stop her hormones from rallying into a cheering squad low in her belly.

"You're welcome." Either the guy was oblivious to the fact he'd made her tongue-tied for the first time in her life, or he was so used to having that effect on women it didn't faze him anymore. "You good?"

It was only then she realized he was still gripping her wrists. Maybe because she was still gripping his. Embarrassed, she withdrew from the contact.

"Yeah. Thanks. And thanks for stopping to check on me." She included the other man in her appreciation, tilting her head back even further to look him in the eyes. They were a soft gray, the deep crinkles at their edges hinting at either a lot of laughter or a lot of time outdoors. His chin carried the same amount of weekend scruff as his friend, only black rather than brown, and a gold stud winked from his earlobe.

He was as handsome as the first guy, but for some reason he didn't garner the same giddy punch in her gut.

Not that it mattered. Her hunky Good Samaritan would disappear down the slope in another minute, lost in a sea of other resort guests, and that would be the end of that. Unless she could think of something clever to say first.

Which, of course, she couldn't.

The man had totally short-circuited her brain.

"Glad we could help." Earring Guy looked at his friend as though impatient for him to say goodbye and get back to their run.

Instead, Good Samaritan said, "I'll meet you at the bottom."

After a brief look of surprise, a wicked smile bloomed, making Earring Guy look entirely too much like a pirate despite the blue knit cap and pricey North Face jacket. With a wink for her, he touched two fingers to his forehead in a salute to his friend and pushed off down the slope.

The wink and smile left Rachel flustered. "You should go with him."

"I think I'll go down with you, if that's okay."

"Oh." Her hormones gave a happy buzz. Then she remembered. Good Samaritan.

The buzz faded. "You don't have to do that. I'd hate for you to waste your last run of the day babysitting me down. I'm fine. Really."

"How can it be a waste? I'll be enjoying the company."

He sounded sincere. But she couldn't keep from poking at it.

"Even if I'm a punter?" She could tell from his reaction he was versed enough in the lingo to understand the slang for a novice with all the right gear but none of the know-how. But even that didn't make him balk.

Brave man.

A grin that rivaled the pirate's tilted his lips. "Trying to scare me off?"

Was she?

Maybe she was. And how stupid was that? Hadn't she just been thinking about not wanting him to disappear into the crowd? Well, here was her chance.

And she was blowing it.

Again.

Get it together, woman!

Buying herself a few seconds to consider her options, she concentrated on brushing the snow clinging to her legs and backside. Should she? If she'd reinjured her leg, she didn't want to be limping down the hill like an invalid in front of him. She shifted her weight with nothing but a twinge from her hip. Everything *seemed* okay.

Oh, what the hell. Why not?

She smiled up at her hunky Good Samaritan. "Sure, I'd love the company, thanks. I'm Rachel, by the way."

"It's nice to meet you, Rachel. I'm Theo."

They took it slow at first. The pain had subsided to a dull ache again, which meant she probably hadn't done any serious damage to her various healing body parts, but she'd no doubt be feeling the brunt of the impact tomorrow. For now, though, she was happy she could ski with her usual skill and form.

Because yeah, silly as it was, she wanted to show off a little. Just enough to counteract the sight of her sprawled face-down in the snow with her butt waving in the air like a big, fat loser flag.

Which was why she started to pick up the pace, finding the lines she would normally use if she were on her own. Not on a training day, but on the days when she skied simply for the enjoyment of it, with no one to please but herself.

To her delight, Theo did more than just keep up.

He actually began to edge her out.

Her competitive nature kicking in, she accepted the unspoken challenge. Luckily, they were on one of the black diamond routes, and it was late, which meant not a lot of traffic on the way down. Even so, she held back.

Not only to keep from putting the other skiers and boarders in danger.

But because she was having *fun*, and she didn't want it to end any sooner than it had to.

Face tingling from the wind and cold, she reached the bottom of the hill in a dead heat with Theo, twin cascades of snow shooting from their skis as they hit the brakes in unison. A joyous laugh broke free as she grinned at him. "You're pretty good."

"You're better." He didn't sound put out by that. In fact, he sounded impressed. "Those were some pretty expert moves."

The observation hit a little too close to things she preferred not to talk about, so she shrugged. "I've been on skis since I could walk. And I guess full disclosure is in order. I'm an instructor here at the resort."

Not a lie. But not the entire truth, either.

His gorgeous lips puckered into a wry grin. "I think I've been sandbagged."

It took a few seconds to tear her attention away from his mouth and give herself a mental shake. Seriously, what was wrong with her?

"And yet you held your own."

"Hmm." He didn't look convinced. "I kind of got the feeling you were going easy on me."

Probably because she was.

Even a black diamond course was child's play when you were used to some of the fastest slopes in the world. But she hadn't wanted to show her Good Samaritan up too badly. He'd certainly made it interesting, though.

Which was when it hit her.

Not once the whole way down had she thought about anything other than the friendly competition with Theo. No worries about falling or taking the wrong line. About making bad times and disappointing everyone. About decisions she didn't know if she wanted to, or even could, make about her future.

Not even memories of the accident had sunk their claws in the way they usually did whenever she hit a trail steeper than the bunny hill she taught on.

She'd just skied and enjoyed it, for the first time since waking up in a hospital not knowing if she'd ever be able to walk normally again, much less ski competitively.

Joy blossomed inside her. Maybe this was the breakthrough she'd been praying for. The hurdle she'd needed to cross before she could get back to what she was before.

Maybe the next time she went to the top of the hill, she'd feel like herself instead of a total fraud.

The urge to jump on a lift and go find out was so strong it was like a string being tugged deep inside her. But she could see from where they stood that the lifts had already shut down for the day.

Damn.

Tomorrow would have to be soon enough.

Disappointing as that was, it still left her with a sense of anticipation she'd been too long without. And it was all thanks to the man at her side.

She beamed a happy smile his way, wanting to thank him for the gift he'd given her, but he'd never understand. Not without a lot more explanation than she was willing to give.

Still, she wanted to do *something* to express her gratitude. Unfortunately, options at the resort were pretty limited. She'd have to make do with what was at hand.

"So, Theo, can I buy you a cup of coffee?"

Chapter 2

THEO BEAUMONT DIDN'T DAZZLE easily, but the smile his little ski instructor aimed his way definitely set him back on his heels.

Not that he hadn't thought she was pretty from the moment he'd helped her to her feet, even plastered in snow and looking annoyed as hell. The crystals that encrusted her dark lashes like diamond dust had emphasized large hazel-green eyes before slowly melting down her light brown cheeks and dripping from her chin.

Being covered in snow shouldn't have been sexy. But there had been a definite pulse of interest between them. Enough that he'd ditched his friends for her.

Shit.

Jesse and Nolan.

"Coffee sounds great, but I need to find my friends." The ones he'd entirely forgotten about. From the slight widening of her eyes, so had she.

"Of course, sorry. Maybe another time."

Oh, no. She wasn't getting away that easily.

"That's not a brushoff, you know. I literally need to find them. They're my ride." Sensing she was still on the verge of bolting, he added, "Besides, don't you want to know what happened with your hit-and-run snowboarder?"

He really hoped Nolan had been able to grab someone from Ski Patrol and catch up to the bastard. The memory of watching Rachel fly off her feet under the impact still made his stomach clench. Accidents were inevitable on the slopes, but reckless assholes like that needed to be stopped.

"Sure, I guess." Although from her tone, she wasn't holding out much hope.

It turned out she was right not to.

"Sorry, I couldn't catch the wanker," Nolan said with an unhappy scowl when they found him and Jesse at their usual meet-up spot a few minutes later and introductions were made.

"It was a long shot anyway," Rachel replied, although she looked disappointed. "Thank you so much for trying, though. I hate that you wasted your last run for me."

"No worries, love. Anything for a damsel in distress."

Theo was usually amused by the way his friend wielded both his charm and his accent like weapons of seduction. Now, he found he didn't enjoy it one bit. He stepped a little closer to Rachel. "Did you report him, at least?"

Surprise, then amusement, danced in Nolan's eyes.

"I did. I wasn't the only one, either. They'd had a few other people stop in making complaints, according to the nice gent behind the desk. Which reminds me." He looked at Rachel. "He wants to talk to you, too, since you were the one injured."

"Oh, but I'm fine," she said, shaking her head. "Really."

"Maybe so, but tomorrow you might feel differently," Nolan replied. "Always better to have the facts on record, just in case. Trust me, love. I'm a lawyer." He flashed her his shark-in-the-courtroom smile, white teeth gleaming.

"Why don't I go with you?" Theo shot a warning look at his friend before giving Rachel a sympathetic smile. "Then we can get that coffee afterward."

She answered with a smile of her own. "We could do that."

"Sounds like a great idea. Count me in." Jesse's tone held an overabundance of humor. At Theo's expense.

The ass.

"Me as well. I could use a nice steaming cuppa right about now."

If Rachel was put off or annoyed by his friends inviting themselves along, she didn't show it.

"Great! It's the least I can do for stopping to help the way you did."

Telling them both to fuck off would only encourage them to make even greater nuisances of themselves. Theo settled for a look that promised swift and terrible retribution.

All it did was get a laugh as they parted ways. Jesse and Nolan went to grab a table in the coffee house at the lodge while Theo escorted Rachel to the security office nearby, skis slung over their shoulders.

Most people, himself included, tended to stomp around in their ski boots. But Rachel moved as though having almost ten pounds strapped to her feet was the most natural thing in the world. Except when they transitioned from snow to the wooden porch of the Ski Patrol hut.

Then he noticed her gait develop a slight hitch. As though she were starting to feel the effects of the crash.

Guilt instantly swamped him. He never should have ignored his better judgement and raced her down the hill.

Stupid, Theo. Really stupid.

And irresponsible. He should have taken better care of her. God, when he'd seen her go down under the snowboarder's impact, everything in him had turned to ice. People could get seriously injured from falls like that. Killed, even.

He shoved the thought away. She wasn't Gavin. She was fine.

And he was going to make sure she stayed that way.

The report only took a few minutes, since neither of them had much to add to what Nolan had already told them. As they departed, though, he got the distinct feeling Rachel was unhappy about more than the fact they hadn't been able to catch the guy who rammed her.

"Everything okay?"

"Hmm? Oh, yeah. Well, no, not really." She sighed. "It's just, Jenks is a friend of my father's, and he's a bit of a blabbermouth, so…" She sighed again. "I'm sorry, I really need to call him before Jenks can get hold of him first."

"Sure, go ahead. I'll wait."

"Yeah, well, this might take a while. I'm afraid I'm going to have to bail on coffee. Raincheck, though?"

Sounded like a pretty lame kiss-off to him.

He put her at a little shy of his own thirty-two. What woman her age had to check in with her daddy whenever they took a spill on the slopes? Especially if this was her job?

One who was hurt worse than she was letting on, perhaps?

An instant punch of panic made his gut clench into a ball of ice.

"Are you sure you're okay? Maybe I should run you to the hospital, just to be on the safe side. Get some tests done or something."

She looked taken aback by the suggestion.

"What? No! God, no. I'm fine." She grimaced. "Okay, I'm a little sore, but it's nothing a good soak in the hot tub won't help with."

"Are you sure?"

"I think I know my own body, thanks."

Great. Now she sounded annoyed.

And yet he couldn't seem to shut himself up.

"I saw you limping a little on the way in. Maybe you should—"

"Stop!" Her expression now matched her annoyed tone. "Look, I really appreciate your help today, but that doesn't give you the right to stick your nose into my personal business, okay? God! I already have one father who hovers like a nervous ninny whenever I stub a toe. I don't need another."

Ouch.

"Sorry."

"Yeah, me too." Not an apology, but a statement of disappointment. "Look, I really need to make that phone call. I'll...see you around."

"Sure. See ya." But he was already talking to her back. It was impossible to miss how stiff her gait was as she walked away, as though she was concentrating on not limping.

Stubborn woman.

Everything in him screamed to go after her, to take care of her since she wasn't taking care of herself. But he wasn't a complete moron. She was more likely to brain him with her skis than listen to what he had to say.

With a curse, he stomped off in the other direction.

The area was filling up with people coming down off of the last run of the day, some heading for the resort, the rest to the parking lot. He was glad to find Nolan and Jesse still waiting for a table at the coffee house.

"Come on, let's get out of here."

Nolan looked confused. "What about Rachel?"

"You screwed it up already, didn't you?" Jesse said with a groan.

"No, I didn't screw it up." But he had the feeling he had. Somehow. "Besides, it was only coffee. It didn't mean anything."

"Dude, I saw the sparks. It was definitely something."

"Jess, you're not in California anymore. You need to stop saying dude all the time."

"I call deflection. Counselor?"

"I concur."

Theo grimaced and picked up his pace walking through the parking lot, heading for Jesse's SUV. "Screw you both."

He ignored the laughter.

His friends were right. There *had* been some kind of spark with Rachel. The first he'd felt with a woman in...well, since before his life had been ripped from its safe moorings and sent spinning into the abyss.

And then, poof. It was gone. *She* was gone.

My fault.

That knowledge sank its claws in as he secured his skis to the roof rack before climbing into the back seat. Okay, yes, his tendency to be protective of the people around him had gotten a little more intense of late. Sometimes to the point of being wicked annoying.

But after Gavin, who could blame him?

Rachel, apparently, judging by the way she couldn't get away from him fast enough.

He dropped his head back against the headrest and closed his eyes on a silent sigh. He needed to stop. He knew he did. His friends might joke about his hyper-protective mode, but he knew it was getting on everyone's nerves. Including his own.

But he couldn't seem to get past the one roadblock that would let him move forward and get on with his life. That would get everything back to normal again.

Which was why he turned down the offer to go to Nolan's place for dinner and a few drinks to unwind, and had them drop him home instead. It might have been a good way to distract himself for a few more hours, but that wasn't going to help.

Only one thing could.

Stripping out of his ski gear, he took a quick, hot shower and got dressed again. From the storage room he grabbed his gear bag and the backpack he'd taken with him on this trip every weekend for the past five months. After tossing them into the back of his Cayan SUV, he made the half hour drive through the late afternoon toward North Table Mountain.

That was one of the best things about Boulder. There might be fresh powder on the slopes up at the resorts, but there were always plenty of rock faces that were climbable almost all winter long. In fact, cold weather climbing was sometimes the best kind. The cooler temperatures increased friction, making the climbs easier and safer. Which should have been a comforting thought.

Instead, the closer he got to his destination, the harder his heart began to pound.

Doesn't matter.

He had to do this.

By the time he'd parked in the lower lot and made his way along the trails to the base of the south-facing cliff route dubbed Pretty Ugly, the pounding had moved from his chest to his head.

Every thud of rushing blood was loud enough to drown out everything except one thought: *just do it*.

Pushing past the fear, he methodically removed his gear from the bag. Strapping on his harness, clipping on nuts, cams, and quickdraws came with practiced ease. He set up his self-belay to the anchors screwed into the boulder on his left and tied in, the hands making the figure-eight knot only shaking the slightest bit. Last came putting on the backpack.

Then there was nothing left to do but climb.

Just do it.

Placing his hands on the familiar first holds of the rough cliff face, a deep shaft of cold sank its teeth into his gut despite the sunbaked warmth still radiating from the stone.

"Suck it up, buttercup." Muttering Gavin's favorite refrain like a prayer, he put his right foot on the lowest rock shelf, just about knee high, and pushed up.

At least, in his mind he did.

His body, however, stayed firmly connected to the ground, not conceding an inch.

"Come on, damn it!"

He visualized the route, one he'd done often enough both alone and with a partner he could probably climb it blindfolded. At a 5.8, it ranked as merely intermediate. Nowhere near one of the most challenging he'd climbed.

That didn't stop it from leaving him frozen with dread. Unable to break contact with the safety of the ground beneath his feet, no matter how many times he ordered his body to follow through on his mental commands to move.

"*Fuck you!*"

Theo threw back his head and shouted the words at the top of his lungs into the echo of the canyon, but even he wasn't sure who he was directing them to. God. The cliff. Gavin.

Or himself.

Chapter 3

"I told you, Pop, I'm totally fine."

"Are you sure? What about your leg?"

"It's fine. *I'm* fine. Really. It wasn't that big a deal."

"That's not what Jenks said."

Damn it, I knew he'd tattle.

"Well, he wasn't there, was he? He only knows what I told him, and I'm telling you the same thing. I'm. Fine." She looked her father dead in the eye as she said it, willing him to believe her.

"Okay."

Rachel blew out a breath and turned to yank open the refrigerator. "Thank you."

"But if you hit your head, maybe we should still go—"

"Don't!" She whirled back and glared. If he said 'go to the hospital', she might just pop a blood vessel. Then they'd have an actual reason to go. "Please. Just...stop."

The honest concern etched into his face made her feel like a bitch for snapping at him. But she'd done her time feeling like a broken doll everyone needed to take special care with. That was over. Bones had set, stitches healed, muscles and ligaments mended. Her body was strong and whole again.

Well, stronger, anyway. Strong enough to take a few bumps on the slopes without needing someone to kiss her boo-boos.

She just needed her father to get that through his thick, over-protective head.

"I'm sorry, Ray-Ray. I can't help worrying about you."

She winced.

The childhood nickname only emphasized the problem they'd been having ever since she'd moved back home with her fathers to recuperate from her accident and subsequent surgeries. And why she was so ready to find her own place again as soon as she could afford it.

Which, with the ski season in Colorado ending, might not be as soon as she'd hoped.

Not having it in her at the moment to go through another round of "I'm a big girl now," she skipped the vitamin water she'd been reaching for and grabbed two beers from the fridge instead. She opened them both and handed him one. "Truce?"

It was obvious he had more to say, but thank the lord for small miracles, he took the beer and sighed. "Truce."

Relieved, she clinked her bottle to his and took a long swallow. One battle down, one to go. At least her other dad would be easier to convince she was fine.

Although a couple for over thirty years, Dellin Long and Karl Miller-Long had very different approaches to parenting. Dellin was the perennial worrier. Karl had more of a 'let her try it once and see what happens' philosophy. Between the two of them, she'd managed to grow up both protected and with a confidence in her own abilities which had served her well on the competitive skiing circuit.

Until that confidence had turned to arrogance and nearly ended not only her career, but her life.

An event, she reminded herself with a long swallow of the tangy brew, which had been just as traumatic for her parents as it had been for her. Probably more so in some ways, since she'd been unconscious for a large portion of it.

Which was why she always cut her father so much slack when he went into over-protective papa bear mode.

Though he sometimes made it harder to be understanding than others.

Looking at him now, signs of what the last fifteen months had cost him were evident. His tightly cropped wiry black hair had gone from salt-and-pepper to almost entirely white. And new worry lines creased dark skin which had once made him look a decade younger than the sixty he'd recently turned. Now, he not only looked his age, but with a few more years tacked on for good measure.

She'd done that to him.

She set her beer down and wrapped her arms around his large body in a hard hug, putting every ounce of unspoken apology she could into it. "Love you."

"I love you, too, baby girl." He squeezed her back more gently than usual and dropped a kiss on her head. "Go have your soak while I get dinner started."

"But I said I'd cook tonight." Not that she wanted to.

Judging by the look her father couldn't hide, he didn't want her to, either.

No surprise there. Her cooking sucked.

"Consider it my terms for the truce." He picked up her beer and held it out.

She rolled her eyes as she took it, trying to seem resigned instead of relieved. "Fine."

After changing into a bathing suit and pinning her hair up out of the way, she brought her beer out onto the back patio. The bite of the March air raised goosebumps on her skin before she stepped into the bubbling water of the hot tub with a happy sigh.

Heaven.

Closing her eyes, she submerged to her shoulders. Inch by tight inch, her muscles unclenched as the heat and jets worked their magic. They couldn't eliminate the aches and pains from today's collision entirely, but at least she wouldn't be hobbling like an old lady in the morning.

No more so than normal, anyway.

Such a stupid thing. If she hadn't been so far inside her own head trying to coax herself into loosening up and feeling the mountain the way she used to, she might have heard the snowboarder coming.

She'd been damn lucky.

Lulled into a state of cozy lethargy by the heat, her thoughts drifted to the other lucky thing that had happened today. Theo. Her Good Samaritan.

Tall. Good looking. Not to mention kind and considerate. And not too bad on skis, either. There had been something compelling about him and his sexy eyes that definitely engaged her interest.

Right up until he started to act like her father.

She groaned and slipped lower until the steaming water was lapping at her chin. Okay, yes, maybe she'd had some kind of knee-jerk reaction to how eerily similar he'd sounded to Dellin when he went all poppa bear on her. And maybe she should have considered he was just being the kind, considerate guy she'd admired him for being and *not* a clueless mansplainer telling her how her own body worked before she bit his head off.

Especially since he'd been right.

She had been limping a little. She just hadn't wanted to admit it.

Brilliant, Rae.

The least she could have done was get his number—or even his full name—so she could text him for that coffee and an apology once she cooled off. But no. She'd stalked off in high snit, leaving the poor guy standing there, probably wondering what the hell her deal was. More than likely, he'd gone off to share a laugh over drinks with his friends about his close call with the batshit crazy lunatic.

Maybe it was for the best. He might have turned out to be a jerk. Or boring. Or married. Or...something. Maybe she'd saved herself from a lot of wasted time and aggravation.

And maybe she was just making excuses.

The truth was, she was about as good at relationships as she was in the kitchen. The two times she'd ever tried, *really* tried, to make time for a man in her hectic lifestyle had been epic fails.

Stefano had expected her to become someone she wasn't to suit his very Sicilian idea of how a woman on his arm should act. And Misha...well, he was Misha. Full of himself, and only interested in her while her star was rising. Once it had come crashing back down to earth, he'd cut her loose and attached himself to someone else who would keep him in the limelight and help boost his own plateauing career.

Both times, it had been her own fault for trying to date within the incestuous circle of world-level competitive skiing.

Not that she'd done much better elsewhere. No man wanted a girlfriend who was off either training or competing more days out of the year than she was home. She'd convinced herself she was okay with putting off having a real relationship and a family until she was ready to hang up her skis. It wasn't *that* much of a hardship to wait.

Her body's reaction to Theo had proven what a liar she was.

It doesn't matter.

She groped for her beer on the ledge and tipped it back for the last swallow. She'd squandered her opportunity to get to know him better. There was nothing she could do about it now except wallow in her own stupidity for a little while longer, then put him and their brief encounter out of her mind.

Easier said than done.

As she lay drowsing in the heat, all she could think about was the way his mouth had looked when he'd smiled at her. Soft. Inviting. Probably extremely talented. An empty throb pulsed deep inside her as she imagined those lips against hers, that body against hers, tall and lean and hard...

"So, how hard was it, really?"

With a startled shriek, she splashed and nearly slid off the seat and under the water at the sound of her other dad's voice. "What?"

As fair as Dellin was dark, Karl's ice-blue eyes pinned her with a bemused look. "The hit you took today on the slopes. How hard was it?"

Of course, that's what he'd meant.

Flustered at her own embarrassment over where her naughty thoughts had been heading, she pushed herself upright on the seat. "Pretty hard, but it didn't do any lasting damage."

As much as she sugar-coated things for Dellin, she could always be brutally honest with Karl. Where her father saw every drop of blood as a failure at good parenting, Karl knew how to separate being her dad from being her coach. A former Olympian himself, he understood a certain amount of damage was to be expected when you committed yourself to the sport of downhill racing.

And if Rachel sometimes wished he'd go a little easier on her, well, that was weakness talking. Karl expected her to be a champion, and a champion was what she would give him.

No matter how much it hurt.

"The leg?"

"Sore, but fine." Although she'd noticed the beginning of some impressive bruises all over her left side when she'd changed. Those were going to be real fun tomorrow.

"Any concussion symptoms?"

"None."

"You're sure?"

"Positive." She would never have driven home otherwise. But she understood his concern. Concussion syndrome had debilitated her for months after the accident. Headaches, vertigo, memory problems, insomnia...it had been miserable.

The last thing she needed—or wanted—was a recurrence.

"Good."

His satisfaction was about more than just her not being reinjured. She had a feeling he saw it as another step in her climb back to competitive form. If she could take a hard fall and suffer nothing worse than a few aches and bruises, it was time to raise the bar on their training regimen.

Something he confirmed when they were sitting around the dinner table a short while later.

"If you come to Copper with me tomorrow, I can get you onto the Super-G course for a couple of runs before they open it to the leagues."

The bite of chicken stuck going down her throat.

Taking a swig of water to keep from choking, she shook her head. "I have work tomorrow, Dad. I'd never be able to drive all the way to Copper, ski, and be back in time."

Not to mention she'd be physically and mentally wiped out even if she could. Not the best condition to be in while teaching novices how not to kill themselves on the mountain after sixty minutes of group instruction.

"Call in. You have more important things to do than show five-year-olds how to snowplow."

Ah, they were doing this again. Fun.

She kept her eyes on her food, carefully cutting a small piece of chicken and popping it into her mouth. "I'm not calling in, Dad."

He made a throaty noise of annoyance.

"You need to take advantage of the offer to train there while you can. There aren't many weeks left in the season, you know."

"I do know. Which is why I need to work every shift I have before it ends." And she was unemployed, living off her sadly dwindling savings.

"If you're going to be ready for next season's Cup circuit, you need to get serious about your training."

The chicken tasted like sawdust in her mouth, but she forced herself to swallow it. "I am serious. I've been going to Copper to train on the downhill runs every day off I've had all season."

Just not on the Super-G course.

Karl shook the drumstick he held in her direction. "But you could be training every day if you'd taken the job there when they offered it to you. Two days a week won't get you back in gold medal contention by October."

He ripped off a bite and chewed with vigor, pinning her with another of those blue-eyed looks that felt like they could see right into her brain.

Which she was sincerely glad he couldn't, because the last thing she wanted was for him to know *he* was the reason she'd turned down the instructor job at the Copper Mountain resort when it had come up, and chosen to take the one at Alta Luxe instead.

It was difficult enough sharing a home with her fathers again after having her own place for so many years. She might be twenty-eight, but from the minute she'd moved into her old room, it had felt like she'd been demoted back to teenager in their eyes.

Not that she didn't love her dads to pieces. She did. She owed them both everything. They'd saved her life—literally.

But work was the only place she could find respite from their constant suffocating, if well-meaning in their own way, attention.

Her decision had absolutely nothing to do with the cold sweat she broke into every time she stood at the top of the Super-G course. Looking down and remembering what the doctors told her at her last checkup.

Pins and rods had put her back together once. They made no guarantees about her chances of walking away from another such catastrophic crash.

Or walking again, period.

As far as her nerves were concerned, two days a week was enough for now.

More than.

To her relief, Dellin turned the conversation to a new topic before Karl could continue to beat the drum of practice, practice, practice. Unfortunately, it wasn't one she wanted to discuss with them, either.

"So, who was the guy who came in with you to make your accident report?"

"How did you...Jenks." She shook her head in disgust. "Pop, your friends really need to keep their noses out of my business." His vast network of friends, acquaintances, and fellow law enforcement officers, both active and retired—like Jenks—were what had made him such an excellent cop.

And made her teenage years hell.

She hadn't exactly had time to do a lot of partying, what with all the training and competing she did. But between everyone Dellin knew in Boulder and everyone Karl knew on the circuit, she was almost guaranteed to run into someone who'd report her every move back to one of them when she did.

That had stifled any urge to go a little wild, like some of her friends.

Dellin brushed aside her complaint like he always did. "He was just concerned. The guy seemed a little too..."

"Too what? Considerate?"

"Focused. On you."

A small flutter of pleasure tickled her belly, but she shook her head. "If Theo was focused on anything, it was making sure I was okay. That's all."

"Theo what?"

"I don't know. We never got past first names."

She didn't miss the slight easing of his expression at the news. Not that she would have given him the name, even if she had it. He'd be on the phone having the poor guy background checked and vetted before the table was cleared.

"He and his friends were some nice guys who stopped to help me out. That's all." And thanks to her little meltdown, that was all it would ever be.

"Just because they seemed nice—"

"Doesn't mean they are. Yeah, Pop, I know."

That sad but true mantra had been drummed into her from the time she was old enough to understand there were bad people in the world. Her father had seen too many of them as a cop to leave her blissfully ignorant about the hard truths. She'd probably been the only kid in the fourth grade to know how to escape from the trunk of a car.

But she wasn't nine anymore, and she was getting a little tired of both her parents forgetting that fact.

Theo saw me, though. The real me.

The thought popped in out of nowhere, but it was true. He'd looked at her like she was a full-grown, attractive woman who'd caught his interest. Just as he'd caught hers.

Before she'd blown it.

She shoveled a forkful of potatoes into her mouth to stifle the groan that wanted to emerge. Being mowed down on the slopes should have been the worst part of her day.

Instead, it was missing her chance with the one that got away.

Chapter 4

Sleep came hard and fast when Rachel crawled under the covers later that night.

Unfortunately, so did the dreams.

She startled awake more than once, panting and bathed in sweat, heart beating like a cowbell, before her brain finally took pity on her and let her sleep the rest of the night until the alarm. She couldn't remember anything from the dreams, but then, she didn't have to.

She'd lived through the real thing.

As predicted, the aches from the previous day's collision bloomed the moment she rolled out of bed. With a groan, she shuffled to the shower, lingering under the hot water to help loosen everything up before the thirty minutes of stretching and strengthening which had been part of her morning routine for as long as she could remember.

By the time she'd eaten breakfast and was in the car heading to work, she almost felt human again. Her hip was still a little cranky, but nothing worth worrying about.

Pushing through the pain had been part of her routine for as long as she could remember, too.

Since her first beginner's class didn't start until an hour after the resort opened, she grabbed the tow rope to the top of Little Hawk, one of the shortest green courses, waving to Raul at the controls as she went by.

He gave her a bemused wave in return.

Okay, yes, technically, she shouldn't be on the mountain for pleasure until after her shift was over. But she needed to find something out, and it couldn't wait.

It was still early enough she practically had the trail to herself. After waiting for a young couple who looked like they could probably benefit from her class to start down ahead of her, she skied over to the edge of the precipice. Set herself up.

And hesitated.

Taking a deep breath, she closed her eyes and just let it all flow over and through her.

The squeak of the fresh snow as she shifted her skis.

The biting kiss of the frigid air as it caressed her bare face.

The almost eerie quiet, every sound muffled and indistinct.

All familiar. All a part of her. Of the mountain.

Concentrating on only those things, she opened her eyes and looked down. It was a gentle slope, perfectly groomed. No obstacles or surprises. Perfect for beginners.

Or for people who might have had their nerve knocked out of them.

Annoyed with herself for having hesitated, she ignored her spiking heart rate and pushed off. The first split-second was sheer terror. Then muscle memory took over. Everything clicked into place. Her balance. Her center of gravity. Her fall line. All of it.

Fear dissolved into satisfaction as she glided through the fresh powder. Yes, it was only a green course. Ridiculously easy. But unlike the start of yesterday's run on the black, and every other run she'd made since getting back on her skis regardless of the difficulty level, there was no blurred vision, no shortness of breath, no disconnect.

Nothing but her and the snow.

Well, that answered that. Not only had yesterday's collision not set her back, mentally or physically, but it seemed her friendly competition with Theo really had shaken her loose from being stuck inside her own head.

It was all she could do not to pump her fist in the air. She allowed herself a shout of laughter tinged with relief instead.

I'm back!

After stopping briefly to give a few pointers to the still-floundering couple on her way by, she finished the rest of the run with a smile on her face. Which faded when she saw the person with the Luxe-blue jacket waiting for her at the bottom of the trail.

Perfect.

Just what she needed to ruin the good mood she'd found.

Resisting the urge to shoot a rooster tail of snow over the woman standing with her arms crossed, she came to a neat stop and planted her poles. "Morning."

Not bothering to return the greeting, Victoria DiBenedetto gave her a disdainful sneer. "Baby Hawk, Rachel? Really? I hadn't realized your confidence was still so shaky you had to ski the kiddy trails to feel good about yourself."

It was all she could do to bite her tongue. A few years her junior, Vicky was a bitch of epic proportions and a massive pain in Rachel's backside. And not just hers. The willowy brunette spread her delightful brand of bitchiness around to everyone.

Rachel was simply lucky enough to be her favorite target.

Unfortunately, Vicky also happened to be the daughter of the owners of the resort, which made her, in some sick, twisted, roundabout sort of way, Rachel's boss.

Sometimes life just wasn't fair.

"Shouldn't you be in Sweden getting ready for the Cup finals?" She couldn't stop the nugget of resentment that knowledge produced.

She was twenty-eight, damaged, and limping toward the finish line of her career, while Vicky was a resilient, up-and-coming twenty-two-year-old with the world at her feet. Every race she missed pulled her further from her goals and allowed Vicky to move up in the overall standings.

And closer to the spot on the next US Olympic ski team they both coveted.

Rather than gloat the way she expected, Vicky looked grief stricken for a brief second before her usual expression of mild boredom returned. "I'll be heading over in a few days after I get some things taken care of." She hesitated before adding, "Claude quit."

It was probably supposed to sound like she didn't care. But off the circuit or not, Rachel heard enough rumors to know that wasn't true. Claude had been a lot more than just Vicky's coach. If he'd broken things off with her, especially so close to the end of the Cup season, something pretty bad must have happened between them.

"Sorry to hear that."

"Yeah, well, his loss. Dad will have him replaced in no time."

Maybe. But there wouldn't be a lot of options available this late in the season. Not for any coaches worth a damn. Or ones willing to take on the circuit's resident brat. Claude had been a saint to stay with her for as long as he had. Probably because of the fringe benefits he'd been getting.

Low, Rae. Really low.

Ashamed of her uncharitable thoughts, true as they might be, she said, "Well, good luck with that."

"And what's *that* supposed to mean?"

"Whoa." She held her hand up. "It meant good luck."

Clearly uncertain if she should take insult or not, Vicky made a point of looking at her watch. "Shouldn't you be giving a class now?"

Tempting as it was to point out Vicky stopping her was the only reason she wasn't already there, Rachel shot her an insincere smile. "On my way."

She started to glide away, then stopped. "Oh, you may want to send someone up to check on the couple I passed on Little Hawk. They looked pretty green. I gave them a few pointers, and the guy insisted they were fine, but since they're still not down yet, I think they might need a little more help."

With her usual compassion and sympathy, Vicky rolled her eyes. "Great."

Satisfied the hapless couple would be taken care of despite Vicky's muttering about clueless punters, Rachel headed the short distance to the area below Tenderfoot where people had already assembled for the first beginners class of the day. Putting her encounter with Vicky out of her mind, she shifted all her concentration to them.

It was a good mix this morning.

Mostly kids, bright-eyed and eager. A few teenagers, which could sometimes be tricky, especially if their more accomplished friends hung around to needle them from the sidelines. And five adults, four of whom looked like couples, with one lone straggler hanging back, as though not entirely sure he wanted to be there.

Clapping her hands as she skied to the front of her motley group, she called, "Good morning! I'm your instructor, Rachel. Let's get everyone lined up right along here, and we'll get started."

She headed for her straggler to make sure he didn't decide to bolt on her. They sometimes did, especially when realizing their instructor was going to be a woman. She nearly fell off her skis when she found herself staring into familiar dark-chocolate eyes she never thought she'd see again.

Shaking herself free of her shock, she blurted, "What are you doing here?"

Watching her with great intensity, a smile twitching the corner of his lips, Theo replied, "You owe me a cup of coffee. I came to collect."

Chapter 5

It was obvious from the way Rachel's eyes widened he'd rattled her.

Smooth move, idiot.

The last thing he wanted was to put her on the defensive. Or weird her out. Both of which were possible with him showing up out of the blue like this. But he hadn't been able to get her off his mind.

Not last night, when he'd done his best to forget everything as he plowed through a six-pack of his favorite microbrew.

Not this morning, when he'd woken with the memory of haunting hazel eyes as vivid as if he'd just seen them, dark lashes dusted with snow like diamond dust.

Not during the forty-five-minute drive to Alta Luxe, when he tried more than once to convince himself to turn around and go to the monthly family brunch at his parents' as planned, instead of making an idiot of himself over a woman he barely knew.

None of that meant he had the right to weird her out, though.

"Sorry, this was really presumptuous of me. I'll get out of your hair and—"

"No, it's okay." The shock in her expression warmed to something a little more encouraging. "I was just surprised to see you. Here, I mean. In my class."

"It seemed like the easiest way to talk to you."

And to divert the keen interest of the woman behind the information desk when he'd asked where he could find the Rachel—*no, I don't know her last name*—who was an instructor at the resort. Signing up for her class made his inquiry seem less personal and more business.

He hadn't realized until too late the class was for beginners.

"I'm...flattered." Although she sounded more like flustered. "But you really don't have to stay. You'll be bored. This is all pretty basic stuff, and well, you're a lot more than basic." Her eyes widened as she realized what she'd said. "Your skiing, I mean. Not you. Not that you're basic, either, of course. I meant—"

Taking pity on her, he grinned. "It's okay, I know what you meant."

"Okay. Good." She smiled back, then muttered a little too loud to go unheard, "Glad one of us does."

Theo felt his mood lighten for the first time since she'd walked away from him the day before. He studied her face, comparing it to the memory he'd been carrying around.

Damn, she really was that attractive.

Her skin practically glowed from the cold air and, judging by the amount of snow on her boots, maybe a recent run down the mountain to get the blood pumping. The deep blue ski jacket with the resort's logo and matching knit cap lightened her hazel-green eyes, making them seem even more luminous against her dark skin and lashes.

Eyes that, if he wasn't mistaken, were looking back with some definite interest.

"I don't want to keep you from your class, so maybe we can meet later for that coffee?"

"Class. Right." She looked almost startled to be reminded of the people shuffling into an uneven line behind her. "Coffee would be great. Or...we could have lunch. Still my treat."

Evolved enough not to argue despite his normal inclination to pick up the tab, he nodded. "Lunch sounds great."

They quickly agreed on a time and place to meet before Rachel gave him a brilliant smile and turned her full attention back to her students. Tempted as he was to stick around and watch her teach, he didn't want to make her self-conscious.

Or, he admitted with sardonic humor, to come off as any more of a creeper than he already had. Showing up like this had been a gamble. Thankfully, though, it seemed to have paid off.

Where it might lead, he'd have to wait and see.

He, Jesse, and Nolan had done three black diamond runs the day before, so he wasn't really in the mood to ski again today. But with a few hours to kill, and no desire to spend them sitting in either the coffee shop or the lodge's massive lobby with only his own thoughts for company, he headed for the lifts.

Too much time to think had been something he'd avoided the last few months. Instead, he filled as many waking moments as he could with hard work and harder play. The time he was left with, when he couldn't do either, he got through with the help of a few drinks.

Not a lot. Never enough to be considered a problem.

He wouldn't let it get to that point.

Just enough to help him sleep, and keep the dreams at bay.

Pushing everything else out of his head, he attacked one of the black courses with focused single-mindedness. Like Rachel, he'd been on skis since he was little. He ate up the tricky turns and steep slopes like they were child's play, but he knew he was only good, not great. Not that it bothered him. He loved sports, all sports, but he'd never needed to be the best at everything he did.

Not like Gavin.

"Fuck!"

A mouthful of snow muffled the curse as he took a bad hop over a mogul he didn't see and went sprawling face-first in the soft powder. Luckily, nothing but his pride was hurt. He was back on his feet and down the trail before any other skiers had to move their line to avoid crashing into him.

That's what he got for thinking.

It happened like that sometimes. One minute he'd be fine. In total control. Then the one thing he absolutely didn't want to think about would pop into his head without warning and take him to his knees.

Though not usually quite so literally.

With resolute grimness, he spent the rest of the run concentrating on the terrain, freezing out any stray thoughts from creeping in. When he reached the bottom, he was cold, tired, and more than ready for a break.

After stowing his gear, he lucked into a seat right next to the immense fireplace in the lodge's lobby. A waitress appeared like magic to take his coffee order. By the time she brought it, his icy fingers were stinging as circulation returned. He wrapped grateful hands around the mug to help speed the thaw.

For several long minutes, he sat with closed eyes, sipping his drink, letting the blissful warmth seep into his body from all directions. It wasn't long, though, before he realized why the chair had been empty despite the crowd, as the heat from the blazing fire underwent a subtle shift from pleasant to uncomfortable to downright stifling.

Needing to remove a layer of clothing or burst into flames, he pinned his mug between his knees and skinned off his sweatshirt, leaving him in just his black, long-sleeved wicking tee.

"I see you've discovered why we call that the hot seat."

Theo looked up into the smiling face of the woman standing beside him. Tall, slender, with a tumble of dark brown hair and looking like she'd stepped off a fashion runway in her designer ski clothes, she was a carbon copy of the ski bunnies he encountered at resorts all around the world.

On a normal day, he'd be more than happy to strike up a conversation with someone like her. Maybe even accept an invitation back to her room if it came, to work up a different kind of sweat than the one the fireplace was causing.

But today was anything but normal, and he had zero interest in a quick tumble.

Not to mention, he already knew this particular ski bunny. Intimately. And he wasn't looking for a repeat performance.

"Hello, Vicky." He tipped his head toward the fire. "It felt good at first, but I'm starting to feel like I should be tied to a spit being basted for dinner."

She gave a tinkling laugh too practiced to be real.

"Mmm, isn't that a lovely image."

Uh-oh.

Warning bells clanged. Their one night in bed had been a mistake, for so many reasons. Not the least of which being he knew her parents. Matt and Maureen DiBenedetto ran in some of the same social circles as he did in Boulder, and while he didn't consider them friends, he did like them.

Finding out the bunny he'd banged after meeting her at the resort two seasons ago was their daughter had been an unpleasant surprise. Especially *how* he learned it, a few months later. As the three of them were seated at his table for one of his mother's many charity events.

Talk about an awkward evening.

For him, anyway.

Vicky had seemed to relish watching him squirm. As far as he knew, Matt and Maureen were still oblivious to their tryst, and he planned to keep it that way.

Just like he planned to never repeat past mistakes.

Although judging by the aggressive invasion of his personal space right now, she had different plans, despite the way he'd avoided her since that unpleasant revelation. Or, more likely, because of it.

Victoria DiBenedetto didn't like the word 'no.'

Walking her fingers along his shoulder, she said in a low purr, "You know, you probably shouldn't stay here and get all sweaty like this. It could be dangerous if you're planning to go out on another run today."

No, what was dangerous was the gleam in her eye.

"I'm fine, thanks."

Her fingertips grazed the sensitive skin of his neck. "Why don't we go somewhere a little less crowded so you can...towel off?" There was a wealth of promise in those two words.

A promise he wanted no part of.

Annoyed, he shifted enough in his seat to break the contact.

"Thanks, but I'm meeting my lunch date in a little while." He emphasized 'date' harder than necessary. It got the desired result. The hungry gleam in her eyes dimmed to disappointment, but not without a flash of anger along the way.

Her hand dropped from his shoulder.

"Oh. Well. Lucky girl." She gave him a smile which was patently false. "In that case, enjoy the rest of your day here at Luxe." With a last raking gaze of his tee-clad torso, she turned and strutted away.

He watched her go in bemused silence. So did a few other men in the vicinity. Judging by the extra swing in her hips, she knew it, too.

Maybe he *should* say something to Matt and Maureen. A preemptive strike in case Vicky decided to do something spiteful. Like tattle to her doting father about them sleeping together, just to cause him grief for turning her down now.

After rolling around the pros and cons for a minute, he decided against it. It wasn't like he'd seduced an innocent. Vicky had been twenty, and the one who'd pursued him. He'd simply made the unfortunate mistake of not asking her last name.

Just like he'd never asked Rachel's.

Way to learn from your mistakes, dumbass.

Well, at least this was one easily corrected over lunch.

Unlike the one who'd just flounced away, and would hang over his head like a ticking time bomb until he figured out how to defuse her. Permanently.

Chapter 6

WHEN HE MET RACHEL near the outside entrance to the lodge's pub-style grill, it surprised Theo she hadn't stowed her gear. Disappointment flashed through him.

Was she bailing on him again?

"Hi." Her smile seemed a little nervous.

Damn it.

"Hi." He gestured to the grill's door. "Should we get a table?"

"Actually..."

Here it comes.

"I was thinking we could go up to Eagle's Nest to eat. If you want to, that is. If not, here is fine, too."

Relief shot through him in a warm wave. She wasn't backing out.

"Eagle's Nest would be great. If we can get in."

The restaurant at the top of the mountain was as popular for its spectacular vistas of the Rockies as it was for its excellent food. Reservations were more than a suggestion.

Of course, depending on the maître d', dropping his name could probably solve that problem easily enough. It wasn't a card he liked to play, but if it would get him lunch with this woman in the restaurant of her choice, he'd do it.

Being a billionaire had its perks.

"It's okay, we're covered. I know a guy."

He loved the smug way she said it, as if pleased with herself. Especially since her words echoed his own thoughts. Then he frowned.

"A guy, huh?" He didn't like the tiny flicker of jealousy that scratched at him.

"Uh-huh. Jacques said he'd hold a table for me, as long as we got there before one." She glanced at her watch. "Do you want to ski back down afterward, or should I stow my things so we can take the gondola both ways?"

Despite the faint burn in his well-used leg muscles, he'd enjoyed skiing with her the day before too much to pass up a chance to do it again. "I'm game to ski it if you are."

Judging by the size of her smile, it was the right answer.

"Great. Let's get your gear and head up."

It was a short ski from the top of the lift to the restaurant, where they both stowed their equipment before Rachel went to find Jacques. Instead of the snooty older man he'd envisioned from the name and title, the guy was close to Theo's age and height.

The side-hug she gave him didn't bother him nearly as much as the enthusiastic cheek-bussing she got in return.

Not that he let it show as he was introduced, shaking hands with a cordial smile. He was in no position to feel anything, damn it. He'd known the woman all of a day. Not even, if you went by the amount of time they'd actually occupied the same space. There was absolutely no logical reason for him to be feeling territorial on such short acquaintance.

And yet, he still had to curb the impulse to crush the other man's butter-soft hand during the shake.

The table they were led to was tucked in a corner. Even so, there were really no bad seats in the entire restaurant. Perched up at close to eleven-thousand feet, with walls made up almost entirely of enormous windows, there were panoramic views on all sides as far as the eye could see, from the Continental Divide to the Great Plains.

The awe-inspiring beauty of it filled him with a sense of peace critically lacking in his life for much too long.

Before his thoughts could spill over into the why of that and ruin what was shaping up to be a great day, he shifted his attention to the woman across the small table. The tiny pucker between her eyebrows as she studied the menu did nothing to detract from her arresting good looks.

Aesthetically, she wasn't any more or less attractive than Vicky. But there was something else, something intangible but very real, which made Rachel a hundred times more appealing to him. More intriguing.

Worth the time to get to know, not just bang up against a wall in a dark hallway somewhere.

He dropped his gaze to his own menu, struggling to erase the mental image of Rachel up against a wall, eyes slumberous with satisfaction, that suddenly engulfed him and made his groin tighten painfully.

Okay, maybe he wasn't quite as evolved as he'd thought.

They both settled on the bread-bowl chili, mild for her, hot for him. As the waitress disappeared with their order, Rachel seemed to become absorbed with the view. There was an almost wistful tinge to her expression.

Like she'd rather be out there than in here with him.

Well, shit.

Maybe he'd misread the situation, after all.

"Is it too weird I came here today to find you? Do you want to go? Or you stay and I can go." The last thing he wanted was for her to feel uncomfortable.

She started, dragging her attention back to him.

"What? Oh, no, of course not." She fiddled with her silverware. "Okay, yeah, it was a little weird when I saw you this morning. But in a good way," she rushed to assure him when he frowned. "To be honest, I'd been kind of annoyed with myself for not getting your name and number yesterday."

Interesting.

"Was that before or after I pissed you off?"

She looked chagrined, then huffed out a small laugh. "After. And I owe you an apology for that. You didn't do anything wrong."

"No, I got a little too pushy about what was entirely your decision."

"And I got a little too sensitive about you trying to help."

"My only defense, if you can call it that, is it isn't just you. I stick my nose into everyone's business. Or so my sister tells me."

Loudly and with great feeling. Lillian didn't pull her punches when she was calling one of her brothers out on his nosy bullshit.

"And mine is that hovering has become an Olympic sport in my family this past year, and I guess it's made me a little overreactive. I need to remember to be grateful I have people who care enough to be worried about me. Not everyone does."

The waitress chose that moment to deliver their food, which gave him a minute to absorb the unintentional blow her words delivered to his gut. He *had* worried about Gavin.

Just not enough.

They both dug into the meal. The chili was hot and delicious. Its spicy bite made beads of sweat break out on his upper lip, but didn't overpower the dark, mellow flavor lent by the cocoa and espresso it was simmered in. He wished he could enjoy it more.

But the reminder of his failure with Gavin had dulled his previous pleasure. Something Rachel was quick to pick up on.

"Is the food okay?"

"Excellent." He dabbed at his sweaty lip with a napkin. "Perfect thing to warm a body up before hitting the slopes again."

She sighed. "Then it's me."

"What's you?"

"I'm boring you. I have zero talent for small talk."

He hated she sounded so sure of that unflattering self-assessment.

"You most definitely aren't boring me. And small talk is highly over-rated. I prefer meaningful conversation to just talking to fill the silence."

"Yes! Exactly!" She made a face. "But it is how people get to know one another on a—um..."

"Date?"

Her eyes widened like a startled cat. She gave an awkward laugh. "Can you call it a date when you don't even know each other's full names?"

Perfect.

"Good point." He reached his hand over the table. "Theo Beaumont."

She hesitated a second before she took it. Enough to make him wonder if she recognized the name. Most people did.

"Rachel Long."

Her hand was strong, her fingers long and elegant as they wrapped around his. Unlike most women he knew, her nails were short and unadorned by polish. No-nonsense, just like her. He liked that.

With reluctance, he let her take her hand back.

A memory nagged at him. "Rachel Long. You know, I feel as though I've met you before. Before yesterday, I mean."

"No, trust me, I'd remember that." She bit her lip and applied her attention to her food as though embarrassed by the admission. "You probably just recognize my name."

Okay, now he was intrigued. That was usually his line.

Dipping his spoon into the chili, he stared at her as he tried to pull up any memory of how or why he would have heard of her. Nothing came to mind. "You weren't on a wanted poster or something, were you?" he joked.

Peeking up at him from under her lashes, she gave him a sly smile that actually made him stop chewing for a second before he realized she was having him on.

Minx.

"I was on the winter Olympic team five years ago. There were nineteen of us from Colorado, so we got a lot of local press, which is probably why my name is familiar."

Probably. But the familiarity tugging at his memory was more recent than that. Damn. He let it go, knowing it would come to him eventually. "I don't think I've ever met an Olympian before. That's an impressive accomplishment."

"It would have been more impressive if I hadn't choked. My performance was less than stellar." Sounding disgusted with herself, she attacked her food with purpose, nearly stabbing a hole in the bowl of sourdough bread with her spoon.

"You're being a little hard on yourself, aren't you? The Olympics are a gigantic stage. I'd imagine the expectations of an entire country can be pretty weighty."

"Not as weighty as having your dad as a coach and letting him down after years of hard work and sacrifice on his part. On both my dads' parts." She rolled her eyes. "Wow, that got more whiney than planned. Sorry."

"Don't worry about it. I know how family expectations can end up being a lot harder to manage than anyone else's."

"That sounds like a story."

"Not really." But she'd shared something personal with him. Only fair to keep the playing field level.

"I work for the family investment business my dad built from the ground up. I have two brothers and a sister, and Dad expected us all to be there to take over when he retires. If he ever does. Sometimes it feels like he's going to hang on to that corner office until the day my mother finally drags him out, kicking and screaming."

Which, judging by the hints she'd been dropping lately, might be sooner rather than later. They were both still only in their fifties, but his mother's good friend had had a serious health scare a few years back. It seemed to have made her more conscious of how capricious life could be, and less willing to delay doing the things they'd always wanted to do.

Something he understood perfectly. Nothing in life was guaranteed.

Except death.

"I can't tell if you're looking forward to him retiring, or dreading it."

"A little of both, I think."

She waved her spoon before scooping out another load of chili. "What about the rest of your siblings? Anticipation, or dread?"

"Well, that's part of where managing family expectations comes into it. Peter and Lillian, my younger brother and sister, both decided to follow their own passions instead of our dad's master plan. Pete's a police officer, and Lil's making her mark in the art world."

Which still managed to both surprise and impress him in equal measure. Lillian had always been a little flighty about sticking with anything longer than a minute. But judging by the rave reviews her last show received, she'd finally found her niche.

"Oh, wow. Great for them. But I'd guess your dad wasn't exactly thrilled?"

"You'd be right. But to give the old man credit, he didn't give them too hard a time about their choices once he knew they were following their hearts. Although my mother probably had a lot to do with that. Dad can have blinders on sometimes when it comes to getting what he wants, but Mom always seems more tuned into what each of us needs most." Whether they knew it or not.

Witness Lillian's fiancé and Richard's girlfriend.

Neither was someone he would have thought his siblings would fall for. But both of them appeared deliriously happy, so what did he know? Clearly not as much as their mother, who took credit for engineering both match-ups.

Which was part of the reason he hadn't brought any woman near her in over a year. He wasn't sure if she'd actually had anything to do with either relationship, but he didn't believe in taking chances. With two of her children safely ensnared, it was only a matter of time before she turned her matchmaking attention to the two who were still single.

Not that Theo had anything against finding The One. He would. Eventually. He'd just prefer his mother not stick her meddling fingers anywhere near his love life.

"Does it bother you they got to do what they wanted, and you didn't?"

He paused with his spoon halfway to his mouth.

"You know, I think you're the first person to ever ask me that." He took his time chewing as he thought about it. "No. Because I *am* actually doing what I like. I have a talent for numbers. My brother makes the money, and I manage it. We're a good team."

One that still butted heads on occasion. Though ever since Richard's girlfriend and her son had moved in with him, he seemed a bit more easy-going. Mellow, even. It was a look Theo was still getting used to seeing on his Type-A big brother, but it suited him.

He scraped up the last spoonful before breaking the bowl open and enjoying a bite of soft, crusty bread infused with the tangy remnants of the chili.

"Getting back to the point I was trying to make. No matter how good Richard and I are at our jobs, or how long we do them, we'll always feel like we're falling just a few inches short of the bar our dad set, even when we're not. *That's* the weight of family expectations."

"Sounds about right." With a sigh, she broke her own bowl open and nibbled on the bread. "I wish there was some way to get past that feeling of inadequacy, you know? Just push it aside and move on."

"If you ever figure that out, be sure to share."

They fell into another comfortable silence as they demolished the last of their bread bowls. By the time they were done, he was feeling pretty good about his impulsive decision to come back to the resort to find her again. His instincts hadn't lied. There was a definite click between them, one he'd like to explore further.

If she'd let him.

Before he could broach the subject, though, she looked at her watch and sighed. "I hate to say it, but we have to get going if we're still going to ski back down. I traded off my first afternoon class, but I need to be there for the other two."

Right. Work. He'd totally forgotten.

Loath as he was to end their meal, the fact she'd planned ahead to make more time with him gave him hope she was feeling the same click he had.

"Then let's go." He held her chair as she got up, which earned him a sideways look he couldn't interpret, but she didn't snap his head off so he figured he was good. "Thanks for suggesting this. I really enjoyed it."

"So did I."

"Good. Does that mean you might want to do it again sometime?"

"I..." She bit her lip. "Yes, I would."

He followed her out of the crowded restaurant with a satisfied grin. Her 'yes' allowed him to ignore the pinch of annoyance when she stopped to say goodbye to the maître d', complete with cheek kisses. *Again.*

But the narrow-eyed look the guy threw his way when Rachel couldn't see gave him pause.

As they went to collect their gear, he had to ask. "So, are you and Jacques..."

She gave him a blank look. Then her mouth opened and closed as she caught his meaning. "God, no. We're just friends. Besides, he's engaged."

It helped when she seemed horrified at the idea. But he hadn't imagined the warning look. "That doesn't always stop a guy from being a dog and sniffing around where he shouldn't."

"If you're engaged to Angelique, it does. She'd castrate him in a heartbeat if he even thought about cheating on her."

"Good to know."

And a little disturbing, given how approving she sounded.

Still, despite her reassurance, he had trouble beating back the primitive need to secure some kind of commitment from her before they left the mountaintop.

"So, how does dinner and a movie sound? Maybe, say, Wednesday night?"

"Wednesday sounds great."

The shy smile she gave him before ducking her head to check her bindings made something tighten in his chest. "Then it's a date."

Since they were under a time crunch, they chose one of the blue intermediate trails down the mountain. Even so, he enjoyed it as much as he had the black diamond run of the day before. Even more so, now that he knew Rachel was actually a world-class skier.

Seeing her maneuver through the snow was like watching a ballerina perform, with skis in place of toe shoes. Every movement she made was graceful yet economical, infused with the easy confidence of someone who was entirely in their element.

They reached the bottom far too soon for his liking.

With only a few minutes left before Rachel's class started, he AirDropped his contact info to her phone and bid a reluctant goodbye before she skied away. As he watched her go, there was a strange tug in his gut that wanted him to go with her.

One he ignored, because acting on it would push him right past creeper and into stalker territory.

During the long ride home, he replayed the day's interactions minute by minute. Every word. Every expression. She had the prettiest damn smile. But had he bored her, talking about his family so much? Did she think he'd been trying to brag? Did she even realize who his family was?

Maybe he should have asked more about hers. Yes, he definitely should have. Rookie mistake, not keeping the focus on her. But she'd seemed interested in what he had to say. Or was she merely being polite? He didn't know her well enough yet to tell the difference.

Then he let out a bark of laughter.

"What am I, fucking sixteen again?"

Which was about the last time he'd obsessively dissected every minute of a first date this way. If today's lunch had been their first date. They never actually reached a decision about that.

Well, at least they'd have something to discuss over dinner.

He stowed his gear in the mudroom to take care of later. Then he braced himself and opened the door leading to the kitchen, where he was instantly mugged by sixty pounds of fur and muscle.

Less than a year old, Roscoe was still all paws and elbows, and hadn't yet figured out his own strength. He might only be dog sitting for his brother, but the crazy mutt seemed to have decided he deserved as thorough a welcome home as if he were Peter.

"Okay, okay, I missed you, too, you furry wrecking ball." He tolerated the excited attention for a minute more before pushing the dog's wriggling butt to the ground with a firm "sit" command. It took a few repetitions, but Roscoe finally complied. "Good boy." Not perfect, but it was progress.

After taking Roscoe out for a much-needed pee, curiosity got the better of him and he found himself Googling Rachel's name on his computer. Dozens of hits came up. He skimmed through a few articles about her winning streak on the Cup circuit in the years following a disappointing showing at the Olympics. The expectation she'd be a contender for gold at the next games if she kept it up.

"Sure, no pressure there," he muttered as he scrolled further down the page. His hand froze on the track pad when one result from fifteen months ago leapt off the screen.

Rachel Long Suffers Major Crash in Super G at Andorra.

Every muscle in his body cramped, that vague sense of familiarity with her name suddenly coming into focus. It was almost impossible not to hear about the horrifying things like that, whether you followed the sport or not. They were the salacious moments news outlets lived for. And exploited ad nauseum.

Despite the dread making him lightheaded, he couldn't stop himself from clicking on the article. Right at the top, under the same blaring headline, was a video.

Leave it alone. Just shut the computer down and walk away.

He clicked play.

It was a clip from the competition's broadcast, beginning with her leaving the starting gate. The two commentators droned on about her need to really push to make the time she needed for a first place finish. And she was doing it. Her time halfway down the course had her ahead of the leader.

And then something went horribly wrong.

Her left ski lost contact with the snow. Suddenly, instead of a perfectly aimed missile shooting down the mountain at eighty miles an hour, she was sliding and cartwheeling like an out-of-control rag doll.

The camera followed every sickening second.

By the time she finally slid to a stop, one leg was bent at an unnatural angle. Even the commentators had fallen silent in horror. The only sounds were the screams of agony the camera's sensitive microphone picked up.

As officials converged on her writhing form, the commentators started up a hushed play-by-play, but he'd seen enough.

Slamming the laptop shut, he sat breathing hard, stomach roiling. Then he stalked to the kitchen, grabbed a beer from the fridge, and emptied it in three long swallows before grabbing another.

Gavin's screams he could almost handle, because they only happened in his dreams. He hadn't been there that day to actually hear them.

Rachel's, however, were going to haunt him for the rest of his life.

Chapter 7

"WELL, LOOK AT YOU, looking like the cat who's gotten into the cream."

Rachel grinned at the sly comment from her friend, not bothering to deny it. She had a mirror. There was no other description for the goofy half-smile tugging relentlessly at her mouth for the past six hours.

Not that she was going to admit as much to Ari.

Well, not in the middle of her store, anyway. There were too many people. Tourists, mostly. No one she knew or knew her. But she'd learned the hard way there were always curious ears and a cellphone camera around when you least expected them.

So, she just smiled even wider at Ari and reached up to pet the lump of fur draped over her friend's shoulder.

"Hey there, Luna. How's the cat business today?"

The Pointed Ragdoll pressed her soft head more firmly into the caress, closing her bright blue eyes and purring hard enough for Rachel to feel the vibration in her fingertips.

Ariel laughed. "Pretty good, if you're her." She gave the cat's cheek an affectionate rub with her own. "I think more people come in to see her than to shop."

Judging by the number of shoppers currently browsing through the tidy aisles of crystals, incense, and other New Age items the Amethyst Dragon sold, Rachel doubted that assessment. Still, Luna was a fixture in the store, as popular with the locals as the other business owners on the blocks-long Pearl Street pedestrian mall.

While some cats were stand-offish and antisocial, Luna was the belle of the ball, eating up any and all attention that came her way.

She also worked well as an accessory to Ari's image when she sat to give Tarot readings in the back room. Between the wild red hair only partially contained by a brightly colored headscarf, her gypsyesque top and skirt, and the string of tiny bells around one ankle which tinkled merrily when she walked, Ariel O'Shaughnessy was the epitome of who tourists expected to find reading cards in a place like the Dragon.

Rachel was one of the few who knew she had a degree in business management from Berkeley, was a certified aromatherapist, and an absolute genius at marketing. Especially when the product was herself.

That's not to say Ari wasn't a little heavy on the woo-woo.

Born and raised in Ireland, she jokingly swore one of her many-times great grandmothers had a touch of fey blood. It might be more fodder for the tourists, but Rachel had learned not to discount her friend's sometimes out-of-left-field advice. It was right more often than it wasn't.

Not because she had 'The Sight' or anything. Because some people were just more intuitive than others.

Which was part of why she was here now.

Brushing long strands of dark brown and white cat fur from her fingers, she asked, "Do you have a minute to talk? I could use some advice."

"Sure. Eddie, can you watch the front for a bit?"

The twenty-something with a shock of purple hair restocking a rack of scented candles gave a wave of acknowledgment.

Ariel led the way to the back of the store and through a door marked "Private" into the small office. Taking Luna from her shoulder, she settled into the leather chair behind the painfully neat desk. "So, who is he?"

Rachel faltered as she took the other chair in the room, a sturdy antique upholstered in a muted brown and gold floral pattern Ari had found at an estate sale. "Who is who?"

"Whoever it is that's put the sparkle back in your eyes." Leaning forward, she studied Rachel more closely and grinned. "And a blush on your cheeks." She sat back, stroking the cat who had taken up a sphinxlike pose on her lap, and pushed hard on her native accent. "Come now, tell your Auntie Ari everything, lovie."

Rachel snorted at the ridiculous moniker, since they were barely ten years apart in age. "His name is Theo, and I met him yesterday on the slopes."

Ariel groaned. "Oh, Lord, not another one of those idiots."

As she'd introduced Ari to both Misha and Stefan, Rachel couldn't fault her for her opinion, no matter how much it stung.

"No, he's not pro. He's a local. He only skis recreationally. Although he does it really well." She couldn't stop the admiration from leaking into her tone. He probably couldn't keep up if she really let loose on the slopes, but he'd kept it interesting. And fun.

Which was exactly what she'd needed.

"Of course he does. God forbid you ever look at a man who doesn't find strapping two planks of wood to his feet and throwing himself down a mountain a good time. No, never mind," she said before Rachel could respond, waving a hand. "We've already had that argument and I lost. Tell me more about him."

"Well, let's see. He's tall. Good looking. Polite. And I don't think he scares easily." She still couldn't believe he'd come back to the resort today just to talk to her after the way she'd acted. That had taken a lot of confidence.

"If that's true, it'll come in handy with your das."

Wasn't that the truth.

Individually, her fathers were intimidating. As a united front 'protecting' their little girl, they were terrifying. At least, that's what she'd been told by more than one boy who'd cut and run on her after she brought them home to meet them.

It was part of the reason she ended up dating guys like Misha. He'd been too full of himself to give a damn what anyone else thought of him.

"Yeah, that's kind of what I wanted to talk to you about. Would it be totally chickenshit of me to not tell my dads I'm going out to dinner with Theo on Wednesday?"

"Dinner, already? He moves fast." She didn't say it like it was a compliment.

"Well, we had lunch today, so no, not really."

Ari raised a brow. "I thought you only met him yesterday?"

It was difficult not to squirm under that deep green gaze. "I did."

"Okay, from the top, please. I want to know everything."

She gave a condensed version of the past two days, from the moment Theo Beaumont pulled her out of the snow to their parting that afternoon. The only thing she left out were the confusing emotions the man evoked in her every time he got within touching distance.

Judging by the thoughtful look on Ari's face as she leaned back in her chair, though, she'd read enough between the lines to figure that part out on her own. "Well, now. Isn't that grand?"

"It isn't grand. It's weird, and confusing, and...and..."

"Scary?"

"Yeah."

"And wonderful?"

She sighed. "Yeah. But it's still so new. This will be the first time I've gone out with anyone since I moved back in with my dads, and I'm not sure how to handle it without either hurting their feelings or scaring Theo off on the first date." Or second. She still wasn't clear on whether or not they were counting today's lunch as a date.

"First off, you're twenty-eight fecking years old, Rae. You don't owe your das an accounting of your love life, whether you're staying with them or not. As long as you're not shagging guys in the middle of the living room, it's none of their business what—or who—you do."

"Lovely imagery, Ari. Thanks."

Because now she couldn't get a picture of a very naked Theo, laying on the oversized sofa by the fireplace as she crawled on top of him, out of her head. She plucked at the neck of her blouse, feeling suddenly overheated.

Luckily, Ariel didn't seem to notice.

"And second, if this guy scares off that easy, was he really worth keeping around in the first place? I mean, when you find the right guy, don't you want it to be someone who can hold his own against them?"

She hadn't been thinking in terms of the right guy. That sounded too...permanent. There were too many things in her life which took precedence over a relationship right now. Training being the biggest.

The past two days had been a good sign—she'd been able to get out of her own head and actually *feel* the mountain again, rather than racing mechanically and overthinking every move. But that was only a start.

She still had to prove she could do the same on the Super G course at Copper tomorrow. And then there were months of grueling work ahead if she was going to be ready to compete when the Cup season started again in October.

No.

To compete and *win*.

Anything less was unacceptable.

Her shoulders started to tense, just like they always did when she thought about it. With effort, she eased them down and pushed her future issues aside to focus on her more immediate problem instead. At least *that* she had a chance of figuring out.

"But is it fair to subject the guy to what they'll do to him? You know how they are. Shouldn't I at least see if we're even going to make it past the first"—or second—"date before I toss him into the shark tank?"

"Hmm, good point." Ariel's head tipped back and forth a few times as she thought. "How about this. Tell him you'll meet him wherever you're going for dinner rather than him picking you up. This way you avoid any confrontation with your das, plus you're not stuck in a car with him on the ride home if he turns out to be a dud."

There was zero chance of Theo being a dud.

A stud, maybe.

Okay, definitely.

But Ari had a point. Nice as he seemed, and as enjoyable a companion as he'd been at lunch, she didn't know all that much about him. Having her own car would be the safer plan until she knew him a little better. You couldn't be too careful these days.

That last bit sounded exactly like her father's voice in her head.

Thanks for the paranoia, Pop.

Paranoid or not, though, it was still a good plan. "That could work. Thanks."

"On the other hand," Ariel continued in a musing tone as she stared off at nothing, "keeping them all apart could be the worst thing you could do."

"Why would you say that?"

Ariel's unfocused gaze cleared. "We need to do a spread."

"What, now? Why?"

"Why not?"

"Not an answer, Ari." She squirmed. "You know I don't believe in that stuff."

But her friend was already rummaging in the desk, bringing out an ornate wooden box from the bottom drawer. From it she withdrew a silk-wrapped object. Her personal cards. Not the ones she used for the tourists, but reserved for special readings.

"And you know it doesn't matter if you believe. What is, is." Opening the loose knot in the silk scarf, she removed the well-worn Tarot cards and fanned them, facedown, across the desk before giving Rachel an expectant look.

She could argue. Or get up and leave. Or just refuse to pick the damn things up.

But instead, she gave in.

To please Ari, she told herself as she stirred the cards before gathering them together to shuffle. Not because she was curious what they'd say.

Okay, maybe she was a little curious.

Ari had told her there was no right or wrong way to shuffle the Tarot, so she kept going until it felt right to stop. She placed the deck facedown on the desk and cut it, laying the top half aside.

Ari dealt the first three cards from the lower half out in a line.

Turning over the first card on Rachel's left, Ariel nodded. "The Hermit. Your goals can be attained, but the journey hasn't always been a smooth or easy one."

Rachel wanted to snort. Talk about an understatement. Her love life was riddled with potholes the size of moon craters.

Second card. "Reversed Five of Wands. There is some discord going on, and it will take some time to work through and fix it."

Okay, that was accurate enough to be a little creepy. Of course, she'd just told Ari all about her concerns when it came to Theo. So it wasn't really news, simply an interpretation of the card that fit the circumstances.

Probably.

Final card. "Ten of Cups. New beginnings. Happiness and long-term joy. Dreams coming true."

That sounded a little too knight-saving-the-damsel for her taste. "So, what? The cards are saying Theo is the man who'll make all my dreams come true?"

There was a long pause as Ariel stared at the spread. Then she smiled and sat back. "Your dreams are yours alone to achieve. Or not. But you do need to know what they are in order to find the right path."

"I thought that's what the cards were supposed to tell me."

"I thought you didn't believe in what they had to say."

Rachel opened her mouth to reply, then laughed instead. "You're right, I don't. But you do, so, what do you think?" She waited with growing impatience as her friend put the deck back together and started wrapping it up in the silk scarf. "Ari!"

Not to be rushed, Ariel placed the deck into the box, arranged several stones of tumbled amethyst and quartz around it, and replaced it in the drawer. Only when she was done did she answer.

"I think this person has come into your life at this particular time because he's important to the choices you're going to have to face."

"Choices? About what? Dating?"

Ariel spread her hands in an I-don't-know gesture. "All new beginnings come with choices. I can't say what they may be. I only know he plays a role."

That she'd said "know" meant they'd strayed deep into woo-woo territory. Time to change the subject.

"I'm going to ski the Super G at Copper with my dad tomorrow." She'd meant to make it sound like no big deal, but the way she'd blurted it out kind of ruined any chance of that.

Rather than seem surprised, Ariel nodded with a thoughtful, slightly sad look. "You knew you'd have to face it eventually. Are you sure you're ready for what might happen?"

She shrugged, trying to dislodge the weight that suddenly seemed to be crushing her, making it harder to breathe. "I got crashed into yesterday and didn't freak out." Although it had been more knocked off her feet than an actual crash. "And I skied with no problems today. Twice." Even though it had only been on a green and a blue. "I think I'm ready."

She ignored Ari's doubtful look. Her friend might be her biggest cheerleader, but she was also a sometimes unwelcome dose of reality.

No one but Ari knew tomorrow wouldn't be the first time she'd visited the Super G course this winter. No one else knew how many times she'd stood at the starting gate on the lip of the mountain. Staring down at the steep slope. Frozen in place by the sickening fist of dread deep in her gut.

Every. Single. Time.

Only Ari understood exactly what was on the line by committing to ski the same style course that had almost killed her, under the watchful eye of her dad in full-out coach mode. What it would mean if she choked the way she had before.

The way she had just last week, in fact.

But fear of failure wasn't the only reason for the uncomfortable nausea that roiled in her belly, though.

Ari might know most of Rachel's secrets.

But she didn't know them all.

Chapter 8

"Want to catch a game tomorrow? The Avalanche are playing New York at the Center."

Cutting through the medium rare steak the waiter had just delivered to the table, Theo grinned. "You mean Amber is actually letting you off the leash for a night?" He chewed the butter-soft meat as he watched his older brother's expression predictably vacillate between gooey-eyed over mention of his girlfriend and annoyed at the dig to his manhood.

Gooey-eyed won.

"She's taking Derek to the movies. She says she doesn't get as much mother-son time now that they're living at my place."

Theo wasn't buying it.

"Or, more likely, she suggested it so you could invite your pathetic younger brother out and pry into his personal life with questions which are none of your business." His teeth snapped on an asparagus tip with a click. He loved his family. He just didn't love the intrusive nosiness that came with them loving him back.

Especially in the past few months.

"You're not pathetic. You've just been...going through a rough patch. Which is understandable, given everything that happened."

Theo shot his brother a look warning he was straying into forbidden territory. Richard's lips pinched, but he silently acquiesced.

And changed his angle of attack.

"Amber said Elena had a good time when you went out a couple of weeks ago. I'm guessing you did, too, since you didn't complain like you usually do after a blind date. So, how about the four of us go out to dinner this weekend? We could try the new TexMex place that opened in LoDo."

Hiding a grimace, Theo sliced another piece of juicy steak and chewed to buy time.

He hadn't complained because she was Amber's friend. Elena had been...nice. But as pleasant as their date had been, there was no spark there.

For either of them.

And despite what Amber might think, her friend was still well and truly hung up on some other guy. The only thing worse than putting the two of them through another evening together would be having the lovebirds along to supervise.

He'd rather stick a shrimp fork in his eye.

"Maybe some other time." Like, never. Wishing it was a beer, he drained his water glass. An attentive waiter was there within seconds to refill it. "So, how is it having Amber and Derek underfoot all the time now?"

As usual these days, his brother was easily diverted by the topic of his girlfriend, her son, or any combination of the two.

"It's a little weird. And perfect." He grinned. "It's weirdly perfect."

Wow. When the mighty fell, they fell hard.

It was still strange seeing his once taciturn brother so cheerful and happy all the time. Not that he wasn't thrilled for him. Finding Amber had been the best thing that could ever happen to Richard.

The problem was, now that he'd drunk the Kool-Aid, he was firmly a minion of their mother, wanting to help spread love and happiness to everyone in his life.

"That's great." He was happy for his brother. He was.

Okay, maybe a little jealous, too. Amber was an awesome lady, and her kid was pretty cool, even if he did prefer video games over sports. But that didn't mean he had the sudden desire to find someone to pick out china patterns with.

Tapping his fork lightly against his plate, Richard said, "You know who else is great? Mimi Kent."

"Who?"

"You know, Mom's personal assistant at the foundation? Tall. Blonde. Glasses." He gestured to his own wire-rimmed pair.

Theo barely resisted the urge to growl. He thought they'd finished with the matchmaking crap. "Wow, weak segue, bro."

A wince revealed Richard agreed. But it didn't hold him back.

"Come on, she's exactly your type."

"And what type is that?"

"Single, female, and into you."

It was Theo's turn to wince.

It was no secret he was a serial dater. While his older brother had dated sparingly and with serious intent, Theo preferred to sample the wide and glorious options available to him. Flitting like a happy bee from flower to delicious flower as the mutual mood struck.

And if that flitting had turned a little more frenetic these past few months, well, it was only understandable. Death made you want to grab onto life with both hands and squeeze out every possible drop.

"Thanks, but I think I'll pass. I prefer not to mix business and pleasure."

While the philanthropic Everbrite Foundation was only tangentially a part of Beaumont Investments, their mother, Patricia, ran it. Which meant even if Mimi Kent was the most amazing woman on Earth, he wasn't going anywhere near her. He needed more than two degrees of separation between his family and his love life.

Ten might not be enough.

Richard looked as though he planned to press, so Theo made a segue of his own. "Speaking of the foundation, has Mom tapped you for the fashion show thing yet?"

Every March, Everbrite partnered with the Avalanche to host a fundraiser for various local sports programs for kids. As with all foundation functions, family members were expected to be visible and hands-on participants.

Of all the events his mother dragooned him into participating in, this was the one he most enjoyed. Besides getting to schmooze with the players from his favorite hockey team, he got to assist in giving kids the joy of throwing a football, swinging a bat, or strapping on a pair of skates or skis. All things he'd loved growing up.

"She tried, but Des already recruited Amber to help with the clothes, and she recruited me." He gave a slow shake of his head. "It's going to be a nightmare. What do I know about fashion?"

Asks the man in the thousand-dollar bespoke suit.

"It'll be fine."

And it would. Because Des wouldn't allow it to be any other way.

The man was a force to be reckoned with, second only to their mother. When he wasn't designing his newest clothing line, he was doing ten other things, all of them with the energy of a class six rapids. Des had no low setting. There was only hyperactive, supersonic, and insane.

Thankfully, the subject of women didn't come up again as they finished their lunch. It wasn't until they were in Theo's car heading back to the office that Richard circled around to his original question again.

"So, hockey tomorrow? You and me?"

"Sorry, I can't."

"Why not?"

Theo repressed a grin at the snap in his brother's voice. He might have mellowed a little, but he still didn't like to have his plans disrupted. "Because I have a date."

"A date?"

"Yeah, a date."

"You're dating someone? And you didn't think to mention this before when I was trying to set you up with Mimi?"

"And miss a chance to watch you fumble your way through playing matchmaker? Why would I do that?" He caught Richard flipping him off from the corner of his eye and grinned. "Anyway, it's a date, not dating. I just met her this weekend."

And hadn't been able to stop thinking about her since.

"Then she won't mind if you cancel, so you can go to the game."

"I'd mind." He shot his brother a sideways glance. "What's the big deal? Pick another night, and we'll go. Why does it have to be tomorrow?"

Richard drummed his fingers on the knee of his black Burberry wool pants. Finally, he sighed. "Because I promised Mom."

"Promised what? You'd take me to a game?"

"That I'd talk to you about...things."

He didn't need to see his brother's uncomfortable expression to know exactly what 'things' he meant. A blast of heat raced up his neck as his slow-burn temper finally ignited.

"You mean she wanted you to make sure I knew how stupid and reckless I'm being."

"Nobody thinks you're stupid. Or reckless, exactly. Granted, we might be a little concerned about some of your more recent recreational choices—"

"You mean Mom is."

"No, I mean *we* are. Everyone. Including me."

Great. Just what he needed. Richard in full-blown big-brother mode.

"Just because you've always been Mister Play-It-Safe doesn't mean how I choose to spend my free time is wrong,"

"I'm not saying it is. Look, everyone knows you've always been the daredevil in the family. You were the one who insisted we could jump our bikes over the pool when we were kids, if we only had the right sized ramp—"

"It would have worked if Dad hadn't stopped us."

Probably, anyway.

He'd calculated all the angles and trajectory, but who knew how accurate his ten-year-old self's math skills had been. It was a good thing Lillian had narced on them when they wouldn't let her join in, although he hadn't thought so at the time.

"And God knows you've done some risky things since then and come out relatively unscathed," Richard continued without missing a beat. "But these last few months, you've gotten a little extreme, even for you. I have to be honest, I'm a little worried about you."

Theo's teeth ground as he forced back the words that crowded his mouth for release. "You can stop worrying. I'm fine." He turned into the parking lot of the Beaumont building, hoping that would be the end of it.

Of course, it wasn't.

"I get the skiing, and the whitewater rafting. I even get the rock climbing, even if the mere thought makes me want to puke." Richard's dislike of heights was legendary. "But what in the *hell* ever possessed you to go skydiving?"

Busted.

It had been too much to hope the posts Jesse uploaded to his social media accounts would go unnoticed. Not that Theo was trying to hide anything. He was an adult and could do whatever the fuck he wanted.

That didn't mean he wouldn't rather avoid the interrogation and familial guilt trip bound to go with it.

"It was perfectly safe."

"*Perfectly safe*?" Incredulity all but lit the words in neon. "You jumped out of an airplane!"

"With an instructor strapped to my back. It doesn't get any safer than that."

"Not unless you'd kept your damn feet on the ground in the first place!"

Theo pulled into his assigned spot in the executive lot. With controlled movements, he turned off the car and gripped the steering wheel, using it to anchor himself as he took a deep breath and got his flaring temper in hand.

He knew his brother meant well.

It didn't mean he couldn't still piss him the hell off, though.

When he was sure he wouldn't say something he'd regret, he let go of the wheel and turned to look at Richard. "I appreciate the concern, but you can all stop worrying. Yes, I like an adrenaline rush with my entertainment. That doesn't mean I'm looking to get myself killed for one."

"Are you sure about that?" Richard asked softly.

Theo stared at him a long second before he got out of the car and started walking toward the building without answering. Because what could he say to a question some days he didn't know the answer to himself?

Chapter 9

"This food is amazing! I can't believe I've never eaten here before."

Theo grinned in both relief and satisfaction as Rachel shoveled another bite of mahi-mahi with *mojo criollo* sauce into her mouth with the enthusiasm of a starving woman. The dish had been his recommendation when she worried about picking anything too spicy from the extensive menu.

A legitimate concern, since the authentic Cuban food at Bayamo ranged from mild to melt-your-eyebrows hot. If you didn't pay attention to what you were ordering, the results could be painful.

Or hilarious, if the unsuspecting person happened to be your brother with no tolerance for heat. Pete still gave him the look of death whenever the subject came up.

Which was why Theo made sure it did.

A lot.

What good were little brothers if you couldn't torment them once in a while?

"I'm glad you like it." He chewed a bite of his own meal. The tender beef of the *ropa vieja* was just the right side of spicy for him. "Save some room, though. The desserts are even more incredible."

That brought a gleam of anticipation to her eyes he had to look away from before his body got the wrong idea. As it was, he'd been at half-mast since the minute she walked into the restaurant.

Which was embarrassing as hell.

What was it about this woman that pushed all the right buttons on his libido? Yes, the deep red sweater she wore over dark jeans made her skin practically glow, and her eyes sparkled with both intelligence and humor. But he'd been around plenty of attractive women over the years. Women who were more overtly sexy and movie star gorgeous than Rachel was, who'd never flipped his switch this way.

It was a mystery he was looking forward to solving.

"Now I know why you eat here so much."

"Why would you think that?"

"Well, the hostess clearly knew you when she brought us to the table." She paused, looking slightly uncomfortable. "Sorry, I just assumed..."

He could tell exactly what she was thinking. That if he wasn't a regular customer, the only reason the hostess would have greeted him so warmly was because they were personally, perhaps intimately, acquainted.

The possibility she was jealous the way he'd been about her friend the maître d' was oddly satisfying.

"No, you're right, I do eat here a few times a month. But the first name thing is more because the owners are my sister's soon-to-be in-laws, so we're technically sort of almost family."

She gave him a curious look. "Technically sort of almost? That doesn't sound like a warm and fuzzy connection."

"It's not, I guess. More of an uneasy détente. Our parents all get along fine, and Lillian and Rafe are totally gone on each other. It's the siblings on both sides that are a little..."

"Oil and water?"

"More like gasoline and matches." He took a swallow of his beer and gave a wry smile at her wide-eyed expression. "My brothers and I had a problem with Rafe when they first got together because we thought he was only after her money. His brother and sisters had a problem with Lil because they thought she was just toying with him and was going to break his heart. Between us, we all did a damn fine job of almost breaking them up."

Not something he was proud of.

"But you didn't."

"No, thank God. In fact, the wedding's next June."

That didn't mean both Lillian and Rafe weren't still making all of them pay in small, devious ways. Like having them all paired up in the wedding party, so they couldn't avoid each other's company.

That was going to be a very long day.

But they'd all earned their penance, so he'd suck it up and hope for the best.

"So, even with the tension between the families, you still eat here? What are you, a glutton for punishment or something?"

"More like a bridge builder." He grinned and gestured to his plate. "Plus, who can resist the food?"

As he'd hoped, Rachel laughed. "Let me guess. Middle child, right?"

"Guilty as charged. Well, technically in age, anyway. My younger brother and sister are twins. How about you, any siblings?"

"No, it's just me." She fiddled with her fork a moment. "My dads adopted me when I was about eight. There were a lot of kids in my foster home, and there never seemed to be enough of anything to go around, including attention. When my dads took me home with them, I was so happy to have a bedroom to myself and parents who loved and paid attention to only me that I never really wanted a brother or sister around. Not until I was older. Now I kind of feel like I missed out."

Dads. So, he hadn't misheard her the other day.

Not that it made a difference to him. But it did make him glad she'd suggested meeting at the restaurant rather than letting him pick her up tonight. Being introduced to a woman's father for the first time was bad enough. Having to meet two of them at once would be exponentially worse.

"Trust me. Siblings can be both a blessing and a curse."

"Come on, I heard the way you talked about yours the other day. You love them."

"Sure, I do. Doesn't mean there aren't times I hate them, too."

"I know exactly what you mean. I love my parents to death, but sometimes..." She made a low growl as she clenched her fists.

The expression and body language spoke of something specific she was still annoyed over. Before he could decide if he should ask, the waitress stopped by the table to see if they were ready to order dessert, and the moment was lost.

After listening to her rattle off a list of the restaurant's most popular offerings, Theo looked at Rachel expectantly.

She hesitated. "Wow, they all sound delicious, I don't know. Why don't you pick? You've done a good job knowing what I like so far."

Normally, he might have thought she was flirting. But as he gave the waitress the names of several choices to bring as a sampler plate, he realized that hadn't been Rachel's intent at all. Which was unfortunate, since his hyper-awareness of her was still as strong as it had been all night.

A problem she didn't seem to have in return.

In fact, it felt like she was barely aware he existed. No, not quite that. More like he didn't exist as a man, merely someone there to hold up one half of the conversation. Given the chemistry he'd felt between them at the resort both times they'd met, this sudden shift to the friend-zone was confusing, to say the least.

Not to mention frustrating.

The dishes were cleared with silent efficiency, and coffee brought. When they were alone again, or as alone as two people could be in the middle of a busy restaurant, he leaned forward on his elbows, giving her the full weight of his attention.

"So, any idea what movie you want to see?" He waited as she took special care adding just a dollop of cream to her coffee and gave it a stir, a bad feeling which was becoming familiar rising in his gut.

His fears were confirmed when she asked, "Would you mind if we skipped the movie for tonight?"

Disappointment filled him. "Sure, no problem." He started to lean back, but was surprised when she reached out and caught one of his hands in hers, holding him in place.

"I didn't mean I wanted to call it a night. I just, well, I had a really lousy day, and I'm not in the mood to sit through a movie right now. If that's okay?"

Relief washed over him at her words. Along with some hope. Maybe the bad day she'd had was the reason for the lack of spark tonight, not disinterest.

Turning his hand so it captured hers in return, he squeezed. "It's totally okay. So is calling it a night, if you really wanted to."

"No, I really don't." She smiled before ducking her head to the side, as though feeling suddenly shy. "I'm having a good time."

"Same." He ran his thumb over the back of her hand in a soft caress, and was rewarded by a slight catch in her breath. Pleased to discover she wasn't as unaffected as she'd appeared all evening, he did it again.

Damn, he should have touched her sooner.

"What would you like to do instead?"

"Um..." Whatever she might have said was lost with the arrival of their dessert.

Reluctantly, he released her hand as the waitress set down a large platter filled with much more than he'd ordered between them. When he raised a curious brow at her, she gave him a tiny shrug and said simply, *"De la Señora."*

Of course it was. *"Por favor, dale las gracias."*

"From the Señora?" Rachel translated with a frown after the waitress departed. "Who's that, your hostess friend?"

Ridiculously pleased at the bite in her voice, he began shifting a few of the decadent offerings onto two smaller dessert plates.

Oh yeah. She was jealous, all right.

"Lucia Delgado, one of the owners. She has a habit of over-feeding the people she likes. It's why I can't eat here more often than I do." He patted his stomach with a grin before he passed Rachel one of the plates. Her fingers brushed his as she took it, and he didn't think it was an accident.

"Oh, I don't think you have anything to worry about." She gave him a quick smile before shifting her attention to the food.

Okay, that time it *was* flirting.

Anticipation zinged through his body.

"Oh, my God." She dipped her spoon back into the small ramekin dish filled with *arroz con leche* and took another bite of the sweet rice pudding. "This is..."

"Incredible?"

"Incredible, amazing, decadent, take your pick."

"If you think that's good, wait till you try the *brazo de gitano*."

He pointed his fork at the piece of rolled sponge cake on his own plate, then watched as she took a bite of her own. Eyes closed, expression rapturous, she made a noise that had his lower body tightening in response.

Holy fuck.

He was in serious trouble.

Tearing his gaze from her, he focused on his own food, glad for the napkin in his lap when the waitress came by to top off their coffees. They worked their way through most of the dessert samples in silence, aside from the occasional happy sounds that escaped whenever Rachel found a new favorite among the assortment.

Which seemed to be all of them.

By the time she put down her fork, Theo had cleared his own plate but hadn't tasted a thing. He'd been too busy running multiplication tables in his head to keep his thoughts from conjuring images of Rachel in more intimate surroundings that would match the sounds she was making.

It had worked, for the most part. But it had been a near thing.

Part of him was annoyed she was so oblivious to the effect she was having on him. Part of him was glad.

And the part he was having trouble keeping in check most wanted to find out if he could get her to make those same noises of pleasure for *him*.

"You were right," she said with a happy sigh. "Everything was delicious. I'm going to have a serious sugar hangover tomorrow and need to double my workout, but it was worth it." As if to prove her words true, she swiped a finger through some of the guava jelly that had leaked onto her plate and popped it into her mouth to lick clean.

It was one temptation too many.

Hands locked around the edge of the table, he said in a low voice, "Do you have any idea what you're doing to me right now?"

She froze, finger still between her lips. Her look of confusion transformed to an expression of purely feminine satisfaction as she slowly withdrew the digit, giving her lips a little lick. "Is it good?"

"Too good." Too dangerous. He wasn't sure his control could handle it.

"Sorry." The smile curving her mouth said the opposite.

With a jerk of his arm, he summoned the waitress and settled the bill. He knew he should make a stop in the kitchen to thank Lucia in person, but he didn't want to take a chance on breaking the sensuous spell that seemed to be working its magic on the two of them. He helped her into her jacket, tugged on his own, and took her hand as they headed outside into the brisk March evening.

Neither of them spoke as they walked down the almost vacant sidewalk, hand-in-hand, until they came to the red Grand Cherokee Rachel pointed out as hers parked at the curb. Taking her face gently in his hands, he said, "I'm going to kiss you."

Heat flared in her eyes before she nodded her consent.

The first touch of his mouth to hers was gentle as he learned the feel of her, the silky texture of her lips. Then they parted for him, and he swept inside, tasting her as thoroughly as she'd sampled each sweet. She groaned and pressed deeper into the kiss, tasting him back, until they both had to come up for air.

It had only been a kiss, both of them fully clothed, with nothing else touching but their mouths. Still, it had set fire to his smoldering body like they'd been rolling naked on the ground together.

Panting, heart racing, he said the first thing that came to mind. "Come home with me."

Looking as dazed as he felt, she stared up at him long enough for him to know he'd overstepped, pushed too far, too fast. Damn it, she was going to say no.

"Yes."

Chapter 10

WHAT WAS I THINKING?

Rachel asked herself that for what had to be the hundredth time since she'd gotten behind the wheel of her Jeep and followed Theo, threading their way out of downtown Boulder north toward the suburbs. What was she thinking to say yes to such an outlandish question, when she knew exactly where it was going to lead?

Where was her sense of self-preservation? Her intelligence? Her pride?

Burned away under the scorching promise of incredible sex, it seemed.

That, and a chance to live in the moment instead of wallow in the misery of her spectacular failure on the slopes. She'd much rather see the passion in Theo's eyes than think about the disappointment and frustration in her dad's earlier today. It was why she'd gone through with the date in the first place, instead of hiding in her room to lick her emotional wounds in private.

After her nerve-free runs at Luxe the other day, her hopes had been high when she drove to Copper Mountain with her dad yesterday morning. Even the cold sweat that had taken up residence along her spine as she inspected the Super G course before skiing it hadn't been able to dent her confidence.

It was normal to be a little edgy under the circumstances.

She would have worried more if she wasn't.

The nausea as she got into the starting gate had been more of a problem. But she'd willed it down, just as she had any number of times before. It was a common symptom of nerves, when a title or a medal could be decided by whether or not she was perfect.

Only this time, there had been so much more on the line.

And she'd blown it.

"Damn it, damn it, damn it!" She slammed her hand against the steering wheel with each refrain, only stopping when a twinge of pain shot up her arm in protest.

She should have been able to run the course.

She should have been in control of her fear, of her body.

But the second she pushed through the gate and started hurtling down the mountainside, it was as if her brain had seized up and her body turned to a block of unresponsive ice. No matter how hard she struggled to force her way past it, to find the ease and joy she'd felt while skiing with Theo, there was only numbing terror.

Wiping out had almost been a relief.

But then she'd had to get back up again. It was the hardest thing she'd ever had to do outside of putting weight on her newly reconstructed leg for the first time, to see if it held. Which it had, making it easier to do the second time, and the third, because it meant things could only get better.

Not so with her training.

Every time she picked herself up and started back down the course, the more paralyzing the fear of 'what if' became.

What if she crashed again?

What if she undid all the good work the surgeons had done stitching and screwing her back together, and this time they couldn't fix her?

What if she'd lost her nerve for good?

What if she couldn't compete anymore?

The fact that last possibility caused her heart to jump a little, not in dismay but in longing, had made her feel like the worst kind of traitor.

Which only forced her to try all that much harder. Her fathers had raised her to be a winner, not a quitter. She'd keep going until she brought home that elusive unicorn, an Olympic gold medal, as tangible proof all their hard work and sacrifices for her over the years had been worth it.

That she was worth it.

None of the subsequent runs had gone any better. By the time Karl called a halt to the day's training, she'd been cold, wet, sore, and humiliated beyond belief.

They'd both tried to chalk her sub-subpar performance up to the fact it had been fifteen months since she'd last run a Super G, but it was a weak excuse at best. Still, they'd returned to Copper this morning hoping to see at least some improvement.

A hope doomed to disappointment.

"Damn it." This time, it was a defeated whisper. "What am I supposed to do now...wow." Tapping her brakes in response to the brake lights of Theo's SUV ahead of her, she stared as the massive wrought-iron gates hung between two stone pillars swung open to admit them. Eyes wide, she followed him down a gently sloping driveway and around the side of a house that, even in the dark, she could tell was huge.

A light came on as they pulled up in front of a four-car garage, pushing back the darkness enough to read "Porche Cayenne" emblazoned across the rear of Theo's SUV for the first time. And see the chunky ski rack on the roof. She blinked at the incongruity of such a utilitarian item on such an expensive vehicle.

Kind of like the man who was walking toward her with his long, rangy stride. His jeans and leather jacket, which she'd thought looked so perfect on him earlier, didn't fit with the gates and two-story mansion—there wasn't anything else to call it—he apparently called home.

Who *was* this paradox?

She popped the door open as he reached the Jeep and took the hand he offered to help her out, even though they both knew she didn't need it.

It was warm and strong, his long fingers curling around hers almost protectively as he led her inside, pausing only to take care of the alarm keypad next to the door and hang up her jacket, which gave her a second to look around.

They'd entered a mud room, although it was way more impressive than the one at her parents' house. It was probably as big as her entire bedroom, with a slate floor, cubby system for hats and gloves, coat rack, and a heavy-duty boot drying rack next to a small bench perfect for taking off your snowy outdoor gear. That, along with the three styles of high-end skis carefully racked in the corner, had her reassessing Theo's level of interest in the sport from recreational to enthusiast.

And wondering again just who this man really was.

Walking down a short hallway with a laundry room on one side and what looked like a gear room on the other, they emerged into a kitchen that would have made Gordon Ramsey weep with envy. It connected to a great room with a soaring fireplace of stacked stone reaching to the vaulted ceiling two stories up.

Although 'great' was an understatement.

The room was freaking *magnificent*. Much like the restaurant, one entire wall was windows. It was too dark now to see it, but they no doubt provided an incomparable view of the Rockies. Likely the same one depicted in the vibrant painting over the fireplace showing them bathed in fire and gold in the setting sun.

"Wow." The word popped out again as an awed whisper.

Theo stopped and looked at her. "What?"

"This." She gestured around them. "Just...wow."

He glanced around the room as though trying to see it through her eyes, then shrugged. "It's just home."

Spoken like a man who'd grown up used to such things. "It's a mansion."

"No, my parents have a mansion. This is just a really nice house."

She gave a small huff of laughter, tilting her head back to look at the immense wood and crystal chandelier suspended between the thick, roughhewn beams. She didn't care what he said. This was a freaking mansion.

"I know you made a few comments about having money, but I didn't realize you meant *money*."

His expression turned guarded. "And that matters?"

Rachel looked at him. She was becoming familiar enough with his handsome face to know her answer mattered to him. More than a little.

She smiled and shook her head. "Not in the least." And it didn't. It had surprised her, but she'd rubbed elbows with lots of rich people during her years on the ski circuit. It just didn't impress her anymore.

It was a few long seconds before the tension leeched from his body.

"Good." He raised their still-linked hands and pressed a kiss to the back of hers, his eyes never leaving hers. "So, what would you like to do? I can get the fireplace going, open us a bottle of wine, put on some music..."

"Ah..." The lingering press of his mouth rekindled the tingles his earlier kiss had started, but his words made her wonder if she'd misunderstood the intent of his invitation. She'd been thinking sex. And he'd been thinking...

Sex. She was sure of it.

There was a hunger in his gaze that belied his offer of a cozy snuggle near the fire. A hunger that matched the one building inside her, wanting, needing to be sated. He'd all but promised her sexual oblivion, damn it, and she meant to collect.

Letting some of that banked heat show in her expression, she smiled. "Or…"

"Or?" The word was practically a growl.

Rather than answer with words, she stepped into him and wrapped her free hand around his neck, dragging his head down for a kiss. He offered no resistance. Once their lips met, it was like it had been outside the restaurant, instant lust welling up, drowning her common sense and leaving her hormones in total control.

Her body approved.

Just as it approved of the rock-hard press of Theo's erection against the cradle of her thighs, awakening nerve-endings which had gotten too little attention for far too long. She gave her hips an experimental roll and was rewarded by a groan that echoed her own.

Yes!

This was what she wanted. And she wanted it now.

Theo kissed his way down her neck to the gentle V of her sweater before ripping his mouth from her skin and panting out, "Are you sure?"

"Bedroom." She rolled her hips again, harder this time. "Now."

Thank God, he took her at her word.

After a look she could practically feel caressing her entire body like a hand, he led her upstairs. Even with her long legs, she had to hurry to keep up with his eager pace. The room he led her to had to be the biggest master suite she'd ever seen, complete with its own sitting area and wet bar.

She couldn't have cared less.

All that mattered was the huge bed, and they were heading for it without delay.

They both stripped, clothes tossed with reckless abandon until they came together again, naked and eager, in another mouth-crushing kiss. The feel of his hot skin, the delicious roughness of his chest hair against her sensitive breasts, was enough to bring her close to the edge.

And they'd barely gotten started yet.

She ran her hands along the strong line of his back, feeling the muscles there quiver like a racehorse ready to run. Emboldened, she explored further south, cupping his firm ass, letting her fingertips stray down to find the warm globes that hung between his legs.

That seemed to be the trigger which finally set him off. He pulled back enough so he could see her face and demand, "Fast or slow?"

"Fast."

Her breath caught as he scooped her up effortlessly and laid her on the bed, coming down over her on all fours. She had a moment of uncertainty when she remembered the scars on her lower body, but it dissolved under the strokes and caresses he was laying against her skin.

Fuck the scars.

He obviously didn't care. Why should she?

When he reached the junction of her thighs, he tested her readiness. She knew what he found. She was almost drenched for him. A fact which pleased him greatly, if the wicked grin that stretched his lips was anything to go by.

He took a second to grab a condom from the nightstand and cover himself before placing his erection against the warm, wet edge of her.

Once again, he gave her a choice. "Hard or gentle."

Her inner muscles clenched in anticipation. "God, hard, please. Oh!" The soft cry was forced from her body as he slid home with one powerful thrust.

Her back arched, lifting her pelvis to meet the next thrust, sending him even deeper, filling the emptiness that had been slowly driving her mad. It was good. So good. But greedily, she wanted more.

"Harder."

He obliged, taking hold of her hips, using his strength to lift her to the angle he wanted before pistoning himself into her with firm thrusts that touched all the right places. There was a rapid sensation of growing tightness in her belly.

Then it burst, her orgasm tearing a scream loose as she fisted the sheets to keep from floating away on the waves of pleasure that rolled over her.

Theo's own shout of triumphant completion was almost lost in the contented haze which came down like a curtain over her senses. She was vaguely aware of him moving to take care of the condom, rousing only when he returned to lie beside her.

She turned her head on the pillow to look at him, feeling drunk and giddy and absolutely *wonderful*.

There was only one thing she could think clearly enough to say.

"How soon before we can do that again?"

Chapter 11

The question, spoken in an almost drunken slur, filled Theo with an absurd sense of accomplishment. Especially since he knew she'd only had one beer with dinner. That meant her condition was entirely because of him. Talk about an ego stroke.

Speaking of stroking...

He ran a light fingertip down her arm, raising faint goosebumps on her silky skin. "I may need a little while to recharge after that. You kind of wore me out."

She grinned. "Ditto. That was a-*ma*-zing."

"No. This—you—are amazing." His fingers rounded her collarbone and slid down to caress her breast. A shiver ran through her body as the already tight dusky tip furled even tighter at his touch. God, she was so responsive. "But there are lots of things we can do to fill the time while we wait."

"Oh, really?" The words were a little breathy.

"Mmhmm." He shifted his hand to her other breast, petite and perky, and slid his body closer. "Lots and lots of things." He ran his tongue over the tip of the breast he'd just abandoned, enjoying the contrasting soft yet stiff texture as it reacted to his ministration.

"I think I like that plan." She gasped as his mouth closed over her nipple and gently suckled. "God!"

Grinning to himself, he continued to lavish attention on all the parts of her luscious body, making mental notes about what she liked best with the noises she made as his guide. Her body was nearly perfection. Toned, trim, a true testament to her years as a professional athlete.

As were the scars.

He hadn't meant to pay them any extra attention. They were inconsequential to him.

But clearly not to her. When his hand casually stroked down her left hip and over the surgical scar there, she flinched for the first time since he started touching her.

It would have been easy enough to ignore her reaction and just pass the spot by, but he had a feeling it would be the wrong thing to do.

"Did that hurt?" He knew it didn't. He'd had a much firmer hold of her there when he'd been driving into her like a man possessed. But he had to ask.

"No. It's just..." She flapped a hand as though to drive him away from the area. "They're ugly."

"Are you kidding? You can barely see them."

Which was the truth. The line running vertically from her hip down along the outside of her upper thigh was a few shades paler than the surrounding skin, but it was hardly shocking or disfiguring. The same went for the one starting at the top of her left knee, ending midway down her shin. Several circular scars around the kneecap were barely larger than a dime.

"And so what if you can? People have scars. It's no big deal."

"Says the man with the perfect body."

Self-consciousness was in clear evidence under the droll comment. Mere words weren't going to fix that.

Taking a page from his brother's playbook, he switched tactics.

"Perfect, hell. I probably have more scars than you do."

"Bull."

"How much you wanna bet?"

Her gorgeous eyes narrowed. "Are you serious? You want to bet over who has the most scars?"

"Why not? Unless you're afraid you'll lose."

As he'd hoped, goading her competitive nature worked where sympathy and reassurance would have failed.

Rachel sat up so they were eye-to-eye. "You're on."

With a grin, he started to point to his shoulder, only to have her shake her head.

"Lay down. I'll find them myself."

Like he was going to argue with that.

Still grinning, he flopped onto his back, arms outstretched at his sides in welcome to her touch. Any excuse that got her hands on his body was a good one, as far as he was concerned. "I'm all yours."

She made a little humming noise that went straight to his cock, which twitched in interest. If she noticed, she ignored it.

Instead, she put all of her attention to the task at hand. She started at his shoulders, running warm, soft fingers across the skin there until she found the oblong patch of rough, rippled scar tissue the size of a silver dollar at the very top of his left shoulder blade.

He obliged her by turning enough so she could see it.

"One of my anchors came loose on a climb, and I dropped about ten feet before the next one stopped me. My back smacked the rock on the way down and took off some skin." Along with a chunk of meat, dislocating his shoulder for good measure.

But they were only talking scars, not injuries.

"Climb? You mean, like mountain climbing?"

"Rock climbing, actually. It's a little different."

She stroked the damaged flesh as though trying to make it better before continuing her search. The next scar was close by, on the back of his left arm, still pink and shiny. "White water rafting. We flipped going through a class five rapid in Australia." He waited a beat. "Damn croc nearly had me."

The shocked look on her face had him hooting with laughter.

"I'm kidding, I'm kidding. Crocs don't live in rough water like that. I caught it on a submerged branch or something."

"You...you jerk!"

She gave him a quick poke in the belly, turning his laughter to a grunt of pain. Damn, the woman had strong fingers.

"Sorry, I couldn't resist."

"Hmph." Despite her sniff of annoyance, the hint of a smile twitched on her lips.

The hunt continued, but the game had changed. As Rachel's fingers slid over his body with ever-increasing eroticism, he realized he might have let himself in for more than he could handle.

Women had run their hands all over him before, sure. But never so thoroughly, or with such focused intent that fire followed in the wake of her touch, scorching him from the inside out.

By the time she reached his feet, he was ready to burst into actual flames. Especially since she'd diligently ignored his now reinvigorated cock on her way past. Her breath touched his skin as she leaned closer to his right foot.

He swallowed a whimper. Either she was more competitive than he'd first thought, or she was making him suffer on purpose.

He was leaning toward the latter.

"Is this scar from a bite?" She caressed the skin near his little toe.

"Yup." The touch seemed connected to nerves that ran north straight to his groin, ratcheting his frustration up another notch.

She pursed her lips as she looked up the long length of his body at him. "Let me guess. Another croc? Or, no, wait, maybe a Tasmanian Devil?"

"Hey, those little bastards have a nasty bite, no joke. But no, that particular bite is from the *Peter Monstercus Minor*, otherwise known as the dreaded little brother."

"Your brother bit you?" She sounded equal parts outraged and amused.

"Yeah, well, we were kids, and I *might* have been sitting on him and forcing him to smell my feet at the time."

"You *what*?"

"Well, Pete had a low tolerance and a high gag reflex for bad smells, and he made the cardinal sin of letting his older brothers know about it." He shrugged. The first rule of survival, in business or life, was to never let your weaknesses show. "The hell of farts and smelly feet he suffered after that was entirely of his own making."

A laugh escaped before she slapped a hand over her mouth. "You're horrible!"

Yeah, he had been.

"It seemed harmless at the time. Who knew he had the bite of a snapping turtle when you pissed him off bad enough?"

"I take back what I said before. I'm *glad* I'm an only child."

"I told you. Blessing *and* curse."

She shook her head, still grinning. As she had with each of the other scars, she caressed this one with her fingertips, sending another shiver of fire up to his cock, which had started to fade a bit as they talked.

"Let's see..." He could see her doing a mental tally. "I think we're all tied up." She ran her hands up his thighs with aching slowness. "Unless you've got more somewhere I haven't seen yet."

He did. One on his lower back and one on his ass—although that was a story he could live without telling.

But as he opened his mouth to reply, her fingers slid high enough on his thighs that her thumbs both came to rest on the base of his cock, which was now straining up from his body at full-mast again.

His breath whooshed out on a shaky gust.

"You were saying?" she asked sweetly.

"Uh, that I—holy fuck!" His hips bucked as she ran those talented fingers up his length in a slow, firm caress. First one hand, then the other, each one straight up and off the engorged tip, letting his erection slap gently back against his stomach as she released it.

"Sorry, I couldn't resist."

"Who wants you to?" He groaned as she took him in her hands and did it again, this time adding a little extra something under the ultra-sensitive edge of his crown that practically blew the top of his head off. "Damn, woman, you're killing me."

His words had exactly the opposite effect he wanted as she moved her hands further down his thighs. "Well, we can't have that, can we? At least, not until we know who won."

"Won?" It took a second for his muddled brain to decipher her meaning. "You did. You totally won. Just please, *don't stop.*"

A smug smile lifted her lips. "Well, in that case, I think I'll collect my prize."

Before he could ask what that might be, she took firm hold of his cock, which pulsed in her hands, and drew him into the warm wet of her mouth. It was so unexpected, and so damn good, he nearly came before she could draw him inside for a second stroke.

Gritting his teeth, he exerted every ounce of control he had, willing the orgasm back. It was a near thing. When he cracked his eyes open to look down his body at her, he realized from the way she was watching him that had been her intent. She'd meant to make him blow.

Competitive little minx.

Well, two could play that game.

He settled his hands behind his head and gave her a smile that said "bring it." Her eyes narrowed as she got the message before applying herself to the challenge. The feel of her tongue curling and playing around his tip had him sucking in a sharp breath, which he let out again in a steadying stream.

Close, so close.

But with the iron willpower that had allowed him to crawl back into their raft in Australia and complete the last two days of their trip down the North Johnstone River with his gashed arm super glued together, he managed.

Barely.

But there came a point where pleasure almost turned to pain, and he couldn't hold back any longer. "Point of no return." He gasped out the warning.

If anything, his words only spurred her on.

Giving in to the inevitable, he dropped his control and let the sensations spill over him as she licked, sucked, and caressed him into a violent, never-ending eruption.

His body bucked, back arching as the release emptied him out in more ways than one. Spent, he collapsed to the mattress in a boneless heap.

Rachel snuggled in against his side, one leg tucked possessively over his.

"I win."

With a tired laugh, he pressed a kiss to her forehead and drew her hand onto his heaving chest. "Sweetheart, I'm pretty sure we both did."

Chapter 12

Who was this sex siren who'd taken over her body?

First, she'd agreed to go home with a man she barely knew. Then she'd had some of the most incredible sex she'd ever had in her life. And *then* she'd turned into this great, big tease and practically ravished him while he lay there helpless in her power.

Okay, so he hadn't been helpless for real. Obviously, he could have called a stop to things any time he wanted. But instead, he'd played along, letting her have her wicked way with him, teasing and tormenting until he'd finally reached the end of his control.

Watching him come, knowing she had done that for him, to him, had been heady enough she'd very nearly come herself.

Sitting on the edge of the rumpled bed, she grinned as she slipped her suede ankle boot on and zipped it closed. Who knew it could be that much fun, giving that kind of pleasure to someone? No wonder people dabbled in a little tie-me-up/tie-me-down sometimes. Control had a very appealing flavor.

And so did giving it up.

A tiny shudder ran through her as she reached for her other boot.

When he'd gone hard and fast, Theo had given her exactly what she'd wanted, even if she hadn't known it at the time. The way he'd gripped her, held her in place, used his muscular body to direct every stroke, every delicious inch of penetration...

She fanned herself, glad the man in question had already gone downstairs while she dressed. The last thing she wanted was to explain her sudden hot flash. If he knew she got turned on just thinking about sex with him, he'd probably be insufferably smug.

After a quick check to make sure she had everything, she descended the remarkable floating staircase she hadn't even noticed on the way up. They'd both been too intent on reaching the bedroom to notice anything except each other.

Following the sound of ice tinkling against glass, she went into the kitchen.

Theo was at the door of the stainless-steel refrigerator, an ice-filled glass held under the water dispenser. He hadn't gotten fully dressed, simply thrown on his jeans, commando, leaving them unbuttoned and hanging low on his hips like a tantalizing promise.

Seeing the long expanse of naked back made her realize she hadn't gotten to explore all of him upstairs. There were still some nooks and crannies left to be discovered.

Her fingers tingled in anticipation.

He smiled when he saw her. Without a word, he held out the glass in invitation. She took it and swallowed the cold liquid in greedy gulps. Good sex was thirsty work. Draining it of every drop, she licked her lips and handed it back to Theo, who was watching her mouth with keen intent. "More, please?"

"Sure." The word sounded a little hoarse.

Smiling to herself, she walked around the perimeter of the massive island which dominated the center of the room as he refilled the glass. Partly to explore. Partly to keep from giving in to the urge of her fingers to check out that small scar she'd missed on his lower back.

Everything from the cookware to the appliances was top-of-the-line professional quality, and every piece had clearly been well-used.

She didn't miss how he made sure their fingers slid against each other when she accepted the refilled glass from him. It made her inexplicable need to touch him less unsettling to know he felt it, too.

"Do you like to cook? Or do you have someone come in to do it for you?"

Because, you know, rich guy.

"Both, actually. During the week, I rarely have the time to do more than heat up what Win, my house manager, leaves for me. But on the weekends, when I'm home, anyway, I like to try out new stuff on my own. You'd be amazed at the recipes you can get off the internet for exotic dishes from around the world. How about you? Do you like to cook?"

She wanted to laugh. "Not really, no. I mean, I can if I have to, but..." She wrinkled her nose. "My father is the chef in the family. He'd love this kitchen."

Theo leaned back against the island. The position tugged at his jeans, letting more of that enticing bit of real estate south of his bellybutton show. "Would that be the father who's your coach, or the other one?"

Pleasure at the unintentional peepshow was blunted by the reminder of the day's earlier failings. Failings she still needed to face the consequences of sometime soon.

"The other one." Needing to move away from the subject before she lost every bit of her afterglow to harsh reality, she gestured to the two metal bowls on the floor in the corner. "I didn't know you had a dog."

After a pause that said her avoidance had been noted, Theo shook his head. "I don't. I was watching my brother Pete's mutt for him last weekend. Guess I forgot to put them away when he came to collect the big pain in the ass."

From the almost wistful way he looked at the empty bowls, though, she got the feeling he'd enjoyed the dog's company a lot more than he'd admit. "Ever think about getting one of your own?"

He shrugged. "Sometimes. But I work all week, and most weekends I'm not home for long, if at all. It never seemed fair to get a dog only to leave it alone that much."

"I know, I feel the same way. Training and competing takes up so much of my time. I'm on the road more weeks out of the year than I'm home. I figure I'll get one when I retire." She caught the surprise as it flashed across his face. "What?"

"Nothing. I, uh, just didn't realize you were still competing. I thought you were working at the resort now."

"Just for this season, when I got cleared to be back on skis but not for racing. But everything's healed enough now to train full time again to get ready for the start of the cup circuit in October."

And there it was.

The perfect opportunity to make it crystal clear what they had—whatever the hell this was—could only be short term. Once she began training in earnest, all of her energy would have to be focused on that. There wouldn't be anything left to give to any relationship, not even a casual one.

The words wouldn't come.

Instead, she sipped her water and glanced at her watch, nearly choking when she saw it was almost midnight. They must have dozed for a lot longer than the few minutes she'd thought. "I have to go."

"I didn't mean to insult you and send you running."

"What? Oh, no, you didn't. I'm not. I just noticed how late it was, and, well, I have work in the morning, and so do you, so..."

Okay, maybe she was running, a little.

"So..." He plucked the glass from her hand and put it aside before tugging her to him. Hands clasped loosely on her waist, he gave her a searching look. "I was planning to take you back upstairs so I could even up the score before you left. I'm usually not that selfish, just so you know. I'm more of a 'ladies first' kind of guy."

She almost laughed, but he seemed genuinely disgruntled by the uneven tally of orgasms given and received. Looping her hands around his neck, she smiled. "You can owe me until next time."

"So, there *will* be a next time."

"Yeah, pretty sure." Her smile dimmed as something which had been nagging at her came back for a few more pokes. "And just so *you* know, I don't usually fall into bed with a guy on the first date. I'm not...this was..."

"I know."

The quiet words cut through her stumbling explanation, leaving her wondering if Theo was as confused by the strength and immediacy of their attraction as she was. "Okay. Good."

He kissed her, soft and sweet. "Are you sure you have to go?"

"Yeah." But he was making it a lot harder than it should have been.

"Then I guess I better make this count."

The kiss that followed kept her in a state of tingling arousal the entire drive home. Like he'd known it would, the sneaky bastard. As she let herself into the house, all she could think about was heading up to her bedroom and making use of the vibrator hidden in the back of her underwear drawer to take the edge off the pulsing need he'd left inside her.

"Do you have any idea how late it is?"

Rachel jumped at the voice coming from the shadows, hand going to her thudding heart. "Jesus, Dad! You scared the hell out of me." She squinted as the foyer lights suddenly blared on, causing spots to dance across her vision. But even those couldn't hide the displeasure carved into Karl's face.

Damn.

"Sorry. I guess I kind of lost track of the time." She could practically hear Ari's voice in her head calling her a wuss. But since she was living under her parents' roof, she figured she at least owed them the courtesy of letting them know she wasn't lying dead in a ditch somewhere. "I didn't mean to make you worry."

"You lost track of time? That's your answer?"

The harsh tone seemed way out of proportion to the offense.

Then she remembered. This was the first time she'd been out on a date since she'd been living there. That, coupled with not having met the guy she was going out with, must have pushed all his protective-dad buttons.

"Yeah, it is. I was having a good time, and just...lost track."

"Oh, I can see what kind of good time you were having."

She barely resisted reaching up to check how messy her hair was. She hadn't bothered with a mirror before she'd left Theo's. Was what they'd done that obvious?

Humiliation swamped her.

"You're twenty-eight fecking years old, Rae. You don't owe your das an accounting of your love life, whether you're staying with them or not."

Ari to the rescue.

It was tough, but she looked her dad in the eye. "I'm an adult, Dad. My private life is none of your business."

"As long as I'm your coach, it damn well *is* my business!"

All she could do was blink. "Are you kidding me?"

"Well, one of us has to take your training seriously."

Another blink. "I'm sorry?"

"You should be."

That was when it hit her. He wasn't upset with her as her parent. He wasn't mad she hadn't called, been worried she'd had an accident or broken down somewhere without cell reception or been with some guy he didn't know.

No, he was pissed *as her coach* because she'd gone out and had a good time—of *any* kind—after her horrible outing on the mountain.

Un-fucking-believable.

Anger began to burn away her earlier embarrassment. "I am sorry if I worried you by not calling to say I was going to be late. But I'm not sorry I went out tonight. Or that I had fun. I think I'm entitled to it once in a while."

"You've had a whole year to goof off and have fun. Now it's time to get your head right and focus on getting back on top."

"A year to..." She almost choked on the anger that swelled up inside her like a geyser. "I had a year of surgeries and physical therapy, learning how to walk again without a limp. Trust me, there wasn't any fun involved."

For the first time, he looked flustered, tugging at his left earlobe. A nervous habit usually reserved for right before a race. "Do you think I don't know how much hard work and dedication it took to come back from where you were to where you are now? Haven't I been there with you every step of the way?"

"Yeah, you have." Literally. "Which is why I don't understand you saying something like that."

Because damn it, it *hurt*.

"I only meant that for the first time since you were twelve, you haven't been fired up to ski a course as many times as you could in a day, then go home and dissect and assess every run so we could figure out what you were doing wrong and fix it."

Maybe because at twelve she hadn't fully grasped how very permanent one simple mistake could be. How much she had to lose.

"What's there to assess? I sucked yesterday. I sucked just as hard today. I know it, you know it, everybody who was there to see me fall on my ass a thousand times knows it. I really don't need to relive it through a blow-by-blow analysis. Let's just focus on moving forward from here, okay?"

Another ear tug. "Okay, kiddo. We'll hit Copper tomorrow morning like the last two days didn't happen."

She stifled a sigh. "Dad, I have work tomorrow."

"What happened to focusing on moving forward?"

"I will. After the season is over. It's only two more weeks."

"That's two weeks of training you'll never get back."

This time she didn't bother hiding the sigh. "Dad, please. It's too late to start this argument again."

He threw his hands up in the air. "Fine. Fine! Go to bed. Go to work tomorrow. Why am I even bothering? I swear, it's almost like you don't *want* to compete anymore!"

Maybe because I don't.

The words were right there, pressing against her tightly clenched teeth. All she had to do was let them out. Tell him she had no desire to throw herself off the top of a mountain anymore. That she was cutting her losses and hanging up her skis for good before she really got hurt. Or died.

If only it were that easy.

Looking at the man who had taken her into his home, made her not only his daughter but his protégé, his *legacy*, she couldn't do it. She couldn't throw all of that back in his face like an ungrateful little brat. They'd both made promises the day he'd strapped her into her first pair of skis and she'd shown a natural aptitude for the sport.

He promised to make her a champion, and she'd promised to let him.

It was far too late for her to change her mind now.

Swallowing down all the words crowding her tongue, she took a deep breath and started up the stairs. "Two weeks, Dad. After that, I'm all yours. Promise."

And she'd keep that promise just like she'd kept all the others.

Even if it killed her.

Chapter 13

"You look like you could use a drink."

Rachel gave a tired smile to the man behind the coffee bar. "Make it a double."

"Wow. That sounds serious." With the deft skill of years of practice, Ben assembled her drink while giving her the lion's share of his attention. "Bad day on the bunny hill?"

No one was close enough to overhear, but she lowered her voice anyway. "Private session. Birthday party. Eight twelve-year-old girls." She shook her head, wondering if there might be any aspirin behind the counter. Or vodka. "It was a nightmare."

Normally, she enjoyed instructing kids, even in groups. But this particular bunch of tweens had managed to work on her last nerve to the point she'd half-seriously considered faking an injury just to cut the lesson short.

It had been Lord of the Flies on skis.

"Well, this should help a little." With a flourish, Ben slid a cup in front of her. "One large hot chocolate, double whip, with an extra pump each of peppermint and vanilla." His other hand came up, a small foil packet of aspirin between his fingers. "And if that doesn't work, maybe this will."

"You're a god among baristas."

"And still you won't go out with me," he teased like he always did.

"I told you at the beginning of the season, lose the beard and I might consider it." She swallowed a chuckle at his expression of horror.

"And look like a prepubescent choirboy? Forget it. I guess you'll just have to wonder what you're missing out on."

"I'll try to survive." She shot him a wink as she dropped her change into the tip jar and took her drink to a small table in the corner. She sipped at the chocolatey goodness with a happy hum.

Sweet perfection.

Swallowing the aspirin, she willed them to work fast. She had another lesson in less than an hour, and her current mood wasn't going to cut it.

Although she couldn't entirely blame her headache or her mood on the birthday brats. Or even on the sugar hangover she'd known she'd pay with after last night's overindulgence on dessert.

No, her pounding head and shredded nerves came courtesy of the mostly sleepless night she spent after the argument with her dad. She'd laid in bed, huddled under the covers, not basking in the afterglow of the incredible sex she'd had with Theo, but instead hearing her dad's harsh words beating at her, over and over, until she thought she'd scream.

You've had a whole year to goof off and have fun.

She knew he hadn't meant it. Not really. And yet the words had stung because they picked at her worst insecurities. Had she stretched her recovery out longer than necessary? Was she making excuses instead of giving it her all?

Was she goofing off?

Rubbing her aching temple, she popped the domed lid off of the cup and used her finger to scoop out some of the whipped cream. As she licked it off, a sudden image of Theo's heated expression when she'd done almost the same thing the night before at the restaurant made her heart pound a little faster.

The image changed to the look of fierce focus he'd had as he pounded into her, using his body to claim every last inch of her with each bold stroke. The memory was so strong, so visceral, she had to close her eyes and bite her lower lip to keep a moan from escaping.

"Ben must be adding something special to your drinks, because I've never gotten one that tasted that good."

Vicky's sarcastic comment sliced through the brief moment of pleasure, bringing Rachel's headache roaring back with a pulsing thud. "What do you want?"

A catty smile curved the other woman's lips. "Oooh, sorry, didn't mean to crash your private little pity party."

Rachel pinched the bridge of her nose. She was going to need a lot more than two lousy aspirin to deal with whatever crap Vicky was clearly itching to shovel her way.

"I've got a headache that could knock a bull moose off its feet, Vick, so can we please cut to the chase for once?"

Had the parents who booked the lesson-slash-party complained? Doubtful, since the father had taken her aside at the end to hand her a hefty tip by way of apology. But why else would Vicky have such an obnoxious grin on her face?

Vicky honest-to-God giggled, a ridiculous sound coming from a grown woman. "Getting knocked off your feet. Good one. I guess you'd be an expert on that after yesterday."

Fuck.

That was why.

Refusing to take the bait, she sipped her drink. "Guess I am." She was pleased with how calm she sounded, because inside she was a roiling mass of anger and humiliation. How the hell had Vicky heard about her training fail so fast?

Worse, how many other people knew?

"Oh, come on, I'm just playing with you."

Yeah, the way a bored lion played with a wounded gazelle before ripping its throat out.

"I don't know what you want me to say, Vick. Yeah, I had a bad training day. Yeah, I wiped out. A lot. But I also got up and kept on going." Even when her mind and body were conspiring to make her stay down. "Next time will be better. And the time after that. And eventually, I'll be right back where I was." She looked into Vicky's eyes. "At the top of the podium."

Some of Vicky's smugness crumbled into surprise. "You're serious."

"Why wouldn't I be?"

"You really think you can come back from an injury like that and ski as well as you used to?"

"I know I can." Probably.

Maybe.

The look Vicky shot her was filled with derision. "Yeah, good luck with that."

"Thanks."

"That wasn't...whatever. You know, I'm actually glad you're planning a comeback."

"Really?"

"Yeah. That means I get another chance to kick your butt and prove I'm better."

"You can try." With a tight smile, Rachel stood, holding onto her cup like a lifeline. It was that, or slap the nasty smirk off the other woman's face.

"Oh, I'll win. Wanna know why?"

"Not really."

"Because I want it more than you."

"You keep telling yourself that." But the words struck the same sore spot her dad's comments had already savaged. Back stiff, she started for the door.

"Hey, I'm not finished yet."

As she spoke, Vicky's hand grabbed her arm, yanking hard enough to make Rachel pivot back towards her, like a yo-yo reaching the end of its string. As a result, hot chocolate cascaded in a dark brown arc from the lidless cup in her hand, drenching the front of Vicky's Luxe-blue sweater. They both stood frozen for a split second, mouths hanging open as they stared at each other in surprise.

Vicky broke the silence first. "You did that on purpose!"

"*You* grabbed *me*, remember? It was an accident." As if to punctuate her words, a glob of whipped cream slid off Vicky's nametag and hit the floor with a wet plop. The urge to laugh was so overwhelming, she had to bite her tongue hard enough to draw blood in order to resist.

Talk about instant karma.

"You...you..."

It was easy to guess what the next word out of her mouth was going to be.

"Guests, Vick."

The soft reminder there were curious eyes and ears all around them was enough to make Vicky visibly swallow down the insult and paste a neutral expression on her face. The anger burning in her eyes, though, was impossible to mask.

Rachel sighed. "I'm sorry. It really was an accident."

Ben arrived in a rush, handing a small towel to Vicky before using a second one to mop up whatever had hit the floor. Which wasn't much. The expensive cashmere sweater had absorbed most of it.

Vicky dabbed at the splashes of hot chocolate on her chin. She didn't bother trying to save the ruined sweater, simply held the towel over her chest like a shield to hide the worst of the mess. "We'll discuss this later."

Getting to his feet, Ben watched with Rachel as Vicky made as dignified an exit as she could back into the main part of the resort. "That sounded ominous."

"Yeah. Just what my day needed."

"Think she'll make trouble for you with daddy?"

"She was pretty upset. Maybe." Almost definitely.

It was a good thing the season was almost over. Being fired now wouldn't hurt her bank account too much. At least her dad would be happy. He'd get his extra two weeks of training out of her, after all.

"I saw her grab your arm, you know. The whole thing was her fault."

"Yeah, well, I'm not sure it would matter. Vicky's used to getting what she wants."

"Well, if you need me to, I've got your back."

"Thanks, Ben. I appreciate it."

The rest of the day passed without being summoned to the main office. Not wanting to tempt fate by hanging around longer, just in case, she put off taking a run down the mountain to test whether her problem was confined solely to the Super G course. It had nothing to do with being afraid of what the answer might be. Nothing at all.

Yeah, you keep telling yourself that.

To her great relief, no one was home when she got there. After a quick shower, she left a note saying she was going to dinner with Ari and headed out. It was a little cowardly, but she wasn't ready to go another round with her dad yet. Not after the day she'd had. She needed a little more time to clear her head and calm her temper.

And if there was a cocktail or two involved, all the better.

Ari opened the door to her apartment before Rachel could ring the bell. "You know, it's creepy as hell when you do that."

Smiling her usual enigmatic smile, Ari closed the door behind her and glided toward the kitchen. There really wasn't a better word for how she moved. It was like she was always in synch with music only she could hear.

Ari epitomized the phrase "dance like no one is watching." Only, she didn't care if people watched. Preferred it, in fact. She was totally comfortable in her own skin, a trait Rachel envied more than a little.

Especially lately.

After hanging her jacket on the old-fashioned coatrack by the door, she followed her friend to the living room, eagerly accepting the offered glass of wine as she settled on the cushy sofa.

Perhaps a little too eagerly, judging by the way Ari studied her over the rim of her own glass. "Want to talk about it?"

Her laugh was abrupt and bitter. "Talk about what? The guy I had the best sex in the world with, but have to give up? The death of my career? Disappointing my dad? The possibility I'm going to get fired tomorrow? Take your pick." She slugged back a swallow of the crisp Pino Grigio, barely tasting it.

"Okay, this is going to take reinforcements." Grabbing the bottle from the coffee table, she topped off both their glasses. "Now, why don't you start from when I last saw you on Sunday. It sounds like you've had a hell of a week so far."

Damn right she had.

And it was only Thursday.

Chapter 14

It took two glasses of wine to get through it all.

Empty Chinese food containers from when Ari had ordered takeout on her phone app to help soak up the alcohol littered the coffee table. Rachel barely remembered eating, but her full stomach said she had.

The cats, who'd joined them about the same time the food arrived, were now draped over their laps, purring like a couple of buzz saws. As she stroked her fingers through Nova's soft fur, she drained the last of her wine and set the glass down with a sad sigh.

"Sorry to dump everything on you like this. I seem to be doing a lot of that lately." She shook her head when Ari lifted the bottle for another refill. "No thanks, I have work tomorrow." Her breath faltered as memory caught up with her words. "Maybe."

"You have work until your boss tells you otherwise. Don't borrow trouble."

"I guess you're right. Besides, getting fired is at the bottom of my list of current problems." Even though it would suck. She liked her job, and her coworkers.

Well, most of them, anyway.

"And what would be at the top?"

An image of Theo in his unbuttoned jeans flashed through her mind, followed by an ache at the thought of never seeing him like that again. Never seeing him again, period. "Figuring out what I'm doing wrong on the slopes, of course. And fixing things with my dad."

"That wasn't your first thought, though, was it?"

Damn woo-woo.

Or maybe her friend simply knew her too well.

"It's what's most important."

"Is it, now?" Ari stroked a hand over Luna's head as she stared at Rachel. She nodded. "Okay, then. Let's take things in reverse order and work our way up. From what you told me about your date, you must really like this guy."

"It was just good sex." She paused. "Okay, really good sex. But like? Ari, I barely *know* him."

"You knew him well enough to have really good sex with him." She flapped a hand at Rachel's sputtered objection. "Face facts, lovie. You wouldn't have gotten naked with a man you didn't know or like. That's not you."

"Not normally, no." But some internal lock seemed to have been turned last night, exposing a side of herself she wasn't entirely comfortable with in the light of day. "Anyway, that's not the point. Whether I like Theo or not is moot. There's no way I can let it be more than a one-night stand."

"Why not?"

"Come on, you know how my schedule is when I'm training. And if my shitty performance over the last two days is anything to go by, I'll be working twice as hard as usual just to get back to where I was a year and a half ago. And then I'll be competing again. Not to mention trying to get my sponsors back. Where am I supposed to fit a relationship into all of that?"

"Wherever you can."

"Right, like it's that easy."

"Hell no, it's not," Ari said on a lilting laugh. "Nothing worth having ever is."

It was the same refrain she'd heard all her life from her dad. Only he'd meant an Olympic gold medal. She didn't think he'd agree with it being applied to dating. Especially not when it might mean borrowing time from her already over-packed schedule to do it.

"I have to keep my eye on the prize." She wasn't sure if the soft words were for Ari, or a reminder to herself.

"Ah, but the real trick is knowing which prize that is."

"There can only be one prize, Ari, and you know what it is. The same thing it's been my whole life. Being the best."

"Who says there can't be more than one prize? Why can't you have your career *and* your man? Plenty of women do."

"I tried that, remember? It didn't turn out so well."

"Because you picked a couple of gobshites. It sounds to me like this one is different."

He was. That was part of what scared her so much.

She'd been with Stefan for six months and never felt half the connection she felt with Theo after just one date. Or two. They really needed to get that figured out. Either way, there couldn't be a third.

Or a second. Depending.

Gee, deflect much, Rae?

"What if he hates coming in second to my skiing?"

"Then you kick him to the curb and good riddance. But the better question is, what if he doesn't? What if he supports your ambitions, is willing to put up with the time you have to spend apart? Wouldn't your accomplishments be that much sweeter if you had someone to come home to and share them with?"

They absolutely would.

A longing she hadn't known existed reverberated inside her. The need for something, someone, in her life that had nothing to do with competing, and everything to do with wanting her for herself. Rachel. Not the athlete, but the woman.

Flaws and all.

Could she do it? Risk opening herself up to a relationship with someone who had the potential of utterly destroying her heart if he decided she wasn't worth the trouble? And even if she did, could she risk angering her dad by not giving her training the hundred and fifty percent he demanded from her?

That thought crushed her burgeoning hopes as effectively as an avalanche.

"I don't think Dad would be happy with me dividing my concentration right now."

Ari made a rude noise. "When are you going to get over this belief that Karl knows everything?"

"He wants what's best for me." That much she was certain of, no matter what.

"You mean for his little mini-me."

"That's not fair. He's my dad. He loves me."

"Oh, I never doubted that. But you do realize he'd love you no matter what, don't you? Even if you never won another medal, never skied another race, that man would love you to pieces."

Her throat tightening with emotions she couldn't quite identify, she grabbed for the wine and poured them both another half glass. She took a deep swallow before attempting to speak. "I know that. But I promised him gold, and I won't go back on my word."

Ari sighed. "Stubborn girl. I swear, sometimes I think you're more like him than if you were his own blood."

The reminder that she wasn't helped fuel her determination to never disappoint her dad again. Even if it meant giving up Theo.

Then she remembered.

"All of this is moot, anyway, if I can't figure out how to find my nerve again." Because whatever was wrong, it was in her head, not her body. That much she'd proven, at least. "I totally sucked on the Super G course."

"You knew your first time back would be hard. Cut yourself some slack."

"I did, the first day. So did Dad. But the second day was just as bad. Worse, even. Every time I managed to stay on my feet and pick up some speed, the fear of hitting a bump wrong or taking a turn too sharp came out of nowhere and had me freezing up and wiping out. It's like I'm being sabotaged by myself."

"Maybe you are. Maybe your subconscious is trying to tell you you're not ready to go back yet."

She shook her head. "I don't have a choice. Not if I'm going to be ready to race in October." Even saying the words made her stomach cramp up.

Damn it, what was *wrong* with her?

Ari was watching her with those witchy green eyes, stroking the cat in long, languid movements. "Remember what the cards said, lovie. The journey won't be a smooth one, but you'll find the right path. You just have to trust in yourself."

That was part of the problem. She didn't.

Not in her love life, and not in her career.

A year ago, even with a steel rod shoved in her leg, she never doubted what it was she wanted. Hell, even in the midst of the most grueling physical therapy she'd ever endured, it had been her guiding light. Her singular goal.

But as she'd worked toward her comeback, something seemed to have shifted ever-so subtly inside her. So subtly she'd never realized it until the time came for her to leave behind the new life she'd built for herself.

Her new friends.

New job.

The time to literally stop and smell the roses growing in her fathers' garden.

Going back to her pre-injury life of constant travel and stress after all of that delicious freedom was like trying to squeeze back into a skin that didn't quite fit anymore.

And despite knowing she had no choice, there was a small, traitorous part of her that didn't want to try. That liked having a home which was more than just a place to rest between competitions. That enjoyed being able to come hang out at a friend's house when the mood struck, without having to work it around her training, travel, and sponsor appearances.

That wanted Theo, so badly she could taste it.

How could she trust herself when she didn't even understand this new person she seemed to be now? One willing to risk her dad's displeasure, to break one of the most important rules she'd lived her entire life by—not to disappoint either of her parents, *ever*—all for a man she'd known less than a week?

Letting herself into the house a few hours later, she was relieved to find no one waiting to ambush her in the foyer this evening. Her feelings were still too tangled up to handle another round with her dad.

The extra glass of wine was going to make her pay tomorrow if she didn't hydrate tonight, so she detoured to the kitchen for a glass of water before heading up to her room. She was about to crawl under the covers when a soft knock came at the door.

For a split second she considered pretending to be asleep, then shook her head at herself and went to answer it. She might be confused, but she wasn't a coward.

Not that much of one, anyway.

She cracked the door. Karl was standing in the hall, dressed in dark green pajamas with a thick matching robe tied over them. From his unrumpled state, it didn't look like he'd been to bed yet himself. His expression was harder to read. "Hey, Dad."

"Sorry to bother you so late, but can I come in for a minute? I need to talk to you about something."

Damn, maybe she should have pretended to be asleep after all.

"Sure." She hesitated, not sure if this was going to be a standing kind of conversation or not, then sat on the edge of the bed. Always hope for the best, right? "So, what's up?"

"I wanted to apologize."

It was a good thing she was sitting, otherwise she might have fallen over. "Oh?"

A quicksilver smile flashed over his face. "No need to look so surprised. I have been known to apologize before."

Rarely. And usually not without some prodding.

"Is Pop making you do this?"

"No." His gaze slipped sideways under her continued stare. "Although he might have made me realize I was out of line with a few of the things I said last night. And I was."

"Yeah, you were."

He met her eyes again. "But nobody's making me apologize. I own up to my mistakes when I make them."

Not that he'd actually said what those were.

In the past she would have just accepted the apology, vague as it was, and called it a day. But that discontented corner of her soul, the part stirring to life the last few months, wouldn't let her.

"And what is it exactly you're apologizing for?"

She'd surprised him. Tugging at his ear, he leaned back against the dresser and crossed his arms. "For implying you weren't taking your training seriously. And for the crack about you, you know. Goofing off." He grimaced as he said it.

So did she. "Yeah, let's just forget that one entirely, okay?"

"Agreed." He cleared his throat. "And I'm sorry if I haven't been supportive of you wanting to finish out the season at Alta Luxe. I know you take your commitments seriously, and it was wrong for me to keep hounding you to treat it like your job there wasn't important."

That sounded more like Dellin than Karl, but she'd take it.

Of course, the fact the season was almost over may have made him a bit more magnanimous than he might have been if it was only December or January. "Thanks, Dad. That means a lot."

"And speaking of Luxe, I had an interesting call from Matt DiBenedetto this afternoon."

"Oh?" The word was a rusty croak.

Maybe she wouldn't have to wait until tomorrow to find out if she was fired, after all. But why would Vicky's father call her dad instead of her? It didn't make sense. Unless the point was to humiliate her, in which case, mission accomplished.

She swallowed hard. "What did he want?"

"He wanted me to consider taking over as his daughter's coach for the last race of the cup season." He seemed amused and a little baffled by the offer. "Can you believe it?"

"Wow. That's...unexpected." Jealousy surged, hot and angry, at the mere idea of her father becoming Vicky's coach, no matter how temporary.

How had she not considered Matt might try to hire him after Claude bailed? Karl was one of the best, and the DiBenedettos accepted nothing less when it came to their little darling.

"What did you tell him?"

"What do you think? Thanks, but no thanks. Sure, Vicky's an up-and-comer, but I only coach one champion, and that's you."

His words didn't soothe her turmoil, but she tried to think past her own petty jealousy. "Are you sure? It would give you a chance to go to Sweden, see some of your friends."

He narrowed his eyes. "Are you saying you *want* me to coach her?"

"No! I mean, I don't know." She tipped her head back with a huff of frustration. "I guess maybe I just realized my injury hasn't kept only me away from the circuit. It cut you off from all of your friends there, too. You haven't seen any of them in over a year."

"There's this thing called the internet? Amazing little invention. Let's you talk to people all over the world as if you're there, without having to go through the nightmare of airport security."

She appreciated his levity, but she'd seen him with his circle of friends over the years. Most were former-competitors-turned-coaches like himself, who sat around swapping stories about their glory days over pitchers of beer.

An email or video chat didn't even come close.

"I'm just saying, if you wanted to do it, maybe you should."

"And what about your training?"

"The race is in what, ten days? That means you'd be back right after my last day at Luxe, so we could still get started on schedule." The more she thought about it, the better she liked the idea of getting a little time without her father breathing down her neck to figure out her issues on the slope.

And what she was going to do about Theo.

Of course, that meant giving Vicky her father for the next week and a half, which totally sucked. She didn't share well with others when it came to her parents. Never had. It was probably one reason her dads hadn't adopted another child when she knew they would have loved a big family.

Something she still felt guilty about.

But she was an adult now, damn it. She should be able to handle her possessive jealousy better than this. Especially when it was something her dad might really want.

The acid churning in her stomach as she waited for his response said she still had a ways to go on that.

"I guess I can talk it over with your father," he said finally.

The fact he was even considering it told her she'd done the right thing. Even so, her insecurities were ripping at her like kitten claws, small but oh-so sharp. "Just don't get too used to her, if you do decide to go. You're only on loan."

With a grin, he walked over and pressed a kiss to the top of her head. "Don't you worry, sweetheart. No one could ever replace you." He closed the door on his way out, leaving her staring after him, emotions churning.

If only she could be sure that was true.

Chapter 15

"Theo, darling, do you have a moment?"

Whenever his mother used that sweetly innocent tone, it was time to run for cover. Only, some imp of bad timing had left him vulnerable in the wide-open space of the hallway between his office and Richard's, with no convenient place to hide.

Or rather, good timing, judging by the determined smile on her face as she approached, a stack of folders in her arms. She'd planned her ambush spot well.

"Like a lamb to the slaughter," he muttered.

"What was that, dear?"

"Nothing." He pasted on his own smile and gave her a dutiful peck on the cheek. "I was just going to—"

"Meet Richard for lunch. Yes, he told me."

The traitor.

"Would you care to join us?" It would serve his brother right to get caught in his own snare. Besides, misery loved company.

"Actually, he asked me to tell you he had something come up and can't make it. But I'd love to have lunch with you, dear. Thank you for asking."

"Ah..." Trapped by his own words, he scrambled for an excuse before giving up. He was well and truly stuck. "Do you want me to drive to the restaurant, or should I have a car brought around?" She wasn't particularly fond of riding in his low-slung Porche Boxster.

"Actually, I already ordered something in for us. I hope you don't mind."

His wary instincts went on high alert.

"Meaning you plotted this ahead of time."

"Plotted sounds so...Machiavellian."

"If the high heel shoe fits."

"Really, Theo. I thought your sister was the melodramatic one in the family. So I wanted to have lunch with my son who's been avoiding my phone calls and skipping family brunches. Is that a crime?"

"One brunch, Mom. I missed one."

But there wasn't anything he could say about dodging her calls. He had been. After his chat with Richard the other day, he hadn't wanted to get cornered into a conversation about his so-called "dangerous" hobbies with her.

Sort of like he was now.

There was no doubt in his mind if he turned around and walked away like he wanted to, she'd be parked in his driveway later tonight waiting to ambush him again. Bowing to the inevitable, he accompanied her toward the executive suites on the other side of the building that mirrored his and Richard's.

One belonged to their father. Their mother had claimed the other to run the Everbrite Foundation out of after his sister had chosen her art over the family business. He pulled out a chair at the small round table in his mother's office for her, where covered dishes from his favorite Italian restaurant were waiting.

Machiavellian indeed.

Inhaling the incredible aroma of the shrimp scampi—also a favorite—as he removed the domed lid, he slid a napkin to his lap and dug in. Maybe if he ate fast enough, he could enjoy some of it before the lecture began.

"So." His mother shook her napkin out and spread it over her lap with precise movements of her elegant hands. "What's this I hear about you jumping out of an airplane?"

Or maybe not.

Swallowing the pasta that had turned to paste in his mouth, he reached for his glass of water. "There was a plane. I jumped out of it. Sounds like you're up to speed." When she shot him a warning look he remembered all too well from childhood, he sighed. "I went skydiving, Mom. I don't know what else you want me to say."

"I want you to say you won't do it again."

He could, but he'd be lying. Dropping through the air towards the ground below had been both the most terrifying and most exhilarating thing he'd ever done. How could he not want to see if he got the same rush the second time around?

Rather than answer, he asked his own question.

"I've been doing extreme sports practically my whole life. Why this sudden concern?"

"If you think I haven't worried about you every time you set off on one of your crazy adventures, then you're quite mistaken." She stabbed a piece of broccoli from her pasta primavera and ate it, not meeting his surprised gaze.

"I'm sorry." And he was.

Making his mother worry was the last thing he ever wanted to do. He studied her as he took a bite of succulent shrimp. Her stylishly cut hair was the same brown as his own, but there was a lot more silver threaded through it than he remembered.

His fault?

"I swear to you, the skydiving company was one of the best out there. They're fully accredited, and have some of the most experienced instructors in the state. They've never had an accident with a student."

"And yet, accidents do happen."

A chill ran down his spine. Damn it, she wouldn't go there, would she?

"Accidents can always happen," he said through tight lips. "Anywhere. Anytime. That's why they're called accidents." The food he shoveled into his mouth had lost all interest for him, but the sooner he finished, the sooner he could escape.

"True. They can even happen when someone is experienced, and very good at what they do."

The comment could have easily been mistaken for a continuation of their discussion about his skydiving, but he knew better. "Mom. Don't."

"An accident, by definition, is unexpected and unintentional. As you said, it's not something you can predict. It just happens. No matter how careful you are or what you do to prevent it."

He slapped his fork onto the table. "We are *not* talking about this."

"We *are* going to talk about it, because you haven't yet, not in all these months, and it's obvious you're still beating yourself up over something which wasn't your fault."

Anger and guilt welled up like twin geysers, propelling him out of his seat and toward the door, words that should never be said to his mother, not even in anger, crowding his tongue. He needed to get out before any of them broke free.

"Theodore Ezekiel Beaumont, don't you *dare* leave this room while I'm speaking to you."

Even at thirty-two, being triple named by his mother in that tone had the power to stop him in his tracks.

Damn it!

Hands clenched at his sides, he swallowed back both the words and anger before he turned. "This isn't the time or the place for this, Mom." But he still retook his seat when she continued to stare him down.

"I know, and I'm sorry, but you really gave me no other choice. We all tried to give you space to grieve after your friend died because it seemed to be what you needed. But I'm starting to think that was a mistake. You've been pulling away from your family, taking crazy risks with your life—"

"I miss one meal and do one skydive, and suddenly I'm, what? Depressed? Suicidal?" The look she gave him said yes even if she didn't.

Shit.

"Let's call it reckless," she said finally. "And it isn't just the skydiving, Theo. The month before that, you skied that ridiculous extreme terrain course in Canada where they have all the avalanches. And the month before, you went whitewater rafting in Australia and nearly had your arm torn off."

"Hardly that." But she didn't let him continue.

"And the month before *that* you flew to the Caribbean and instead of relaxing on the beach, you ended up swimming with a bunch of sharks. With no cage." Her voice had gotten slightly shriller as she spoke, betraying her agitation. "All these outlandish...*adventures* of yours started right after Gavin's accident, and they've become progressively more dangerous every time. So, you tell me, what am I supposed to think?"

His knee-jerk response was *I'm a grown man and don't have to explain myself to you*, but hearing the last four months of his life laid out that way gave him pause.

Yes, he'd always enjoyed extreme sports. But in moderation. One crazy trip a year, maybe two if something extra special and unique came up, like snowmobiling into the northern wilds of Canada to catch a total solar eclipse. The rest of the time, he limited his adrenaline-inducing fun to the activities he could find closer to home. Especially rock climbing.

Something that had been impossible for him to do since the day he got the call about Gavin being killed on one of their favorite rock faces.

Which was when everything on his mother's list had started.

"Maybe after seeing how easily life can be snuffed out in the blink of an eye, I wanted to feel as alive as I possibly can."

She shook her head. "I know you think you're somehow responsible for what happened—"

"I am responsible, Mom. I'm the reason he was out there by himself."

"No, *he's* the reason. Nobody forced him to climb that morning."

Part of him agreed with her.

But the other part, the part that couldn't forget the way Gavin's mother and sister had looked at him at the funeral, knew better. They saw what he did every time he looked in the mirror: the man who could have prevented tragedy from occurring, if only he'd cared enough to be there.

But he hadn't.

He'd chosen a few extra hours of sleep instead, and now Gavin was gone. Forever and always. And Theo was left with the guilt and knowledge that by changing one simple, selfish decision, he wouldn't be.

"If I'd been there, things might have gone differently."

She laid a hand on his arm, her voice softening. "Have you ever considered if you'd been there, the thing that might have been different could have been *your* anchor breaking loose instead of his? That it could have been you who died?"

No, not really.

Because he never would have used the inadequate anchor points to set his nuts that Gavin did. He'd spoken with the park rangers who investigated the accident, trying to wrap his head around how such a senseless and tragic thing could have happened. And they'd both said the same thing. Every one of Gavin's anchors that day had been set poorly. Almost like an amateur had done them.

Or someone who'd been spitting in the eye of fate.

Since Gavin was an even better climber than he was, that knowledge had left him with one possible conclusion.

Theo might not be suicidal. But Gavin just might have been.

And no one had noticed. Not Theo. Not his family.

Nobody.

That, more than anything else, made it impossible for him to shake the guilt which had ridden him ever since. Not that he'd shared his suspicions with anyone. The last thing he wanted was to taint Gavin's memory and cause his family any more pain than what they were already going through.

The official report said it was a tragic accident, and that's what it would remain.

One more burden he carried alone.

He put his hand over his mother's where it lay on his arm, concerned by how cold it felt. That proof of how worried she was for him made him choose his words with care.

"Mom, I promise you, I'm always careful, no matter how it might seem to you. I plan to live a long, healthy life and kick the bucket exactly like *arrière grand père* Beaumont did."

His crappy accent brought a flicker of a smile to his mother's face. "At ninety-nine, in bed with a glass of wine in one hand and a woman in the other?"

"Not a bad way to go." They shared a grin at the much-exaggerated family legend of his Cajun great-grandfather, and he felt some of the tension seep out of her. "I'll cut back on my 'crazy adventures' if it will make you feel better."

"It would."

"Okay. Consider it done." He patted her hand and released it. "Now, if you don't mind, I've got work to get back to."

"But what about your lunch?"

One look at the half-eaten meal in front of him and his stomach clenched the way it had the split-second before the parachute had snapped open. "I guess I'm full." He gave her a cheek-peck and retreated before she could call him on the lie.

It took every bit of self-control he had not to head for Richard's office and rip him a new hole for throwing him under the mom-bus. Instead, he went to his own suite, told his PA to reschedule anything on his afternoon calendar for Monday, and did something he'd never done in all the years he'd worked at the firm.

He ditched work and went home early.

But no matter how fast his road-hugging little sports car zipped through the winding roads to his secluded neighborhood, he couldn't shake the guilt that clung to him like sticky cobwebs. Or the litany of "what-ifs" which beat like a drum inside his head.

What if he'd said yes when Gavin called that morning instead of saying he was too tired and hungover?

What if he'd offered to climb later in the day, once his head had cleared, instead of flat-out refusing?

What if he'd heard the desperation in his friend's request instead of bitching at him for calling so damn early and waking him up?

Once home, he stripped out of his suit, dragged on sweats and a t-shirt, and went to the small but well-equipped gym in the basement. Music blaring over the speakers, he attacked his workout with all the pent-up pain and anger that had chased him home.

Once his muscles began to burn, he slowed down, but not by much.

An hour later, body dripping with sweat and aching, he grabbed a sports drink from the mini fridge in the gym and gulped it down on his way up to his bedroom. A long, hot shower under the pounding spray of the multi body-jet system he'd splurged on went a long way toward making him feel human again. But it couldn't stop his mind from continuing to pick at the things his mother had said.

Was he being reckless?

He hadn't thought so. He'd thought he was simply grabbing life by the throat and draining every drop out of it he could. But maybe...maybe he'd been trying a little too hard to thumb his nose at death. Maybe it was time to dial it back, just a little. At least until his mother stopped riding his ass, anyway. Then he could go back to pushing the envelope, albeit a bit more carefully.

A dark blue towel wrapped around his waist, he was halfway to his closet when the phone in his suit jacket on the bed rang. He ignored it. He wasn't ready to deal with his brother just yet.

Once dressed in faded jeans and a flannel shirt over a tee, he felt a little better. But there was something still twitching right below the surface. Some deep sense of dissatisfaction he couldn't put a name to that the punishing workout hadn't fully quenched.

When the phone rang again, he cursed and dug it out of his suit, ready to give Richard the grief he deserved until he saw the name on the screen. A smile broke across his face.

"Rachel, hi."

"Hi. I, um, hope it's okay to be bothering you at work like this." She sounded adorably unsure of herself.

"No, it's fine. I'm actually not at work. I took the afternoon off."

"Oh, so you already have plans. Never mind, then."

"The only plan I had was to not be at work." And not kill his brother, but she didn't need to know that part. "What's up?"

"Well, I was wondering if you might want to do something tonight."

Stretching out on the large bed, he relaxed with his back against the headboard. The restlessness inside relaxed with him. "I thought we had a date for tomorrow night?"

"Maybe I don't want to wait that long to see you again."

He adjusted the pillow behind his back. The one she'd used. It still carried the faint scent of her. He pulled in a deep lungful of it. "Maybe I don't want to, either."

"Thank God." A quick laugh followed the faint words. "Oops. Didn't mean to say that out loud."

"Would it help if I said I was thinking the same thing?"

There was a slight pause. "Yeah, it would. Thanks." She cleared her throat. "So, um, what would you like to do?"

"You." It was his turn to give a self-conscious laugh. "Yeah, didn't mean to say that out loud, either. Sorry." The silence from the phone was unnerving. "Rachel? I didn't mean to offend you."

"You didn't." Her voice was low and a little breathy. "You made me hot."

He groaned. "Do you want to come over now?"

"I wish. But unlike you, I'm still at work. And now I have to give my last lesson while I'm thinking about doing all sorts of naughty things with you."

He groaned louder as his lower body pulled taut in his jeans. "You're killing me."

"Just making sure you're thinking about me, too."

"Like there was any doubt." He wouldn't be able to do anything else. "Come over when you get off work. I'll make us dinner."

"You don't have to go to all that trouble for me." Her voice lowered to a whisper. "I'm a sure thing, remember?"

For some reason, her words bothered him.

"It's no trouble. Do you like lasagna?"

She hesitated long enough before answering he was certain she was going to protest again. Then she said, "That sounds wonderful. What can I bring?"

"Just you. And your imagination," he added, getting the whimper of reaction he was hoping for.

"I'll get even for that."

"I'm counting on it."

After ending the call, he stayed stretched out on his bed, replaying the nuances of the conversation in his head. Rachel was turning out to be a delightful distraction, but she was also something more. He just wasn't sure what that was yet.

But he had a feeling he was going to enjoy finding out.

Chapter 16

"I think we ruined dinner."

Rachel's droll comment brought a smile to his lips. Rolling his head slightly on the pillow, he pressed a kiss to the warm, firm skin of her arm.

"It'll keep. But even if we did, it was worth it." He kissed her again, teeth scraping lightly over the gentle curve of her shoulder as he inched his way up toward her neck. "Don't you think?"

"I, ah..." She seemed to lose her train of thought as he found the throbbing pulse at the side of her neck and he ran his tongue along it.

"You were saying?"

"I was saying, um, that you went to all the trouble to cook, so we should probably—ooooh." It came out as more sound than word as he closed his mouth over that tender spot and suckled gently.

Not hard enough to mark her. But enough to tease the nerve endings just under the delicate layer of skin to life.

It didn't matter that he'd spent the last two hours delighting in every inch of her delectable body. Every sound of pleasure he could drag from her was still a victory. Every discovery of another erogenous zone—like her neck—another quiver in his arrow for future sensual forays.

Of course, she'd done her share of making him groan as well.

One hand slid over her right breast, caressing it in soft circles as his mouth nibbled up under her chin, causing a shudder. He found her mouth with his. She returned the kiss with an almost drugged lassitude. When it was done, she lay passive against the pillow, her mesmerizing eyes blinking up at him with a glaze of total satiation.

"Fuck dinner."

Her unexpected words made him tip his head back and laugh.

Without warning, he grabbed her around the waist and rolled onto his back, bringing her with him so she was lying flush on top of him. "I'd rather fuck you. Again. But in order to do that, we need to keep our strength up, which means I have to feed you first."

Not to mention his cock needed a little recovery time. Even with her delightfully naked body sprawled over his, there was barely a twitch.

As surprise from the quick change of position bled away the lethargy in her expression, Rachel pushed herself upright to straddle the overused body part in question. Hands braced on his sweat-dampened chest, she gave him a smile that reminded him of his friend Nolan's cat after a hit of catnip.

Even more so when she stretched her upper body, neck and shoulders reaching up and back as her palms stayed anchored, like some erotic yoga pose. Her firm breasts with their tight, dusky nipples swaying tantalizingly close yet just out of reach of his mouth.

Planned or not, the pose also pressed her mound more intimately against his groin. Which suddenly showed a spark of life where a minute ago he'd been certain it would take an hour or two to recharge.

"Or we could just stay here." He groaned as her lower body did some sort of shimmy, but as he reached for her, she slid away and climbed off the bed.

"I thought you were going to feed me first? You know, to keep up my strength." She ran her hands up her ribcage and over her breasts before throwing them up over her head in another sexy stretch.

The little tease.

Well, two could play at that game.

He stroked a hand along the length of his growing erection. "And what am I supposed to do with *this* now that you woke it up?"

The hungry look she gave his body said she'd be happy to show him. Then a smile tilted her lips as she scooped up his discarded t-shirt from the floor. "Why don't you use your imagination?"

She slipped the shirt over her head, the hem coming down like a curtain over her exquisite ass as she exited the bedroom, laughter trailing behind her.

He stared after her in disbelief for a second before dropping his head back onto the pillow with a laughing groan. Then he was off the bed, dragging on a pair of sweats before following her. She was already in the kitchen, peeking under the cover of the casserole dish he'd hastily thrown back in the oven on warm earlier.

She threw him a saucy grin over her shoulder. "Looks like it stayed nice and *hot* for us."

"Okay, okay, you win," he said with a laugh. He hugged her from behind. "I shouldn't have teased you while you were at work."

The grin turned smug. "Told you I'd get even."

"Yes, you did." His lips brushed her ear. "And I enjoyed every second of it." Pressing a kiss to the delicate shell at the same time he pressed another, more insistent part of his body against her ass, he felt her breath catch.

Mission accomplished.

He reached for the potholders hanging limply in her hands, transferring the hot dish to the table he'd set before she arrived. After serving them both, he forked up a sample bite. The noodles were a little dry around the edges and the cheese had congealed somewhat, but overall not too bad considering how long it had been left in the oven.

"This is really good."

The surprise in her voice was too endearing to be an insult. "Told you I could cook."

"You didn't lie."

The praise shouldn't have made him feel as pleased as it did. He hadn't cooked to impress her. He'd used it as an excuse to get her to his house with the hopes of coaxing her back into his bed.

Not that she'd required any persuading. They'd barely gotten "hello" out of the way before they fell on each other like a couple of sex-starved teenagers.

You don't have to go to all that trouble for me. I'm a sure thing, remember?

The memory of her earlier comment still rankled. Maybe that was why it mattered so much she like the meal.

No one should ever feel they weren't worth a little extra effort.

With that in mind, he sought a safe topic of conversation to help counter the almost visceral sexual tension simmering between them. "So, how was your day, dear?"

"Definitely better than yesterday. How about yours, sweetheart?"

"It was definitely worse than yesterday. But"—he looked across the table at her with a slow grin—"it's improving by the minute."

The look she gave from under her lashes sent a lance of fire straight to his groin.

"Oh, I can almost guarantee it's going to get even better."

So much for a safe topic.

Determined to get through the meal without self-combusting from lust, he applied himself to his food and tried again. "What movie do you want to see tomorrow night?"

"I don't care. Whatever one you pick is fine."

"Come on, you must have a preference. Action? Thriller? Comedy? Sci-fi?"

She shrugged. "I like it all. Streaming channels were my new best friend while I was recovering from the surgeries on my leg and knee. I became a bit of an omnivore, watching anything and everything."

The reminder of her accident sent a feeling of a different kind snaking through his belly, but he fought to keep it from showing. "Okay. But just so you know, if you're into chick-flicks you're out of luck. That's where I draw the line."

"Duly noted," she said, grinning.

They ate for a few moments in silence. It felt weirdly normal, sitting at his table with this woman, eating a meal as though they weren't both mostly naked. His t-shirt hid all the curves he'd only recently explored, but he remembered each of them. Intimately. They were forever burned into his memory, along with every other part of her delectable body.

What would she think if he stripped the shirt away and laid her across the table for dessert?

"If you keep looking at me like that, we're never going to get through the meal."

Her throaty words cut through the fantasy. His eyes swept up to meet hers. "Like what?"

In answer, her bare foot touched his, then slid up his leg like a warm caress until it found the erection his sweats did little to hide. "Like that."

He growled as her toes curled against him. "If you wanted to get through the meal, you wouldn't be doing that."

When she pressed her toes against the length of him again, he dropped his fork with a clatter. He stood, sending his chair skittering back, eyes never leaving hers, which were dancing with heated triumph.

With a toss of her head that was all dare, she slowly got to her feet.

That was all it took to snap the leash.

She let out a squeal of laughter as he lunged around the table, sliding out of his reach and scampering from the room. He stalked after her, following the sound of her laughter back up to his bedroom, where she was waiting for him, gloriously naked on her knees in the middle of the bed.

He stripped off the sweats and joined her, the fever they both seemed in thrall to leading the dance. Their lovemaking was swift and fierce. But as he lay sated in the aftermath with her curled into him as she dozed, he had the feeling no matter how many times he had her, it would never be enough.

Chapter 17

She wasn't supposed to like him this much.

After she'd dragged herself home the night before, body limp as a well-wrung rag, she'd been sure she finally managed to screw the man right out of her system.

But no.

He'd been the first thought she had when the alarm yanked her from sleep this morning. The image that made her linger far too long in the shower, daydreaming. The person she'd counted the minutes until seeing again after work today.

Canceling their movie date tonight would have been the smart thing to do.

Keeping her distance in the future smarter still.

But as she'd been working up the nerve to call and tell him that, the emptiness of the house had pressed in on her, reminding her not one, but both of her parents were now halfway around the world. Matt DiBenedetto had offered the option of bringing Dellin along as a little extra incentive when Karl told him he was reconsidering his offer.

Or an outright bribe, since even Matt wasn't entirely blind to what a raging bitch his precious little girl could be.

Whichever it was, her fathers had taken both the bait and the job, and hopped onto the DiBenedetto private jet and flown off for Sweden yesterday before she'd even gotten home from work.

Logically, she understood why. Her dad had little enough time to work with Vicky and evaluate what needed to be addressed before the race. Every day he got with her was important. More important than delaying just so she could hug her daddies goodbye.

But logic didn't rule the insidious little voice which whispered inside her head.

See, it's starting already, just the way you knew it would. She's already more important to him than you are, because she's a champion and you're a loser.

She knew it wasn't true. She did.

But those whispers were controlled by pure emotion, born of a lifetime of worry, and no logic in the world could silence them.

Which had been the driving force behind her impulsive call to Theo, asking if he wanted to get together last night. She needed something to take her mind off of her ridiculous insecurities, and a night of mind-blowing sex seemed the perfect solution.

And she'd been right. The sex *had* been mind-blowing, and she hadn't thought about her dad flying off to coach Vicky even once.

She just hadn't expected it all to backfire on her quite so spectacularly.

Because while the sex was fierce and joyful and thoroughly distracting, there had been moments when things strayed a little too close to being something else.

Something more.

That was why she had put an end to the far-too domestic feeling of sitting at his cozy kitchen table, eating a meal he'd cooked for her himself as they chatted about their days. One touch under the table, and she'd set the evening—and their relationship—back on its proper track.

Or so she'd thought.

The fact she had just spent two hours in a dark movie theater holding hands with him proved otherwise.

So did giving in to his suggestion to join his friends for trivia night at one of the local pubs afterward, instead of heading immediately home for another round of scorching sex. She could have said no.

She *should* have said no.

Instead, she was wedged around one of the tall pub-style tables with high stools, playing a bar game with three of the best-looking men in the place. None of whom were too shy to let her know how much she sucked at it.

And she was enjoying every minute.

Except for the minutes she remembered she shouldn't be.

"We're getting our asses kicked," Jesse groaned as the quizmaster announced a break before the next round of questions.

The dark-haired pirate looked even more the part tonight than the last time she'd seen him on the slopes. The gold stud in his ear had been replaced by a silver cuff, which was joined by several thick rings and a leather necklace anchoring a chunky silver medallion in the notch of his throat. Swap out his black Henley for something with billowy sleeves, and he'd look right at home on the deck of the Black Pearl.

Although finding out he was a pediatrician had kind of blown that Jack Sparrow fantasy right out of the water.

Nolan, on the other hand, looked exactly like the lawyer he was. His closely cropped black hair and neatly trimmed beard and mustache gave him a polished finish not even the jeans and gray sweatshirt that proudly proclaimed him a Harvard alum could diminish. It took no imagination at all to picture him holding a courtroom spellbound with his commanding presence and cultured voice.

But no matter how attractive she might find both men, it was the one sitting next to her that held her complete attention.

Like Jesse, he wore jeans and a Henley, although his was a dark forest green that made his brown eyes seem even richer and more intense despite the dull bar lighting. Unlike Jesse, though, he'd taken the time to shave his weekend scruff away, leaving the line of his jaw bare and dangerously chiseled.

For her, he'd whispered when he kissed her at her door on picking her up. So he didn't leave any whisker burn in sensitive places later. She squeezed her thighs together to combat the tingle thinking about that unspoken promise caused.

Nolan, mistaking the reason for her squirming, patted her hand with a grin.

"Don't worry, love. Jess likes to bitch to hear his own voice. We're only in third place and there're still two rounds to go. Plenty of time to make a comeback."

"Hey, if anyone likes the sound of their own voice, it's you, *mate,*" Jesse replied with an exaggerated roll of his eyes.

"Well, he does have that nifty British accent."

Jesse gave her a disappointed look. "Not you, too."

She smiled and shrugged. What could she say? Accents were hot.

As Nolan continued to needle Jesse, Theo ran a hand down her thigh to clasp her knee under the table as he leaned closer. "If I didn't love him like a brother, I might have to punch his lights out for making you smile that way."

Turning her head so her lips pressed intimately to his ear, she murmured, "He may have made me smile, but you're the one who's going to make me scream later."

His hand tightened on her knee for a second before relaxing again, the only outward reaction he gave to her words. Until she pulled back and could see his eyes, which had heated to something dark with intimate promise.

"Count on it."

They stared at each other for a few long seconds from only inches apart, close enough for her to smell the sexy scent of slightly heated man underneath the woodsy cologne he wore. Jesse cleared his throat.

"If you can tear yourself away from your lady for a minute, bro, this round is yours."

She sat back in her seat, heat stinging her face at being caught acting like a besotted schoolgirl.

Theo leaned back to give the waitress holding a tray of drinks room. "Sorry, Celeste." He reached for his wallet as the empty beer pitcher on the table was swapped for a full one. But when Celeste placed a tall blue beer can that read Blonde Bombshell Ale in front of him, he froze mid-motion. "What's that?"

"Compliments of the lady at the bar." She shot an apologetic look at Rachel before continuing. "I told her you were drinking draft, but she said this had special meaning for the two of you."

A sick sensation that might have been jealousy burned away Rachel's earlier embarrassment as she watched Theo's face blank of any emotion.

While Jesse cursed under his breath, Nolan snatched up the can and put it back on the tray along with some money, since Theo was still frozen in place. "We won't be needing this, thanks."

Celeste hesitated, as though waiting to see if Theo would protest. When he didn't, she asked, "Any message you want to send back?"

Jesse replied for him. "She's not expecting one."

Curiosity lit her expression, but when no one said anything else, she shrugged and left to deliver the rest of her drink orders.

And still, Theo said nothing.

Instead, he shifted his gaze toward the bar.

Rachel knew the second he saw who he was looking for, by the way the muscle along his clean-shaven jaw jumped. Her stomach did a flip, but she forced herself to follow his line of sight and find his mystery admirer.

It wasn't hard to pick her out of the crowd. She was the only one staring back with an expression of raw hatred on her face.

Rachel swallowed. The woman was in her thirties, her short hair that rare natural shade of white-blonde no salon could quite match, her body painfully thin under the oversized sweater and leggings. She was pretty, or she would have been if she hadn't been exuding such malevolence from every pore of her being.

Ex-girlfriend? Spurned lover? Whoever she was, it was clear she loathed Theo with the strength of a thousand suns.

Theo started to slide off his stool, only to have Jesse grab his arm. "What do you think you're doing?"

"I should talk to her."

"The hell you should!"

Nolan was more eloquent, but no less vehement.

"Theo, as your lawyer, I strongly advise against it. She's clearly trying to provoke contact. Don't give her what she wants."

Theo let out a harsh bark of unhappy laughter. "What she wants is her brother not to be dead, and I can't give her that, now can I?" The muscle in his jaw ticced again. "The least I can do is give her the satisfaction of calling me a bastard to my face."

"Not tonight, you don't." Nolan shot a meaningful look at Rachel before pinning his friend with a stare that probably made witnesses quake on the stand.

Theo remained rigid for several seconds before his shoulders slumped and he nodded. He turned to her, his expression no longer blank, but bleak.

"I'm sorry about this. You didn't need to get pulled into my drama."

Jealousy was quickly being overridden by curiosity. "I'm not even sure what 'this' is. Anyone care to enlighten me?"

All three men shifted uncomfortably. Theo finally broke the awkward silence. "Loretta's brother, Gavin, was a friend of mine. He died in a rock-climbing accident a few months ago. That was his favorite beer."

Her mind went immediately to the scar on his shoulder he'd said came from a climbing accident, but the scar tissue was a lot older than mere months. A different accident, then.

Still, the specter of what might have been chilled her.

"And she blames you?"

He nodded once, the movement tight and controlled.

"Which is utter bullshit, since he wasn't even there when it happened," Jesse said as he filled everyone's glasses. "But that doesn't stop her and her equally batshit mother from harassing Theo every chance they get."

"But if you weren't there..." She looked to Theo for an explanation, but he was too busy staring into the amber depths of his drink to answer. Nobody else did, either.

The feeling she was being shut out left a bad taste in her mouth, but it was just the reminder she needed. This wasn't a relationship. She was only here for the sex.

The music level dipped as the quizmaster announced they'd be starting the next trivia round in a few minutes, breaking the quiet tension around the table. Everyone was getting their answer sheets ready when Loretta slammed the blue can down at Theo's elbow, making them all jump.

"You do *not* get to just send this away like it doesn't matter he's not here," she said through clenched teeth. "Like *he* doesn't matter."

Theo looked stricken. "That's not—"

"You don't get to forget what you did. Ever." Tears choked her words.

"He didn't do anything, you crazy bitch," Jesse growled, coming out of his seat. Theo's raised hand stopped him.

"Loretta, if I could go back and change what happened that day, I would. Believe me. I miss him, too. Every day."

"Right. You're *so* torn up about it. That's why you're out laughing it up with your buddies, having a good time, and he's—" A sob ripped away further words.

Rachel almost pointed out Loretta was out at a bar having a good time herself, but the naked pain in the woman's eyes stilled her tongue. Instead, she tried to diffuse the tense situation by saying, "I'm very sorry for your loss."

The quiet sentiment seemed to confuse the other woman. She hesitated, her angry expression beginning to crumble before she reformed it into a snarl. "Go to hell."

All four of them watched in varying degrees of shocked silence as she shoved her way through the people trying to make it back to their tables for the next quiz round. Jesse shook his head and picked up his beer. "Told ya. Batshit crazy."

Rachel started when Theo's hand touched hers under the table, their fingers twining together in an almost painful grip. He wouldn't look at her, but she could read the desperation in his grasp, the need for an anchor in the wake of Hurricane Loretta.

She gave it to him.

As wordlessly as he had, she squeezed his hand. A slight tremor ran through him in response, but the subtle tension remained.

"We can go," she whispered.

He shook his head and reached for his beer with his free hand, draining the pilsner glass in several large gulps. Then he reached not for the pitcher, but the can Loretta had left behind. He stared at it, blinking rapidly as though holding back some stronger emotion.

"Gavin loved this pale ale crap." His fingers tightened around it.

Just when she thought the metal was going to dent under the pressure, he set it down and released her hand so he could pop the beer open and pour it into his empty glass. "A toast. To friends gone too soon."

Jesse and Nolan exchanged subtle looks before raising their glasses.

"To friends."

They all drank, but Theo was the only one to drain his glass dry. Again.

Unfortunately, it wasn't the last time, either.

Chapter 18

By the time the pub quiz was over, their team had dropped to a dismal fifth place.

Surprisingly, Jesse wasn't bitching about it.

Even more surprising, their lousy finish hadn't all been her fault.

Rachel eyed Theo with concern as he drank down the last of his beer. Everyone else had switched over to water when their last pitcher was empty, but he'd ordered another of those tall blue cans for himself.

And then another.

And one more for good measure.

So, it didn't surprise her when he wobbled like a first-time skier trying to find their center of gravity as he slid off his stool to leave. She caught his arm as he bumped the table, the empty beer and water glasses littering its surface rattling ominously, until he found his balance.

"Bro, you're in no shape to drive," Jesse said, frowning. "You should have stopped drinking when we did. This isn't like you."

So, it seemed getting shitfaced-drunk in public wasn't the norm. *Good to know.*

Taking a deep breath and straightening as best he could, Theo replied with over-exaggerated care. "I'm perfectly capable of driving home."

Yeah, not so much.

She reached into his jacket and took his keys, holding them in front of his face so he could see them before she put them in her own pocket.

Not missing a beat, he said, "I'm perfectly capable of being driven home."

"That's more like it. Come on, big guy." Jesse and Nolan each took an arm and somehow wrangled Theo out of the bar without making it obvious they were doing it. Rachel followed behind.

"I'm parked down this way," Jesse said, nodding to the right. "I'll take you both home."

She shook her head. "No, it's okay. I'll drive him to his place. I know where it is."

The two men looked at her in surprise.

Fair enough, since she'd surprised herself. But the memory of how tightly Theo had held onto her earlier, like she was the only thing keeping him from flying apart into a million pieces, made it feel important she be the one to get him home.

That if he finally shattered, he wouldn't want to do it in front of his friends.

"Are you sure, love?" Nolan asked.

"Yeah, it's fine."

After they got him buckled into the passenger seat of his Cayan, Jesse asked, "You gonna be okay getting him out again on the other end by yourself? I can follow you, if you want."

"Thanks, but I think we'll be good." She looked at Theo, knees a little too close to the dash, since no one had thought to adjust the seat back before cramming him and his long legs in. "As long as he's awake, anyway."

Jesse laughed and pulled her into a quick hug. "Drive safe."

"You, too." She looked at Nolan, expecting a similar friendly sendoff, only to find him studying her with a pensive frown. "What?"

The frown dissolved into a smile. "Just thinking Theo's a bloody lucky bastard, is all. Most women would have called themselves an Uber and left it to one of us to drive his drunken ass home."

"Yeah, well, I guess I'm not most women."

The smile turned wistful, almost sad. "Like I said. Lucky bastard." He dropped a quick kiss to her cheek and followed Jesse back down the street, turning to walk backwards so he could add, "Call if you end up needing help. My number's in his contact list."

After adjusting the driver's seat and mirrors, she began to doubt her ability to follow through on her self-appointed task. Yes, she'd been to Theo's house before. Twice. But she wasn't a hundred percent sure she could get there from here without some help.

A quick glance at her inebriated passenger confirmed she wouldn't be getting it from him. So, she fished out her phone and opened up the mapping app she'd used the night before, hoping the address was still in it.

"You're so beautiful."

The slurred words had her rolling her eyes. "You're so drunk."

"I know. I'm sorry." He sounded so forlorn she couldn't get mad at him.

"Don't be sorry. Just don't be sick, and we'll call it even."

Nothing squicked her out more than the rancid smell of vomit. Just the sound of someone heaving was enough to get her going, too. If Theo ended up puking while she was driving, they were both in serious trouble.

Glad she'd stopped at two beers since she had work in the morning, she followed the directions as her phone called them out. Eventually, the streets started to look familiar.

There was a moment of panic when the big black gates loomed in front of her, but as she tried to remember the guest code Theo had given her the night before, they swung open on their own. Thank God, the car must have had a transponder in it. She eased through, checking in the rearview that they closed again.

One obstacle down.

She looked at Theo.

One big one to go.

Prying him out of the car once she parked was the hardest part. But once he was upright, he only needed a little support to keep him that way. He was able to pick out the right key for the door so she didn't have to try them all, but shutting the alarm off turned out to be a bit trickier. After fumble-fingering through two incorrect codes, he finally just told her what it was so she could do it for him.

"You're going to need to change that tomorrow," she said, directing him through the kitchen and into the great room, where she deposited him on one of the long sofas. It was a good thing they were so big, because this was where he was spending the night. No way she was trying to get him up those stairs to his bedroom.

"Don't go," he said when she started to leave.

"I'll be right back."

In the kitchen, she searched the cupboards until she found the drinking glasses, then reconsidered. Opening the fridge, she grabbed a bottle of electrolyte-infused water and brought that to him instead. Much as she hated using plastic bottles when a glass would do, it was the safer choice to hand a drunk. "Here, drink."

He did, only to make a face after a few swallows. "This is shitty beer."

"That's because it's water."

"Oh." Frowning at the bottle, he asked, "Did we drink all the beer already?"

"Yes, Theo, you drank all the beer. Which is why you're going to have the hangover from hell tomorrow if you don't drink the water now. Where do you keep your aspirin?"

"What?"

"Aspirin. For the hangover."

"Oh. Umm...medicine cabinet. Bathroom." He made a vague gesture toward the stairs with the bottle, water sloshing.

It felt strange walking through his bedroom, past the neatly made bed where just twenty-four hours earlier they'd spent an entire evening laying naked in each other's arms, doing all kinds of delicious things to one another.

Her body thrummed at the memory.

Much as she'd been looking forward to a repeat performance this evening, that obviously wasn't happening. Instead, she was playing nursemaid to a man she was supposed to be getting less emotionally involved with, not more.

The smart thing to do would be to give him the aspirin and leave.

But did she do that?

No.

She went back downstairs with not just aspirin, but a pillow and blanket from the bed, and a pair of sweats and a t-shirt from his obscenely large walk-in closet. All so he'd be comfortable sleeping on the sofa.

"You're such a sucker, Rae," she muttered, shaking her head.

Theo sat in a different place on the sofa than where she'd left him, water abandoned on the coffee table. In his hands instead was a black-framed picture. A quick look around the room showed an empty spot on the wall beside the fireplace, right below a framed Colorado Avalanche jersey covered in signatures from their 2001 Stanley Cup winning team.

She wanted to yell at him for taking the risk of bashing his head in on the stone hearth if he'd stumbled and fallen, but the look on his face as he gazed at the picture stopped her cold. He looked...gutted. There was no other word for it.

Dropping everything on the second sofa, she shook two aspirin from the bottle into her palm and gave them to him. "Here."

He popped them in his mouth, accepting the water she handed him next to wash them down, never once looking away from the picture. She took the water back, hesitated, then sat gingerly beside him so she could see the photo.

It showed Theo and another man dressed in climbing gear. Filthy, exhausted, covered in sweat, arms looped over each other's shoulders as they grinned at the camera like a couple of conquering heroes, thumbs in the air.

"That's you and Gavin?" Not that she needed the confirmation. The white-blond hair identical to his sister Loretta's was a dead giveaway.

He nodded. "This was taken the first time we summited El Capitan. Biggest damn climb of my life. I almost called it quits three-quarters of the way up, but Gavin called me a pussy and told me I'd always regret it if I got that close to the top and chickened out."

He laughed, a sad, bitter sound. "He was right. I would have. It was one of the best days ever, conquering that mountain. I felt like I could do anything." His thumb stroked over the glass covering Gavin's grinning face. "I fucking miss him, Rae. I really fucking miss him."

Her heart pinched at the anguish in his voice. "Of course you do. He was your friend."

"He was. And now he's dead, because of me."

Feeling as though she were treading on shaky ground, she said, "I thought Jesse said you weren't there the day he died." Or had she misunderstood?

"I wasn't. That's why he's dead."

"That makes no sense."

"No, it doesn't. It never has." He laid his head against the back of the sofa and closed his eyes with a weary sigh. "He called me that morning, out of the blue, wanting me to go with him to North Table Mountain. I'd been out late the night before at my mother's charity masked ball, and it was barely freaking dawn out, and he wanted to go climbing."

"And you said no."

"And I said no. And he died."

"That's not your—"

"I think he killed himself. And I think he was hoping I'd stop him."

She stared at him, trying to absorb the import of the whispered words. "Why would you think that? Did he say something? Leave a note?"

"No. He was just…he was reckless. He went up a cliff we've done a hundred times. He knew where the bad spots were to anchor in, and he picked them anyway. Thumbing his nose at fate, deliberately. And fate won."

She wanted to argue bad choices didn't equal suicide, but it was doubtful anything she said would matter. "Even if that's true, it doesn't make it your fault it happened."

Eyes filled with grief and self-loathing pinned hers. "He reached out to me for help. And I blew him off." He looked down at the picture laying limp in his hand. "His mother and sister have every right to hate my guts."

She didn't agree. If Gavin really had been suicidal, his family should have been the ones to notice, not Theo. Something they probably already knew. That would explain the huge hate hard-on they had for him. If they could convince themselves it was Theo's fault, then it couldn't possibly be theirs.

Assholes.

Grieving ones, but still. It was totally unfair to make him carry that weight.

Sliding off the sofa to her knees, she started working on his shoelaces. "Why don't we get you more comfortable so you can get some sleep." It was a little troubling he sat so docile as she tugged off his shoes. She undid the button on his jeans, but hesitated before going for the zipper. What might have been sexy any other time now felt awkward.

"Nope, sorry."

Leaving his jeans intact, she helped him swing his legs up onto the sofa, sliding the picture frame from his hand as she did. He didn't seem to notice.

As she was sticking the pillow behind his head, he closed his eyes again. "There's another reason they hate me."

She grabbed the blanket and shook it open. "And what's that?"

"His last wishes were if he ever died on a mountain, he wanted me to spread his ashes on top of it, as a sort of cosmic fuck-you to the place." His words were getting slurry again as sleep edged in.

Well, that was a weird thing for someone to ask of a friend.

She draped the blanket over his long body. "Why are they mad at you for that?" When he didn't answer right away, she thought he'd fallen asleep.

But as she picked up the picture from where she'd laid it aside, he mumbled, "Because I can't. I can't get my damn feet off the ground. I've tried, and tried, and tried. But every damn time, I just can't do it. Not one inch. And I hate myself for being such a fucking coward more every time I fail."

His words hit such a personal place inside her she actually had to press a hand to her chest to hold in the pain.

How did he know?

But he couldn't. He didn't.

Logic reasserted itself. Clearly, he'd been talking about himself, not her. But his contempt for his own weakness mirrored her own, and for that, she felt like a strange sort of kinship connected them.

It was a horrible thing to find yourself ruled by your most irrational fears. Even more so when you knew you were letting someone else down because of it.

Light snores from the sofa told her he was asleep for real. Time for her to go.

Past time.

Staring at the picture in her hand, she studied Gavin's grinning face and shook her head, angry at the man she'd never met. Whatever happened that day, only he knew for sure.

And he wasn't talking.

Chapter 19

Something died in his mouth overnight.

It was the only explanation for the foul taste that greeted him the second his brain chugged over from sleep to semi-wakefulness. He tried to swallow it away, but it took several attempts just to work up enough saliva to unstick his sandpaper-dry tongue from the roof of his mouth.

That only made the taste worse.

With a groan, Theo cracked one eye a sliver and winced.

Why the hell was his bedroom so bright? Had he forgotten to close the drapes before going to bed? The thought ping-ponged around for a few seconds until he realized he didn't remember going to bed.

Hell, he didn't even remember coming home.

Forcing his eye open a bit wider, a bottle of water came into focus in his direct line of sight. Saying a prayer to the gods who took care of fools and drunks, he batted the blanket out of the way and grabbed it, drinking down every precious drop.

Better.

But Jesus fuck, he really needed to do something about the sunlight pouring through the patio doors before it split his head in two.

There was another ping-pong session as his brain lost some of its fuzziness and his thoughts solidified.

Patio doors?

Blinking against the harsh morning light, he slowly swung his legs off the sofa. What the hell was he doing down here? But even as he thought the question, bits and pieces of the previous evening were already filtering back into his memory like water refilling a wrung-out sponge.

Going to the movies with Rachel.

Trivia afterward at the pub.

The ugly scene with Loretta.

And beer. Lots and lots of beer.

"Son of a bitch." Even the soft words hurt his head.

Okay, that was most of the night. Everything that came after, though, was still hazy. Whatever it was, he had a feeling he wouldn't like it.

Urgency from his bladder got him on his feet and into the downstairs bathroom. Once that was taken care of, he was debating between going upstairs to shower or into the kitchen for coffee when he noticed the piece of paper filled with loopy handwriting on the low table between the two facing sofas.

A quick peek at the signature told him it was from Rachel.

"Oh, this can't be good." He sank onto the sofa to read it.

Theo~

Sorry, but I had to borrow your car so I could get home. It's at my house, you can come get it anytime. Or I can pick you up after I get off of work this afternoon and drive you to get it. Text me and let me know.

~Rachel

He blew out a breath he hadn't realized he was holding. At least it wasn't a 'drop-dead and never call me again' letter. But the fact he'd left her in a position of either getting a ride home from one of his friends who she barely knew, or borrowing a car she wasn't familiar with driving, made him furious at himself.

A wispy memory surfaced. Of her driving, telling him not to puke.

No, begging him not to.

He groaned.

"Beaumont, you are one sorry bastard."

Disgusted with himself, he tossed the note back onto the coffee table. And saw the picture frame laying there, facedown. His already queasy gut clenched as he reached for it, knowing what it was before he turned it over to see Gavin's face grinning up at him.

The sight caused more memories to bubble up from the quagmire of his beer-addled brain. Telling Rachel about climbing El Capitan. About Gavin's call. His death.

Hell, he'd even bared his soul about how he hadn't been able to fulfill his friend's final wishes because he was too damn scared to climb anymore.

Jesus, had he fucking *cried* in front of her?

Coffee. He definitely needed the coffee first.

Before that, though, he replaced the picture on the wall where it belonged. As he turned away, his eye caught on the collection of smaller photos scattered across the live-edge wooden mantle over the fireplace. All of his "adventures," as his mother had called them. The most recent addition being of him and his skydiving instructor in freefall.

Yeah, he should probably hide that one the next time his mom came over.

Maybe she was right to worry. Jesse might have suggested it, but he'd gone willingly. More than. Because if he could do that, jump out into space at twelve-thousand feet, how could he *still* have problems with climbing up a mere two-hundred-foot cliff?

He'd gone the very next day to Pretty Ugly, pumped with confidence. Only to come away a miserable failure.

Again.

Padding to the kitchen in his socks, he threw a pod of dark roast in the machine, not wanting to waste any of his precious Hawaiian Kona on hangover-compromised taste buds. While it popped and gurgled, draining steaming liquid gold into his mug, he grabbed another bottle of electrolyte water from the fridge and guzzled half of it down. And realized something important.

He'd been spending far too many Sunday mornings exactly like this lately.

Hungover. Missing pieces of time.

Miserable.

Which was the first step in admitting he might be in a little bit of trouble.

He hadn't believed it. Hadn't *wanted* to believe it. Thought he had it all under control. But knowing he'd gotten so drunk he needed to be driven home and put to bed by his date finally cracked his hardened shell of denial.

Waiting for the guilt and pain about Gavin's death to fade away on their own wasn't working. He just didn't know what else he *could* do.

How did you fix the unfixable?

A long shower and a few more cups of coffee made him feel human enough to attempt some food. As he sat down to his egg white omelet and dry toast, his brain circled back to how badly he'd fucked up last night.

Seriously, *spectacularly* fucked up.

And he wasn't sure what it meant for this thing building between him and Rachel. Her note had been almost painfully neutral, so no clues there. But she had offered to come pick him up after she left work.

That had to be a good sign, right?

"Of course it is," Jesse said when Theo called and asked him. "If she's willing to go all the way out there and collect your sorry ass after last night, then she can't be too pissed. Not that she doesn't have a right to be." His tone was disapproving. And Jesse rarely disapproved of anything.

"I know. Believe me, I know." He pinched the bridge of his nose. "I'm just...I don't know what to say to her."

"Well, 'sorry I was a dumbass' would be a good start."

He laughed. "Dumbass?"

"I thought it sounded nicer than asshole."

The words came across as angry rather than joking, and he realized his friend was well and truly irritated with him. "I'm not sure what you're getting pissy about. It's Rachel's evening I ruined, not yours."

"If you think watching my best friend rip himself to shreds over blame that isn't his to take wouldn't ruin my night, then you're both a dumbass *and* an asshole." He made a disgusted sound. "I know Gavin was your friend, but you aren't responsible for his choices. You need to let it go before it hollows you out."

Let it go.

His jaw clenched at the familiar refrain. How many times had he heard those unhelpful words over the past five months? A dozen? A hundred?

"If it was that easy, I would."

"I know. I'm sorry." And he sounded it. "I'm just worried about you, dude. I thought this thing with Rachel meant you were finally moving past everything that happened and getting back to normal."

He wasn't sure what this thing with Rachel even was, much less what it meant. What he did know was he didn't want to let it end. Not without a fight.

After ending the call with Jesse, he brought up Rachel's contact and typed out a long, rambling text of apology. His thumb hovered over the send button.

Then he deleted it and typed out *I'm sorry about last night. I'd love it if you came by after work so I can apologize.*

Some things were better said in person.

There was no immediate reply. Logically, he knew she probably wouldn't check her phone until she had a break, or even lunch. That didn't stop him from sweating out every minute until he heard the tinny *ping* of an incoming message two hours later.

See you then.

His breath left in a relieved whoosh.

It wasn't absolution, but it was a start.

Chapter 20

Too on edge to stay cooped up in the house for hours waiting until Rachel arrived, Theo pulled on boots, grabbed his leather jacket, and went through the mudroom into the garage. The four bays currently housed his Porsche 718 Boxster sports car, Ducati Diavel 1260 motorcycle, and a trailered snowmobile.

The empty spot his Cayan normally occupied was like a bitch-slap reminder of everything he'd done wrong the night before.

The bike didn't get much use in winter. But the itch to get out, to do something fast and fun and a little dangerous, was riding him too hard to ignore. And while the Boxster was a great car, there was something undeniably exhilarating about having a powerful machine like the Diavel at your command.

The thrum of the engine, the rush of wind caressing your body as you hurtled down the road at breakneck speed. The knowledge one wrong move, one tiny mistake, was all that stood between a great ride and an epic wipe out.

It was exactly what he needed.

He headed along one of his favorite routes, curling through the foothills and around several canyons before winding upward toward the summit. The tension knotted between his shoulder blades eased in direct relation to the speed he picked up. The roads were dry and virtually deserted, so he tweaked the throttle even more.

It wasn't smart, but he needed to feed the part of his soul that craved the challenge.

The danger.

There were three cars already in the gravel parking lot at the top of the elevation when he pulled in. People milled around the edge of the observation area, some with their phones up, taking pictures of the awe-inspiring view, others merely staring in silent wonder.

He parked his bike as far from all of them as he could. Normally he didn't mind chatty tourists. It was something you got used to, living in a high-traffic tourism area like Boulder.

But today, he knew he was lacking any of his usual aplomb.

Pulling off his helmet, he ran a hand through his hair to unstick it from his head, the cool breeze sending an invigorating chill through him as he unzipped the leather jacket partway. The last remnants of the hangover blew away like so many cobwebs. He felt good.

He felt alive.

He sometimes stayed at the lookout for hours. Absorbing the views and contemplating his navel, as his younger brother Peter called it when he wanted to rag on Theo for his love of sitting in the middle of nowhere, watching the horizon and clearing his head.

Which was working.

But as time ticked by, the peace he found slowly unraveled. The same sense of restlessness which had pulled him from his house now put him on his bike, roaring back down the mountain roads toward home before he could rationalize why.

But he knew.

It was because that's where she would be soon.

By the time Rachel drove her Cherokee through the gates, he'd convinced himself it was just guilt and the need to apologize fueling his urgency to see her. But when she got out of the Jeep and gave him a tentative smile as he leaned in the open doorway, waiting, he knew he was full of shit.

He'd missed her, plain and simple.

Somehow, in one short week, she'd become important to him. Enough so that simply being in her presence again soothed the restless itch which had settled under his skin all day, that not even his ride or the mountains had fully satisfied.

That strange power should have worried him. Terrified him, even.

For some reason, it didn't.

Her welcoming smile made it easy to brush aside the awkwardness of the moment and meet her halfway to the door. Taking a chance, he opened his arms. His heart thudded with relief when she walked straight into them without hesitation.

Holding her tight, the faint vanilla scent of her shampoo already familiar enough to be comforting, he rocked them slowly in place. "I'm so sorry about last night."

"It's not a big deal."

"Yes, it is." He pulled back enough so he could see her face. "I lost control and let myself get so drunk while we were out that I couldn't get you home safely at the end of the night. There's no reason in the world good enough to excuse that."

She pursed her lips in a half-frown. "I'd say being verbally attacked by a crazy woman in public is a pretty decent one."

Loretta's twisted expression as she spewed her rage-fueled accusations made him flinch from the memory, but he refused to take the out Rachel was offering.

"No. I don't blame other people for my own failings. I screwed up. Me. I'm sorry, and I promise you, it will never happen again." His heart pounded hard inside his chest, the echo pulsing thickly in his ears and throat as he waited.

She stared up at him for long seconds. He felt caught in her gaze, the intensity almost hypnotic as she studied him. Finally, she put a hand to his cheek and smiled.

"Okay."

That was it. A single word, and it dropped the weight of the world from his shoulders.

He mirrored her, placing his hand to her soft cheek. "Yeah?"

"Yeah."

Never breaking their gaze, he leaned in to kiss her. She did the same.

The kiss was light. Chaste. But with their eyes open, it was somehow more intimate than if there had been tongue and teeth and other body parts involved.

When he pulled back, he was encouraged by the fact her lips chased his for a second before retreating on a soft exhalation of breath that might have been a sigh.

"Do you want to come inside? I think I owe you another dinner, at the very least."

She hesitated, worrying at her lower lip with her teeth. "I came straight from work, so I still need to shower and change. I was thinking maybe we could just go get your car?"

Disappointment swamped him, but he did his best not to let it show.

"Sure, I understand. Let me lock up first." He turned back toward the house, but her hand on his arm stopped him.

"No, I meant...maybe this time I could make dinner for *you*. At my place. Where your car is." She tucked her lip under her teeth again and looked at him through her lashes. "And maybe breakfast, too?"

Blood rushed south at her soft-spoken almost-invitation, making his jeans suddenly too tight for comfort. "Very tempting."

She must have sensed his hesitance. "Why do I hear a 'but' coming?"

"*But* I thought you were staying with your dads? I don't see any scenario where me staying for breakfast in their house would end well."

Showing up at their door with an overnight bag in his hand was *not* the first impression he wanted to make on the two most important men in Rachel's life.

She gave him a look one part defiant, one part uncertain. "How about the scenario where they're both away for the next week?"

Huh.

Didn't see that one coming.

It would explain a few things, though. Like why he hadn't met them when he'd picked Rachel up last night. Something he'd prepared for, and felt oddly deflated when it didn't happen. But now...

A slow grin stretched his lips.

"In that case, breakfast sounds...wonderful." He made the word into a sexual promise. One rewarded when her pupils dilated with arousal. Unfortunately, he had to bring a little reality to their game of innuendo. "I know you're off tomorrow, but I'm afraid I still have to go to work. So I'll need to leave pretty early in the morning."

Not the way he wanted to end their first full night together.

He'd prefer some slow, lazy wakeup sex, followed by a gourmet breakfast they could take their time burning off again afterward.

Judging by her disappointed frown, she'd been thinking along the same lines.

"You're the boss. Can't you just take the day off when you want to?"

"I'm one of the bosses, not *the* boss. And I'm afraid I already used my 'goof off from work' card the other day."

And gone radio-silent all weekend with his family, not returning any of their calls. He had a feeling one of them would be on his doorstep before noon tomorrow if he didn't show at the office in the morning.

He looped his arms around her waist and tugged her closer until her front was tight against his. "What if I make it up to you?"

Her lips parted on a soft inhale as his erection nudged at her.

"I think I could be persuaded."

It took less than ten minutes to pack up what he needed to bring, and they were on their way. The ride gave him time to wonder if maybe he was making another mistake. He'd only just apologized for his grievous lapse of control the night before, and now they were planning their first overnighter.

Was that too fast?

Or was he overthinking things again?

Desperate to get out of his own head, he cast about for a safe topic. "So, where are your dads, anyway? Off on vacation someplace?"

"Not exactly."

If he hadn't been looking at her, he might not have noticed the way her hands tightened on the steering wheel as she answered. Okay, not as safe a topic as he'd hoped. Before he could come up with something else, though, she sighed and loosened her grip.

"It's kind of a working vacation, I guess. Sort of. My dad, Karl, stepped in as a last-minute replacement coach for another skier for the World Cup final next Sunday. My other dad, Dellin, went with him, because there's only so much Vicky anyone can take at one time. He's going to need a break."

She was probably trying to sound neutral, but failing. Badly.

"I didn't realize he coached other skiers besides you."

"He doesn't." Another mini-stranglehold on the steering wheel. "This is a one-time favor."

O-kay then.

It was pretty obvious she didn't like the situation. Or she didn't like Vicky.

A lightbulb went off.

"Wait, Vicky? As in Victoria DiBenedetto?"

She shot him a suspicious glare. "You know her?"

There was definitely a right way and a very wrong one to answer.

He chose carefully.

"I know her parents, so yeah, we've met." Technically true. "And I, uh, ran into her at the resort last weekend."

The part about her hitting on him was better left forgotten. As was the rest of their previous association.

Thankfully, she didn't press for more, and they both let the entire topic drop, continuing the rest of the ride with only the radio to break the quiet. Once she parked in the driveway next to his Cayan, he grabbed his garment and overnight bags from the back seat, which she took from him after they got inside the house.

"I'll put these upstairs and grab a quick shower before I start dinner. Make yourself at home. The kitchen is at the end of the hall on the right if you want to get something to drink, and the tv's to the left in the den."

More curious than anything, he took himself on a walking tour of the house. It was less than half the size of his, but it had a warm, lived-in feel which made it cozier than his had ever felt. There were dozens of family photos running down the length of the main hall.

He walked the timeline of Dellin Long and Karl Long-Miller's life together.

First came the pictures of the two of them together. Vacations, holidays, backyard barbeques. Then, about a quarter of the way down, Rachel appeared for the first time. Her eight-year-old face stared with solemn eyes at the camera despite the flower-encrusted birthday cake in front of her and the sparkly party hat on her head.

There were more of her from that first year after her adoption, some of her alone, some with her fathers, love and happiness shining in their eyes. But in all of them, she held the same stoic look on her face.

It was the same one he'd seen on other kids he met through his mother's charity foundation, kids from broken homes and foster care. And it broke his heart to see it on Rachel's younger self. It was a look that said she wasn't ready to let down her guard just yet, no matter how good things seemed to be.

That she was waiting for life to kick her in the teeth again at any second.

It wasn't until the next birthday party picture he saw the first smile appear. Small, tentative, but real, it changed her entire face, from cautious waif to adorable imp. After that, it was like watching a flower bloom as he followed the progression through the rest of her journey to adulthood.

He could literally see her happiness and confidence grow from picture to picture. The last few picture frames hung in a single line rather than grouped the way the others had been, as though they were placeholders for future pictures to come.

It didn't dawn on him until he was done that there hadn't been a single photo of Rachel skiing. Which seemed strange.

Until he stepped into the den.

One entire wall had been turned into a huge collage of photos hung around shelves and shadow boxes. Each picture showed Rachel at some skiing competition. Each display held medals and awards she'd won. Junior World Ski Championships. US Championships. World Cups. World Championships.

There were a lot of them.

"I see you've found the shrine."

He turned at Rachel's amused words as she walked to him and slid her arm around his waist, leaning into him, smelling warm and sweet from her shower. She'd changed into a soft pair of dark navy velour sweats and matching long-sleeved tee which hugged her trim body, leaving her feet bare except for thick fuzzy socks.

She looked and smelled positively edible.

He forced himself to return the embrace without falling on her like a starving dog.

"The shrine?"

"It feels that way, sometimes. Like, hey, look at me, I'm so great." She shook her head. "But it makes Dad happy to show my medals and globes off, so I let him do what he wants with them."

And it was clear he'd been doing it for most of her life. Odd that she would hand the awards she worked so hard for over to him rather than show them off herself. But maybe she just wasn't the pretentious type.

"Are these pictures of all the races you've been in?"

"God, no. Just the ones I won. No one wants to look at a loser." They came out of her mouth, but he had a feeling the words were Karl's.

It made him think a little less of the man.

"What goes there?" He pointed to a bare spot left in the middle of all the photos and awards like a bullseye. He felt her take in a slow, deep breath and let it out.

"That's for the Olympic gold I owe my dad."

"*Owe* him?"

"Yeah. I blew my first chance, and I missed last year being injured. But I've got another shot to get it right in three years." She slid out of his loose embrace and took his hand, tugging him away from the display. "Come on, I need to get dinner started."

He should let it drop. But something about the word "owe" really bothered him. He sat at the kitchen island brooding over it as she put a pot of water on the stove before taking a container of what looked like homemade sauce out of the freezer.

She paused in the act of popping it into the microwave. "I hope you like spaghetti. That's kind of my only halfway decent meal."

"Love it. Can I do anything to help? Set the table?"

"No, I've got it, thanks. You get to sit and relax this time." She set the microwave to defrost before moving to a cabinet for the plates.

"But you're the one who worked all day. At least let me do something."

"How about you get us something to drink from the fridge?"

"Done." He pulled open the door and studied their options. There were several bottles of local microbrew, a bottle of decent vintage red wine, and a pitcher of what looked like iced tea, which was what he grabbed. After last night's fiasco, alcohol was off the menu for a while.

Maybe a long while.

After he'd poured the iced tea and Rachel had put the sauce in a pot on the stove to heat the rest of the way, he circled back to his earlier thoughts.

"So, about this gold medal. Did you mean you owe him because of the family expectations thing we talked about once before? Because that's a pretty heavy obligation to hang around anyone's neck. No pun intended."

"Not really. I mean, it is, but why else would I work as hard as I have all these years if I never earned the ultimate prize? What would be the point?"

"You mean all of those successes"—he gestured toward the den—"would mean nothing if you don't get Olympic gold?"

"No, of course not." She turned to stare at the pot of water as though willing it to boil.

Her body language said shut up, but he couldn't. "Then what?"

She answered without turning. "I owe him because I made a promise, okay? The day he committed to being my coach, mine and nobody else's, I promised I'd never disappoint him. That I'd get him the gold he didn't get because of me."

"What? Because of you, how?"

"Because he chose to coach me rather than train for his final Olympics."

The water wasn't quite boiling yet, but she shoved the pasta in anyway as he stared at her stiff back. He didn't know a lot about Olympic skiing—okay, anything—but he knew a lot about professional competitors.

And if Karl had thought he'd had a chance in hell of grabbing the gold, nothing would have stood in his way. Not even a prodigy daughter.

"Did he tell you that?"

"No. Not in so many words."

"Then what words?"

Turning, she crossed her arms over her chest, her expression bordering on hostile. "That wall in there? It used to be his. All of his medals, his awards. The day I won my first race, he took them all down and put them away, and told me it was my wall now, and it was up to me to fill it back up again."

What a bastard.

"Let me guess. There was a blank spot for a gold on his wall, too."

She gave a jerky nod. "So no, he never actually said it. But I still know what I have to do. I always have. I don't have a choice."

There was a sense of resignation in her words that made it feel like there was a much wider obstacle between them than just the kitchen island.

With slow movements, he approached her the way you would a skittish animal, not wanting to spook it into running. He didn't bother trying to pry her arms loose from herself, just wrapped her in a hug and held her there until she unclenched and slipped her arms around him in return.

"You have a choice, Rachel. You always have a choice."

Chapter 21

You always have a choice.

The words were spoken with such sincerity they almost made her believe they were true. But she knew better. From the day she'd stepped onto her first slalom course, her path had been set.

Winning made her dad happy.

Making him happy made her feel safe.

Therefore, she'd set out to win enough medals for that damn wall to make him downright ecstatic and guarantee he'd never give up on her and leave.

But the missing gold hung over her like an albatross. Once she got it, the wall would be complete. She'd finally be able to give him the one thing he really wanted. And she could retire without any guilt.

Unfortunately, the opportunity for gold was three long years away. That meant three more years of training and races to push through first.

No matter how much she'd prefer not to.

The warmth from Theo's body radiated through his thin sweater and into her, chasing back some of the chill thinking about that caused. She snuggled deeper into his embrace, inhaling the tangy scent of his cologne mixed with a touch of leather and sweat. "You smell really good."

His laughter was a soft rumble in his chest against her ear. "I think that might be the spaghetti sauce."

Tilting her face so she could breathe in deep at the warm curve of his neck, she sighed. "Mmm." She raised her head further so she could look at him. "Nope, definitely you."

From this close, she could see a faint nick on the curve of his chin, fresh enough she could tell he'd shaved before she picked him up. Which was kind of a shame, since she'd liked his weekend scruffy look the one time she saw it.

Unable to ignore the effort he'd gone to for her, she pressed a gentle kiss to the tiny wound. Then another a little closer to his mouth. Then another.

With a throaty groan, he covered her mouth with his, sweeping in and driving her crazy as his hands kneaded her butt through the almost non-existent barrier of her sweats. She clung to him, running a hand through his soft hair, knocking it into disarray as she met him kiss for kiss, touch for touch.

Somehow, they managed to turn off the burners on the stove before they stumbled upstairs to her bedroom. Clothes came off, giving her only a second to be grateful she'd put on one of her few lingerie sets before that, too, was gone and she was lying naked on the bed, Theo poised over her on all fours.

The look in his eyes tore a sound of need from somewhere deep inside her.

"Now. *Please*."

The press of his hard flesh into her was exactly what she needed, but it was just a tease before he was gone again, leaving her empty and aching.

She whimpered at the loss.

"Condom." His voice was deeper, almost a growl. "Where's my bag?"

"By the closet." She flapped her hand in the general direction, shocked at her lapse and grateful Theo had had enough functioning brain cells to think for the both of them. Then he was back and sliding home again, and there was no time to think about anything other than the incredible sensation of him filling her to perfection.

Her entire focus narrowed to just the two of them.

Their bodies.

Their pleasure.

No room left for guilt, or obligation, or confusion. All of it squeezed out and forgotten as he stroked her higher and higher toward the bright, shining promise of release. He kept her there, teetering on the knife's edge for what seemed like an eternity as he did all kinds of delicious things to the rest of her body with his mouth and hands.

Even under such a deluge of pleasure, lying passive wasn't her style. She did her own teasing and touching as well, everywhere she could reach. Hours naked together had taught her he enjoyed having his testicles caressed and fondled, how sensitive his nipples could be while he was aroused.

She took one hard peak between her teeth and tugged, ever-so gently, and was rewarded by a full-body shudder and a groan that marked the end of his patience.

Good. She'd already long passed hers.

Hiking her right leg up over his hip, Theo adjusted his angle and found that spot inside, the one that was like hitting the switch on a detonator. The one she hadn't even known existed until he found it their first night in his bed.

His mouth ate at hers as they both raced toward orgasm, only breaking free as it burst over them, both gasping for air as his hips continued to move, to drag over that spot, prolonging the pleasure until it was almost unbearable.

It took a few minutes before either of them had the strength to move from where they finished, although Theo had shifted his weight to the side so he wasn't crushing her. He recovered first, as he always seemed to, getting up to take care of the condom before returning to spoon against her body.

The feel of him, strong and warm at her back, was quickly becoming one of her favorite things. She knew it shouldn't. Knew she wouldn't get to keep him much longer.

But in the quiet aftermath of their lovemaking, her body still heavy and languorous and tingling inside and out, she couldn't find it in her to worry all too much about it.

"We seem to be making a habit of this." Theo's amused words tickled her ear.

"What, ending up in bed? I have no complaints."

His chuckle touched things deep inside her body, making her shudder in response.

"None here, either. But I was talking about ruining meals *because* we keep ending up in bed."

"Still no complaints." She ran her hand along the arm he'd wrapped around her belly, enjoying the play of muscles beneath the firm skin as they flexed at the caress.

He was so deceptively lean, she sometimes forgot just how strong he really was under all that honey-tanned skin. His face and arms were slightly darker than the rest of him from his trip to Australia. But he was delightfully golden everywhere else, too, thanks to what he'd referred to as his mixed bag of genes.

At least he knew what his bag contained. His parents could trace their family lines back at least three generations to half a dozen European countries via Louisiana and Georgia.

She envied that sense of family. Of belonging.

All she remembered about her mother was that she'd had beautiful dark skin and a lilting island accent that had made the bedtime stories she read seem extra magical. About her father, she knew nothing.

Her mother had never mentioned him, and Rachel had been too young to think to ask. After her mother died and she'd been dumped into the foster care system, though, he'd become that mythical thing all orphans dreamed of: the heroic parent who never knew their child existed, riding to the rescue and taking them away to live happily ever after.

Only, like with most fantasies, it never happened.

She'd spent two long years in the system, years where her hopes and prayers went unanswered. Until finally, when she had almost no hope left, someone *had* rescued her. Not her nameless, faceless father, but Dellin and Karl. Two strangers who'd taken her into their home and their hearts.

They'd saved her.

More than that, they loved her, when she'd all but forgotten what that felt like. Even so, she hadn't felt secure in her new home for a very long time. Too many kids had come back to the foster homes when the people who'd considered adopting them decided they were too much trouble, or 'not a good fit' for their lifestyle.

Like they were shelter puppies rather than damaged, frightened children.

It had taken her almost a full year to stop waking up every morning wondering if today was the day she'd finally have her happiness snatched away again. If today she'd be shipped back to her fosters because she hadn't been good enough to keep.

It had been twenty years, and there were still days she marveled at her good fortune it had never happened.

And yet...

The traitorous part of her that didn't want the life she'd been crafting this past year snatched away wondered if maybe twenty years of being the most dutiful daughter she could be was finally enough.

True, she still hadn't won that stupid gold. But maybe it wasn't meant to be. Maybe the accident had been a sign. Maybe everything she'd already accomplished could be enough.

You always have a choice.

Did she? Maybe?

Theo pressed a kiss to her shoulder. "You sleeping?"

She answered before she could censor herself. "Thinking."

"About what?"

Dare she tell him the truth? Hadn't he confided his own personal demons to her last night? He might have been drunk when he did it, true, but it still seemed like it somehow made it okay to share her own issues in return.

Safe, even.

Like some kind of cathartic quid pro quo.

The words trembled on her lips, the need to confide her deepest, darkest secret to someone almost making her throw a lifetime of caution to the wind. How hard could it be?

I'm not sure I want to race anymore.

Eight little words, and she could get the weight of the world off her chest. She opened her mouth—

—and couldn't do it.

She wanted to, God how she did.

But the old fears rose up to choke her into silence.

Fear of giving someone a piece of herself. Of handing them something they could use against her. To shove under her emotional armor and rip her open with her own words. Lessons she'd learned hard and fast at the hands of the older, more streetwise kids in the foster system. And a few of the adults as well.

Never tell anyone your secrets.

It had been Ivy's number one rule.

Her internal debate must have been going on too long, because Theo said, "Never mind, you don't have to tell me."

The tender thread of disappointment in his voice made her feel even worse about not trusting him enough to be honest. Maybe she could give him a partial truth and still keep her secret safe.

Turning, she slid her leg between his and laid her head on his outstretched arm so they were face-to-face. "I was thinking about how much I'm enjoying this time with you, and how much I'd miss it. Miss you." Something flared in his eyes that made her pull back a fraction. "Is that too weird? I know it's only been a week, but—"

"No, it's not weird." He ran a fingertip along the curve of her cheek and smiled. "I feel it, too. This connection. It's special. I'm just relieved to hear you feel the same way, and it's not only me wondering what the hell it is."

Damn it.

She hadn't meant to make him think that. Now it was going to be even harder when the time came to break things off.

Unable to stay in his arms while he was looking at her with such tenderness and wonder, she managed a smile. "I don't know about you, but I'm starving." She untangled herself from him and scooted off the bed.

Not the most graceful way to change the subject, especially considering what that subject was, but it was all she had.

Knowing he was watching her every move made her all thumbs as she pulled her clothes back on. Struggling with the hooks on her lacy black bra, she cursed her earlier choice of lingerie. She never had these kinds of problems with her sports bras.

Then his fingers were there, brushing hers aside and doing up the hooks like he was a pro. The thought should have cooled the heat that rose at his touch, but when he kissed her shoulder before moving away to grab his own clothes, it was all she could do not to melt into a great big puddle.

That was when she realized the truth.

It wasn't the sex with him that was dangerous. It was the intimacies like that little gesture which were going to make it so hard to let him go.

The sauce turned out to be salvageable, although they had to throw the mushy pasta out and start over with new. Theo declined the offered wine, but she needed a little liquid courage to get through the meal and the rest of the evening. This man made her resolve weak, and she couldn't have that.

"That was fantastic," Theo said as they stacked the dishes in the dishwasher later. "I thought you said you couldn't cook."

"I can't take credit for the sauce. My father made it."

"The one who likes to cook, not the coach. Dellin?"

She smiled, pleased he'd remembered. "Yeah. After he retired from the police force, he needed to find things to keep him busy. He took a cooking course and loved it."

"And what do you love to do?"

She paused in the process of rinsing out the sauce pot. "What do you mean?"

"Besides the obvious—skiing—what do you like to do? I want to know what Rachel Long does for fun."

"Not much, really. Training and racing don't really allow for a lot of free time." There. She'd said it.

"But when you do have some?"

He was persistent, she'd give him that.

She sighed and thought about it. "Reading, I guess. And listening to music. There's a lot of travel and hotel downtime to kill during the Cup season."

Far too much.

The lonely evenings. The long drives and flights from race to race. The unexpected weather delays and cancelled races after days of prep.

All of which had started to wear thin long before her enforced hiatus had hammered home just how lonely and isolating that life could be.

As they tidied the rest of the kitchen, they talked about favorite books and bands. Some of their tastes overlapped. Some were miles apart. The conversation flowed easily to other topics as they snuggled under a fleece throw on the sofa to watch one of the tv crime shows she'd become addicted to, her head on his chest like a pillow.

Somehow, it seemed easier to say whatever came to mind that way. As though not looking at him granted a sense of anonymity to the words. Aside from Ari, she couldn't remember being this comfortable talking about herself to someone, ever.

When they went to bed, Theo made unhurried, intense love to her in perfect counterpoint to their earlier mad frenzy. When she came, it was in a long, slow rush of warmth and pleasure that rolled over her like a lazy wave and pushed her under toward sleep.

She felt safe, and warm, and loved.

Tucked against his side, her face in the curve of his neck, one arm flung over his lightly haired chest, she felt his breathing even out and fall into the deep rhythm of sleep.

Pressing her lips to his skin, she breathed out in the softest of whispers, "I'm not sure I want to race anymore," before she followed him into the land of dreams.

Chapter 22

"Glad to see you decided to grace us with your presence today."

Richard's sarcastic words jarred Theo back from where he'd been staring sightlessly at the computer screen on his desk. He refocused on his brother, who was looming in the open doorway, hand still on the brass knob, and scowled. "Don't you ever knock?"

"I did. You didn't answer. Which is why I wasn't sure you'd be in here, even though Sabrina assured me you were. Care to tell me why?"

Normally, Richard's heir-to-the-throne attitude pissed him off when he threw it around at the office. But leaving in the middle of the day without a word on Friday had probably earned him a few free shots.

But only a few.

"I didn't hear you, that's all."

"Really?" Closing the door for privacy, he prowled towards the desk and Theo. "Must be some mighty interesting reading to keep you so distracted you could miss something like that." He stepped around the desk and turned the laptop so he could see the screen.

His "ah-ha" expression fell away when all he saw was the interest report Theo had stopped reading—he checked his watch—twenty minutes ago.

"What were you expecting, porn?"

Richard ran a hand through his hair, looking bemused. "Honestly? I don't know what I was expecting. Some answers, maybe."

"To what?"

"To what the hell is going on with you. First you up and walk out of the office without even telling me—"

"Yeah, after you helped Mom ambush me."

"—then you won't pick up your damn phone all weekend when people are trying to make sure you're okay. That was a dick move, by the way."

It had been. But he'd been in no frame of mind to deal with any of his well-meaning family. "I was busy. I didn't have time to keep explaining myself to everyone."

"Oh, fuck me, were you off doing something stupid and dangerous again?" Richard glared. "Swear to God, if another video shows up online and Mom sees it, I'm going to kick your ass."

"No, I wasn't doing anything dangerous." Unless you counted the risk he was taking to his heart. Then, because Richard was wearing on his last nerve, he added, "Not that it's any of your business if I was."

"Then where the hell were you?"

"Again, not your business. But because I know it's the only way I'm going to get you out of my office, I'll tell you. I spent the weekend with a woman." He had the satisfaction of watching his brother's mouth drop open in surprise.

Which quickly morphed into suspicion. "All weekend?"

"Not forty-eight hours continuously, if that's what you mean. But most of it, yeah. Happy now?"

"Who was it? Did you hook up with Elena, after all?"

"I'll say it again. Not. Your. Business. Now, can I get back to work, please?"

But Richard wasn't about to be deterred. "Wait, this isn't the one you said you had a date with last week, is it?"

"What if it is?"

His eyes narrowed. "Who is she?"

"No one you know. Drop it."

"What do you know about her? How did you meet?"

His brother's demanding tone put his back up, but refusing to answer would just make Richard more persistent. The man hated any puzzle he couldn't solve.

That didn't mean Theo couldn't fuck with him a little first.

"I met her at one of the resorts last weekend. She's a professional."

Richard's expression closed down. "A professional what?"

With a smirk, Theo let him think the worst until he couldn't hold back a laugh any longer. "Jesus, you're easy. She's not a hooker, you ass. She's a ski pro."

"Oh." Richard didn't have the decency to look embarrassed. If anything, his expression grew even more suspicious. "What's her name?"

"Why, so you can give it to security and have them do a background check on her? Forget it."

"But you said you only just met this...person, and suddenly you're spending the whole weekend with her? What do you really know about her?"

Theo's temper snapped. "No. Do *not* go there. We swore we'd never stick our noses into each other's love lives again after we nearly ruined Lillian's life fucking around with her relationship with Rafe. So back the fuck off."

Though he put his hands up in surrender, Richard didn't relent.

"I know. But you haven't exactly been yourself lately. And I'm just worried maybe you're a little more vulnerable right now than normal, which would mean you're not being as cautious as you should be."

"I know exactly what I'm doing."

Although that might have been a bit of an overstatement.

He was in relationship waters he'd never tread before. It did make him vulnerable, just not in the way his brother meant. Past experience had given Richard a jaded viewpoint, where everyone was a potential gold digger until proven otherwise. And while he might not have the rest of it figured out, he knew for a fact Rachel wasn't that.

"I appreciate the concern, but stay out of it, Richard. I mean it."

He didn't look happy, but his brother nodded. "Fine. I'll leave it alone." He waited until he was halfway out the door to add over his shoulder, "For now."

The door thudding shut covered the curse Theo sent after him. Big brothers were a pain in the ass—he should know, he was one himself—but Richard was worse because he always thought he knew best, simply because he'd been born first. Which was compounded by the annoying fact he usually *was* right about most things.

But not about this.

No, Theo's problem with Rachel wasn't about money. It was the words she'd breathed against his neck last night when she thought he was asleep. Words that had haunted him all morning and left him staring off into nothing, searching for answers.

And finding none.

I'm not sure I want to race anymore.

What the hell was he supposed to do with that kind of confession?

Especially when he wasn't supposed to have heard it. If she'd wanted him to, there'd been more than enough opportunities to bring it up. So why whisper it into the dark like some dirty little secret no one was supposed to know?

Possibly because that's exactly what she thought it was?

She'd spent her entire adult life competing at the highest levels around the world. *Winning* at the highest levels. To think about ending her career before age or loss of skill forced her to went against everything he knew about her.

But then, as Richard had so obnoxiously pointed out, he didn't really know all that much, did he?

So, what would make Rachel even consider changing the trajectory of her life like that?

The image of her cartwheeling down the mountainside sprang in screaming technicolor to mind, bringing with it the familiar rise of bile to burn his throat.

Fuck.

That would do it. As horrific as her injuries had been, it was no small wonder she'd have thoughts of hanging up her racing skis for good. It still shocked—and terrified—him that she planned to go back to it.

The fact she could still make herself ski on any mountain at all was incredible. How hard must it have been for her the first time she'd gone down anything higher than the bunny hill she taught on? How much strength had it taken to even attempt it?

More than he'd been able to find, that was for sure.

He still couldn't climb anything other than the practice walls at the club. There, he was fine. They were his bunny hill. But put one foot on an actual rock face, and he still froze.

Every. Time.

And he hadn't even been the one to fall.

So, if her doubts had anything to do with her accident, he understood. But he couldn't do anything about it. Not without admitting he'd heard her midnight confession. And he had a feeling that wouldn't be in his best interest.

Might, in fact, drive a wedge into their still forming relationship.

So, much as he'd rather not, he would keep the knowledge to himself and wait for an opportunity when he could use it to help her. Maybe that way at least one of them could get past their issues and finally find some peace.

Chapter 23

SHE WASN'T GOING TO watch the race.

Lying next to a sleeping Theo, she stared at the ceiling of his dark bedroom and tried to convince herself that was the right choice. Getting up in the middle of the night to watch the World Cup finals live would be an exercise in futility.

Not only because she had to be at work in the morning—her last day—and needed the sleep, but also because it would be recorded in the DVR when she got up. That way she could fast-forward past all the other racers, commercials, and commentary fluff.

Plus, it was sure to be playing all over the resort when the US time-delayed coverage was broadcast, just like all of Vicky's races were.

How many times was she supposed to torture herself?

Decision made, she rolled on her side and snuggled closer to Theo under the covers. He made a soft noise and threw an arm over her waist. She'd noticed that about him. How even in sleep, he was possessive about keeping her close.

It should have felt claustrophobic.

Instead, she'd had some of the best sleep of her life this past week.

Not that they'd planned to spend every night together. It just seemed to happen. Like the shift back to his house had.

Theo might have joked her dinky full-sized mattress was the reason, but she had a feeling it had more to do with the fact it was her parents' house, not hers. And it made him uncomfortable to be sleeping with her in it. For an adventure-seeking wild man, at his core he had some very old-fashioned tendencies.

Not that she thought he'd ever admit such a thing.

And while his king bed and fancy shower were definite draws, they weren't her main reasons for preferring his house to hers. No, if she was here, that meant she wouldn't have to look at that damn shrine her dad had created.

Because when she did, she didn't see a decade's worth of accomplishments. All she saw, all that mattered, was the big blank spot in the middle staring back at her. Reminding her she was still a loser where it counted most.

She glanced at the glowing clock on the nightstand.

Almost four a.m. Noon Swedish time.

The race would be starting any minute.

Her dad was there because she'd told him it was okay to go. Shouldn't she at least watch a little of it? When he called later, she knew he'd ask if she had, and what she'd thought of Vicky's performance.

With a tiny growl of irritation in the back of her throat, she tugged the covers higher around her neck. Stupid freaking Vicky. For four years she'd been nipping at Rachel's heels like a puppy determined to play with the big dogs. And for four years, she'd been gaining ground. Not just in rank, but in experience and skill.

One day soon, she was going to be more than an annoyance.

She would become a true rival.

So no, she didn't want to get out of her comfortable bed and watch, unless it was to see her fall on her skinny ass.

The uncharitable thought made her sigh.

Vicky wasn't any different from a dozen other up-and-comers who hit the circuit every year. They were all cocky, unwilling to listen to the advice of the more seasoned veterans, so sure they knew it all already.

But there was something extra irritating about Vicky that rubbed Rachel on the raw. Some drive, some single-minded determination that said she knew where she was going. To the top, no matter what.

Rachel recognized it, because she'd had that same drive once.

She just couldn't find it anymore.

And without that spark, that all-consuming focus, she would never work her way back to the top of the standings. Never make the Olympic team. She'd be left in the powder by people like Vicky, who simply wanted it more than she did.

She yanked the covers from her neck as it suddenly got hard to breathe.

Damn it!

Why hadn't she kept her mouth shut? It was her own fault her father was in Sweden coaching someone else to the podium.

She should have left well enough alone. Should have let his "no" to Matt stand. Now he was five thousand miles away, sharing the expertise that had always been for her alone with Vicky freaking DiBenedetto.

"Just go watch," Theo mumbled, startling her.

"What?"

"Watch the race. The tv's set to the right channel."

Another plus to Theo's house. He got every sports channel known to man. Still, she'd already made her decision.

"I told you before I wasn't going to."

He opened one eye to stare at her from across the pillow. "And yet you've been a whirling dervish for the past half hour. Clearly, I didn't do as good a job of tiring you out as I thought."

A blush heated her cheeks. He'd done a marvelous job tiring her out.

Three times, in fact.

But it seemed not even orgasmic oblivion had been enough to shut her overactive brain off. "I don't know what to do. I want to watch, but I don't."

"Then watch it in the morning like you planned."

"You're right. I should."

"Okay, glad that's settled. C'mere." He tugged her close, wrapping her in the safe cocoon of his embrace, and slipped beneath the line of consciousness again, his even breath soft puffs of warmth against her skin.

She tried to do the same. She really did.

She lasted five minutes.

Carefully crawling out from under his arm so she didn't wake him, she grabbed his robe from the chair by the bed and padded quietly downstairs. Making sure the volume was low before she turned on the massive tv, she settled on the sofa, legs drawn up under the flannel robe to cover her bare skin.

It was stupid to be doing this.

But she still couldn't make herself turn it off and go back upstairs.

Instead, she scoured the names as they flashed onscreen, showing who was racing in what order. A tiny pang of sadness hit her. She knew almost all of these people. Spent most of the past ten years with them.

What did it say that she hadn't really missed most of them at all?

Intent on the screen, she didn't notice Theo until he stepped into the small pool of light thrown by the tv. Bare chested, wearing only a pair of gray sweatpants which hung low on his hips, he was adorably rumpled and sleepy looking.

He spread the blanket he carried around his shoulders like a cape and slipped in behind her on the sofa so she was sitting between his legs. As he wrapped it around them both, the warmth of the blanket immediately dispelled the chill she didn't realize had seeped into her bones.

Or maybe it was the man who did that.

Which was a much deeper thought than she had time to examine right then, so she pushed it away.

"You didn't have to come down and lose sleep because of me." But it was a half-hearted denial at best. One he didn't bother to respond to. He just tucked her to his chest, his head against hers, and watched with her in silence.

Until he asked a short time later, "Is it bothering you to watch this?"

It was tough to tear her attention from the action on the screen. "What do you mean?"

"You keep flinching."

"I do?" But even as he said it, she realized he was right. And wrong. "I guess my muscles are following the rhythm of the course out of habit."

"Oh, you mean like when you see skiers close their eyes and pantomime what they're going to do before they race?"

"Yeah. You inspect the course the morning of the race, looking at the lines and falls and gate placements and a million other things so you can memorize your moves in advance."

"Makes sense." He hesitated. "I thought maybe it was uncomfortable for you to watch."

"Why, because I'm not there myself?"

"Partly. But I was thinking more like it was the same race you got hurt on. That was the Super G, too, wasn't it?"

A tiny frisson of something cold shivered through her. "Yeah, it was. Huh. I hadn't thought of that." Maybe there was more than one reason she'd been conflicted about watching. "Wait, how did you know that?"

"I, um, saw a clip of it online."

She forced herself not to cringe. There had been a time she couldn't turn on a tv or go online without running into some version of that damn video playing. If she never had to listen to herself scream again, it would be too soon. "I'm not surprised. Most people have."

His hand smoothed down her left hip under the blanket, covering the scars hidden beneath the robe. "You were damn lucky."

"It didn't feel like it those first few months." It was a hard admission, but true. "But yeah, the fact I got such good medical care and they were able to put me back together again makes me extremely lucky."

"Some people might not want to tempt fate a second time after a crash like that."

The way he said it, slow and hesitant, like he was trying to reach a point he didn't think she was going to like, made the hairs on her neck stir in warning.

"And some people need to make their own fate," she said, trying to derail whatever it was he was going to say. "As soon as my dad gets back tomorrow, we'll be starting my training."

There, it was said. She was committed. She was keeping her promise.

So why didn't she feel any better?

Theo didn't say anything for a few long moments. He simply held her as they watched another skier run the course to the quiet droning of the commentators at low volume. After she passed the finish line, he asked, "But we still have a date for Saturday morning, right?"

She wanted to say no.

He'd played dirty, asking her to attend his mother's charity brunch/fashion show while she was still in a post-coital stupor the other night. But a promise was a promise.

"Yes, it's still a date."

Her dad wouldn't be happy about losing a whole day of practice. Especially so soon after they got started. But since the event raised money for sports programs benefiting underprivileged kids in the area, she hoped he'd at least be a *little* understanding.

There were a lot of kids who weren't as lucky as she'd been to have parents who could afford for them to participate in sports.

He kissed her ear and squeezed her tighter. "Good."

The level of satisfaction in that one word put her a little off-kilter. Before she could read too much into it, she saw the name they'd been waiting for flash on the screen. Grateful for the distraction, she said, "Vicky's next."

It was kind of surreal, rooting for someone who was usually her competition. But just this once, she hoped Vicky did well. If she didn't, Rachel wouldn't put it past her to try and lay the blame on her dad's coaching. It wouldn't matter he'd only had her for a week. Vicky was the queen of deflection.

One of the many reasons she went through coaches like used tissues.

Because Theo had pointed it out, this time she was aware of every jerk and twitch her body made as she followed Vicky's progress down the course. Super G was a wild cross between downhill racing and giant slalom. It required someone fast, agile, and a little bit ballsy. Who didn't flinch at attacking the tricky gates at upward of eighty miles an hour on rutted and sometimes icy snow.

Rachel hadn't been able to do anything *but* flinch since she'd started working the course at Copper. That knowledge made it hard to watch the flawless performance on the screen. Harder still to see the look of satisfaction on her dad's face when the camera flashed to him for a few seconds at the end of the run.

The total opposite of the disappointment he'd shown for the pathetic performances she'd given him last week.

The tv clicked off, pulling her from the dark swirl of emotion threatening to drag her under. Theo tossed the remote to the cushion and scooped her up, blanket and all, like she weighed nothing.

"You watched her race. You can find out where she finished in the morning. Now, you need sleep."

She should have argued. Lashed out at his high-handedness.

Instead, she let herself be distracted by the strength he displayed carrying her upstairs. She might have let him continue to distract her with that body of his after the blanket and sweat pants came off, leaving him deliciously bare.

If she hadn't remembered she needed to send her dad a congratulatory text.

Grabbing her phone, she turned her back to him as she typed out a quick message. No way could she look at him naked and talk to her dad at the same time. A very masculine chuckle from the bed told her he knew exactly what effect he had on her, and he liked it.

Arrogant bastard.

She couldn't keep from grinning as she thought it, though.

Since she didn't expect an immediate reply, she put the phone back on the charger, took off the robe, and climbed into bed. The sheets had cooled in their absence, but the furnace that was Theo's body quickly warmed her skin back to a toasty glow as he tucked himself around her.

Like she was something precious he was afraid of losing if he didn't hold on.

Placing her hand over his where it rested on her belly, she turned her head enough to kiss him softly. "Thank you."

The words were purposely vague. They could have been for any number of things he'd done for her tonight. But right that minute, they were because he was there with her when she needed him, for no other reason than because he wanted to be.

Precious, indeed.

Chapter 24

"WHAT DO YOU MEAN, you're not coming home tomorrow?"

Dellin's deep voice rumbled over the phone Rachel had pressed to her ear as she huddled in a corner of the noisy employee locker room, trying for privacy. "Well, Matt was so pleased with his daughter's performance he gave your dad a nice bonus for a job well done, and a pair of open-ended first-class tickets home. So, we thought we'd take advantage of the chance to spend a few days playing tourist."

Something ugly slashed through her belly.

She had checked the standings as soon as she'd gotten up. Vicky's time hadn't landed her on the podium, but no one had expected it to. Except maybe her. But she'd been in the top twenty, which was better than any of her other finishes that season.

Rachel had tapped out a second congratulatory text for that to her dad before jumping in the shower where she could cry without Theo hearing. She hadn't even been sure what she was crying about.

"That was nice of Matt." She tried to keep her tone neutral, but couldn't pull it off. It wasn't nice. It was another bribe.

She should have expected him to pull something like this if Vicky did well. A man with that much money would offer just about anything to get what he wanted, and what he wanted was Karl coaching his precious princess. Now more than ever.

Her father must have caught something in her tone.

"Is everything all right, baby girl?"

No, not at all.

"Sure, of course. It's just...I thought Dad was totally focused on getting back here to start my training. So, I'm kind of surprised he'd decide to blow that off in favor of some impromptu vacation."

There was a long silence on the line.

Long enough, she wondered if the call had dropped out. She was pulling the phone away from her ear to check when her father spoke again, his tone the one he usually reserved for the heart-to-hearts they'd had when she was a teenager.

"Sweetheart, you and your dad are two peas in a pod when it comes to skiing. Both of you are so hyper-focused that you can lose sight of everything else around you. You're right, he's anxious to get your training started. But I convinced him taking a few days to enjoy ourselves before getting back into the grind of that wouldn't change anything in the grand scheme of things. Might, in fact, be something we need after the last year or so."

Guilt washed her pique away like a sad rain.

It hadn't only been her life turned upside down and backwards after her accident. Both her fathers had put their lives on hold for months while they took care of her. Turning the den into a bedroom for her, complete with a hospital bed, until she was able to climb the stairs again. Taking her to doctor appointments. Making sure she did the exercises the physical therapists ordered, even when she got sullen and depressed and didn't want to.

All that—and more—and she was getting pissy about them taking a few days of vacation time for themselves.

What an ungrateful bitch she was.

"You're right. I'm sorry. That was totally selfish of me. You both deserve to relax and have some you-time."

"It's not selfish, baby girl. Hyper-focused, like I said. Something you and your dad both need to work on. None of us is getting any younger, you know. You both need to enjoy life a little more."

Her mind inappropriately flashed to the enjoyment she'd been having with Theo. "I'm trying."

"Good. And how is that young man of yours?"

Total panic froze her brain. How did he know she'd been talking about Theo?

More important, how *much* did he know about Theo? She might be well above the age of consent, but that didn't mean she wanted her fathers to know she'd been all but shacking up with someone while they were away. "Uh…"

"You know, the one you had dinner with last week. Have you seen him again?"

She would *not* think about just how much of Theo she'd been seeing.

Every delicious inch.

Focus, Rae.

"Yeah, we've been out a few more times."

"Sounds like it could be something serious."

She didn't like the hopeful note in his almost-question. "Pop, you know I won't have time for any kind of actual relationship once I start training. It's more of a just-for-now kind of thing."

And if she said it enough times, maybe she'd stop hating the sound of it.

"So much like your father," he muttered. "Baby girl, anything's possible if you want it bad enough.

"Now *you* sound like Ari."

"You've got a smart friend, then. A little weird with all that crystal and incense stuff, but you should listen to her on this. And me."

"Pop…"

"Okay, okay, I'll stop. Besides, this isn't a conversation for over the phone. But let me say one more thing before I go, and I want you to really think about it."

"Okay." She braced herself.

"Your father and I were together for almost ten years before we adopted you, and we've had twenty more wonderful years together since. And somehow, both of us managed to have full-time careers, and a marriage, *and* raise a daughter along the way. If we can do it, why can't you?"

Why can't you?

Her father's words rang in her ears long after she said a distracted goodbye and hung up. It was a good question. One she didn't have a ready answer for. Or maybe one she just wasn't ready to answer yet.

The resort was open year-round, and some of the snow-sport staff would stay on as long as the snow lasted, which might be another few weeks or a month, depending on the weather. But the season for most of the staff ended when they closed the chairlifts for the day and cleared the last of the guests off the mountain.

Even though he wasn't there, Matt had arranged the usual end-of-season party for everyone. The emotional upheaval of goodbyes blocked out her father's nagging question for a while.

But once she was on her way home, the silence in the car let it seep right back in, chasing her like a slowly building avalanche the entire way. By the time she let herself into the house, a headache was pounding behind her eyes that just begged for a glass of wine, the hot tub, and Theo to make it better.

It was the last part that made her grab her phone and tap out a quick text telling him she wasn't feeling good and wouldn't be coming over tonight.

She'd finally gotten used to wanting him.

Needing him, however, couldn't be allowed.

It was far too dangerous.

She let out a small yip when the phone still in her hands rang. Surprise turned to resignation when she saw the caller ID.

Of course, he wouldn't let her take the easy way out. "Hi."

"Hi yourself. I got your text, and I wanted to make sure everything was okay." When she didn't say anything, he asked, "*Is everything okay?*"

"Sure, it's fine. I just…it was a long day, and I didn't get much sleep last night, and I have this monster headache coming on, so I thought I'd take some aspirin and lay down."

"Is there anything I can bring you to make you feel better?"

You.

Squelching the whiney thought, she pinched the bridge of her nose. "Thanks, but I'm good."

Liar, liar.

"I just need a good night's sleep. Besides, you have work in the morning, and I plan to sleep in on my first day of unemployment. So, I'll, um, I'll call you tomorrow, okay?"

There was a momentary silence. "Sure. You take care of yourself, Rae. Sweet dreams."

"You, too."

She had to put the phone down to keep from calling him right back and begging him to ignore what she'd just said and please come over. They'd been together every night for over a week. It had created an unrealistic sense of intimacy that was messing with her judgement.

About everything.

If she was going to really consider her father's question, she had to do it without the narcotic effect Theo seemed to have on her. A little bit of distance was exactly what she needed to clear her head.

No matter how much her heart said otherwise.

Chapter 25

A LITTLE BIT OF distance hadn't done a damn thing except make her cranky.

After the worst night's sleep she'd had in weeks, Rachel was forced to admit the truth: she missed Theo. And not just for the sex, although yeah, she'd kind of missed that, too.

A lot.

But it was the warmth of his body next to hers in bed. The weight of his arm holding her close. The feel of his breath on her skin. Those were the things she missed most.

And she had no one to blame but herself.

Checking her bindings one last time, she glided to the starting gate and stared down at the Super G course below. When she had stood here with her father two weeks ago, she'd felt like she'd been punched in the chest. Now, she just felt annoyed.

At herself. At her fathers. At Theo. Hell, at the world.

She was good at this. Damn good.

There was no physical reason she should be sucking at it so badly.

It was a mental block, plain and simple. One she needed to get over, and fast. Especially when Vicky was out there right now, skiing the races Rachel should be winning. Inching her way closer to the spot on the Olympic team Rachel coveted. Getting pointers and encouragement from Rachel's dad while she did it.

Basically, she was living what should have been Rachel's life.

And that was totally unacceptable.

But the only way to reclaim it was to get her shit together and start racing again. And to do that, she needed to get out of her own head.

Ari had said maybe her subconscious was sabotaging her efforts because she wasn't really ready yet. Well, she was ready now, and her subconscious or her nerves or whatever it was better get the hell out of the way.

With the fire of that thought burning deep in her gut, she pushed off.

The beep of the timer sounded as her body broke the gate's plane, but she wasn't interested in how fast she went. Not this time. This run was to prove to herself she could make it to the bottom of the course one time without landing on her ass along the way.

She struggled through the first few gates, going too wide, then cutting too tight as she passed between them, almost losing her balance as her center of gravity became misaligned. With a curse she recovered, but barely.

The fire inside her flickered, then burned hotter.

I can do this.

Her concentration narrowed, blocking out things she shouldn't be thinking about. Vicky. Her dads. Theo. None had a place here on the mountain with her.

The next few gates came easier, but still weren't as smooth as they should be.

She narrowed her focus even further, until there was only her breathing, her skis, and the snow. It was all about balance. Harmony. Connection.

Somewhere about halfway down, something clicked inside her, like a compass that had finally found its direction again. The gates flew by as she whipped between them, skis and body in perfect synchronization, no thoughts except the next gate, the next turn, the next shift.

It was just her and the mountain, and it was glorious.

When she hit the end of the course, she almost shouted in triumph, but settled for a silent fist-pump. It hadn't been pretty, and it hadn't been fast, but it was her first complete Super G run without a fall since her accident, so it was worth celebrating.

But one run proved nothing.

She needed to see if she could do it again.

She did. Several times, each run smoother and faster than the last. Until by the final one, the afternoon was waning and her legs felt like the over-cooked pasta from the other night's dinner.

For the first time in a long time, she was sorry for training to end. As she hiked to her car and strapped her skis to the roof rack, the silly grin seemed plastered to her face. Stupid to overdo it like that, but so worth it.

She'd proven two things to herself.

The first was that she had broken through her mental block. When her father came back, she'd be able to show him she could handle whatever training schedule he wanted to throw at her. She was ready.

Her high lasted until she got home and finally allowed herself to think about the second thing she'd proven: that she could ski well even if it wasn't what her heart desired anymore. Because as much as she had felt the connection to the snow, as in-tune as her body had been with the course, it hadn't been the same.

There was something missing, some indecipherable feeling that had always been there before, but now wasn't. The runs had been amazing, her form improving every time, but deep inside, she knew she'd only been going through the motions.

She could feel the course again, but she couldn't *feel* it.

It doesn't matter.

As long as she'd mastered the issues that were keeping her from performing, she could fake the rest. Enjoying herself had never mattered as much as making her dad proud. Being able to do that again was all she cared about right now.

That, and seeing Theo.

Stripping off her sweat-dampened clothes, she collapsed onto the bed with a groan. She could lie to herself all she wanted about the skiing, but when it came to Theo, it seemed only hard truths would do.

And the truth was, he'd begun to mean something to her. Something more than a temporary fix to a lifelong sense of loneliness.

Her father seemed to think that wasn't a problem. So did Ari.

So why the hell was she fighting it so hard?

Swiping the phone up from the nightstand, she started to type out a text to Theo, then changed her mind and dialed his number instead. Her mouth went a little dry as she listened to it ring.

"Hello, Rachel."

She winced at his neutral tone. Not that she could blame him for it. The last time they'd spoken, she'd basically blown him off with the "I have a headache" excuse. It didn't matter that she'd really had one.

"Theo, hi." When he said nothing, she added, "I hope I'm not interrupting your work."

"No, I'm just leaving the office for the day, actually. What's up?"

She closed her eyes, picturing him in his tailored suit and power tie, looking all corporate and sharkish, and had to bite her lower lip to keep a tiny sigh from escaping.

The man was a treat for the eyes no matter what he was wearing, but she'd started looking forward to stripping him out of those designer suits when he came home from work. It was like peeling away the layers of civilization he had to wear as camouflage during the day and finding the earthy, sensual man he hid underneath.

"Rachel? I asked what's up?"

Because she was thinking it, she said it. "I was laying her naked wishing you were, too."

He made a small choking sound that was half-laugh, half-surprise. "What?"

"Are you wearing the black suit today, or the blue Armani?"

"I...the gray Burberry. Why?"

"Mmm, I love how that one makes your ass look, but I still want to peel it off you nice and slow until you're wearing nothing but skin."

"Jesus, Rae." There was a slightly muffled sound of voices around him.

"Where are you?"

"I just got in the elevator, so I can't really talk at the moment."

"Can anyone hear me?"

"No." The word was strained.

She smiled, settling more comfortably against the pillow, eyes still closed to better picture her own words. "Good, then you can still listen."

"If you wait two minutes, I'll be in the car, and we can—"

"I want to slide your tie off, nice and slow. Then unbutton your shirt, all the way down, so I can lick my way along that line of hair all the way from your chest to your navel."

"Rae." There was a command in that one word to stop.

Which she ignored.

"Off comes the jacket, and the shirt, and then the belt, just as slow as the tie. One. Tug. At. A. Time." She bit her lip again, feeling a tug of her own low in her belly as she painted her hypothetical seduction.

"Fuck."

Hearing him apologize to someone for the muttered curse only made her hotter, knowing he was surrounded by people who had no idea she was talking dirty to their boss.

"No, not yet. Fucking comes later, after I peel your pants down those long legs of yours, leaving you all hard and ready, with only your briefs keeping me from taking you in my mouth. *Are* you hard, Theo?"

His swallow was audible. "Yes, damn you."

"Are you ready for me?"

"You're in so much trouble when I get there."

"Are you?"

"Yes." It was a growl of need and frustration, laced with anticipation. "Happy?"

"Not yet, but I will be. All I have left to do is tug the band of your briefs over the tip of you, all swollen and needy, and give it a kiss. Or maybe a lick. Would you like a lick better?"

Her only answer was the sound of Theo's rapid breath sawing into the phone. She squirmed on the comforter, caught in her own web of words as arousal sparked along her nerve endings, waking her body from its earlier fatigue.

"Yes, definitely a lick." His quick intake of air said she'd chosen right. "But it's not enough. I need more. So those briefs have to go, so I can touch all of you. Every delicious inch hot and hard in my hand as I take you into my mouth. Slow or fast?"

"Jesus fucking Christ. Just...just wait two seconds." There was the chirp of a car alarm, then a door slamming.

"Slow or fast?"

"It doesn't matter. I won't last long either way," Theo growled. There was a change in the ambient noise that said he'd switched over to the in-car Bluetooth. "But I'm not going to go in your mouth, sweetheart. I have other plans for you."

Her heart rate sped up at the dark promise in his voice. "Do tell."

"Are you really naked?"

"The only thing I'm wearing is a smile of anticipation." Which widened at his groan.

"Where are you?"

"Lying on my bed. Thinking of you."

"Are your nipples hard?"

A shiver ran through her body, but she was far from cold. In fact, she was close to breaking a sweat again. "They are now."

"Touch them."

The command made her open her eyes in surprise. She gave a shaky laugh. "What?"

"Touch them. Run your fingers over them and imagine it's me doing it."

She could have lied. He'd never know the difference.

But she let her eyes drift close again and sent her free hand gliding along her own ribcage, up to her breast, to the rigid peak that hardened even more as she slowly circled it with her fingertip.

"Are you doing it?"

"Mmmhmm."

"Does it feel good?"

"Yes." She let the word draw out in a hiss of pleasure.

"Now, wet your finger."

"What?"

"Wet your finger, and do it again, and think of my mouth sucking on those luscious, hard tips, all hot and wet."

His words were too compelling to disobey.

Feeling only a little self-conscious, she stuck her finger between her lips to moisten it. Then applied it to the breast that had been neglected, running it over the hard bumps of her areola as she circled inward to her aching nipple.

In her mind's eye, she saw Theo's head bent over her breasts, worshipping at them. Every tug of her fingers was his mouth suckling, every pinch his teeth tugging.

She groaned.

"That sounds like it feels good." Theo's voice rasped in her ear.

"It does."

"How good?"

"*So* good." Good enough she was close to going up in flames, burned by her own game, and she didn't even care.

"Are you wet for me?"

"Yes." How could she not be, when every touch was sending tingles straight from breast to groin?

"Touch yourself there. Tell me how hot and wet you are thinking about me touching you."

The command should have made her at least hesitate. But she was too caught in the sensations to care who won this particular battle.

Her hand skated down her torso and between her thighs. A small gasp escaped as her fingers brushed over her swollen clitoris on the way to where she was damp and aching, and far, far too empty.

"You're ready, aren't you?"

"So ready."

"For who?"

She whimpered. "For you. I need you, Theo. I need you to come fill me up." Another brush of that sensitive bundle of nerves made her groan, ratcheting the tension in her body even higher as her legs moved restlessly on the bed. She was close. So close.

"I'm going to, sweetheart. I'll fill every inch of you, and make you feel so damn good you're never going to remember what it was like before you were mine."

Something echoed deep inside her aching body at his words. Something other than mere arousal. But she was too far gone to recognize it or care.

"I'm so close. I need...I have to..."

"No! Wait for me. I'm almost there."

The growl of command in his voice was enough to make her still her hand and rest it low on her belly, but it couldn't stop the aching pulse of need threatening to draw it back again. Being on this teetering edge was like standing at the lip of a mountain slope.

Where the thrill of anticipation lasted only until the lure of the drop grew greater and you had no choice but to push yourself over the edge.

"I need...I need..." Her head whipped back and forth on the pillow as she fought the growing demand of her body.

"I'm here, baby. Come down and let me in."

His words made her realize the pounding she heard wasn't only her heart in her ears. Moving like a drunk in a fog, she hurried down the stairs. Only the fact she was stark naked made her think enough to check it was really Theo before yanking the door open, staying to the side, hidden from anyone who might be passing by.

Theo froze at the sight of her naked body. Nostrils flaring like a stallion catching the scent of a mare, he slammed the door behind him and stalked her way.

A thrill ran through her at his heated expression, at the intent in every panther-like movement of his body. Something about the predatory way he approached made her back toward the stairs.

Not to run away, but to continue the game they'd started.

He matched her step-for-step, gaining on her because of his longer legs, until when she finally turned to take the first step up the staircase he was on her, claiming her mouth with hot, hungry kisses she met with equal fervor.

His clothes disappeared from his body, not in the slow reveal she'd earlier described but in a flurry of graceless yanks and wrenched buttons. It didn't matter how they got there, as long as the end result was nothing between them but air.

His skin was hot on hers as he kissed her again. This time with hands roaming over her as though he'd been away too long and needed to reacquaint himself with the landscape of her body.

The bed was too far for either of them to wait.

She sank to her knees on the second step, bracing her hands on the one above as Theo drove himself into her body from behind with one strong, sure thrust.

Oh, yes!

This was what she'd wanted. What she'd needed.

She pressed back, meeting each frantic thrust with one of her own, ensuring he went as deep as possible, filling every inch of her exactly the way he'd promised.

The fire had already been burning long enough in them both that it was a quick rise to the point of full immolation. She cried out as her release exploded through her body, the tightening of her inner muscles bringing Theo with her.

He groaned as he continued to thrust through the orgasm, making her curl her fingers into the carpet as she writhed and gasped from the prolonged sensations.

Limp, lazy, and sated, she pressed her cheek to the step as he collapsed against her back, glad he seemed as undone as she felt. Because she was pretty sure once the afterglow passed, she was going to find she'd done something very, very stupid.

She'd pushed over the edge, all right, but it was a freefall into something a lot scarier than any mountain, any race, had ever been.

She just might have let herself fall into love.

Chapter 26

How could it keep getting better every damn time?

After cleaning up the aftermath of not using a condom, they'd gotten into the hot tub, where he let his fingers play in lazy circles on her shoulder as they relaxed in the soothing waters in blissful silence. Thankfully, that mistake wouldn't have consequences, since Rachel was on birth control.

Which didn't excuse his lapse. All he'd been able to think about when he walked through the door was getting inside of her. Claiming her. Putting on a condom, always an automatic move for him, had never even entered his mind.

Pill or not, they'd agreed in the beginning to use condoms, so he'd do his damnedest to never make that mistake again.

Which sucked, because now he knew what he'd been missing. The feel of sliding into her bare had been beyond exquisite. Even the thinnest bit of latex made wouldn't come close.

A disappointment he'd just have to deal with.

The risk far outweighed the reward.

And with as often as they made love, it would be like waving a red flag at fate and daring it to do its worst. Kind of like doing it on the staircase. Too much chance of someone walking in and—

His hand tightened on her shoulder. "Aren't your fathers coming home today?"

There was a hesitation before she answered, stoking his tension.

"They were supposed to, but they decided to take a few days of vacation first. They'll be back Friday instead."

The rush of relief almost made him dizzy. "Good." He gave her a searching look when she didn't echo the sentiment. "Or, not good?"

"No. It's fine."

"See, your words say that, but your face doesn't look like it agrees." He puzzled over her almost mulish expression. "Wait, is that what last night was about? Being upset your dads changed their plans?"

"No." She groaned. "Okay, maybe a little."

"You could have just told me."

Why did it hurt so much she hadn't? That she'd made up an excuse instead?

"I know, I'm sorry. But I really did have a headache. It was just...brought on by a lot of different things. Saying goodbye to everyone at work. Vicky's stupid race. My dads. Us. I just needed a night to myself to try and sort everything out in my head."

He wasn't sure how he felt about that "us" being included on her list.

"And how did that go?"

"Honestly? Not as well as I'd hoped." She leaned her head on his shoulder. "I didn't like sleeping alone."

"Neither did I." Which was strange, because it had never bothered him before.

In fact, most of the time he was relieved to have his own space back again once a relationship had gotten a little too cozy. Sometimes even before that. Growing up in a big, nosy family made privacy a valued commodity.

What did it mean that instead of relief, last night his house had felt empty and, damn it, lonely because she wasn't in it?

Clearly, he had some "us" things of his own to sort out.

"I'm not really sure what comes next."

Her words echoed his own thoughts.

"Neither am I." He started drawing lazy circles on her shoulder again, as much for his comfort as hers. "Well, I do know I want to keep seeing you. But I also know you plan to start training once Karl is home. Meaning your time will be more limited, which means *our* time will be more limited."

He paused, giving her an opening to bring up her whispered secret. Clearly, it had been weighing on her. When she didn't, he pushed, just a little. "If that's still the plan? To start training again?"

"It's still the plan." She sounded resigned.

So, he pushed a little more.

"And you're sure that's what you want?"

Eyes narrowed, she leaned away from him. So far that the only thing left touching were their knees beneath the roiling water. "Why wouldn't it be? Of course, it's what I want. Racing is my life. It's the only thing I have that makes me special."

Her tone and body language screamed he'd pushed a little too hard. Right into "you fucked up" land.

He tried to deflect and deescalate. Something he was usually good at as the family's unofficial mediator.

"I'd have to disagree. I think you're pretty damn special just being you."

As she often did when he paid her a compliment, she brushed it aside and ignored it. "Why would you even ask something like that?"

Because I was awake when you confessed your secret to me and I'm trying to figure out how to help.

But he wasn't stupid enough to tell her that. Not when she already looked like she wanted to shove his head underwater. "I just want to make sure you're happy."

"I'm happy."

"Okay." What else could he say when she clearly wasn't?

"I *am*. As a matter of fact, I ran the Super G course at Copper today, and it went great. Dad's going to be really pleased with my progress. That makes me *ecstatic*."

Her wording only reinforced his earlier suspicions her happiness was somehow inextricably entwined with pleasing her dad. "That's great. Really. I'm glad it went well. I want you to be happy." He slipped his arm back around her shoulders and gave an encouraging tug in his direction.

She resisted for a second before giving in with a sigh, bringing her body back against his, and laid her head on his shoulder. "I can't give up racing just to spend more time with you, Theo. I just can't."

"I would never ask you to." But was that really true? If her training schedule kept them apart for more hours than they were together, would he start to resent it? Or would he start to obsess over her health and safety every time she was somewhere beyond his reach, like he had that first day they met?

He hoped not.

But the truth was, he didn't know. He'd never been invested enough in a relationship to not be able to walk away without regrets at any time. This relationship with her, though...

The idea of walking away hurt more than he thought it could.

"So, what do we do, then?"

"I guess we figure it out as we go. Find a way to make it work." He pressed a kiss to her steam-dampened hair, inhaling the vanilla scent of her shampoo. "I want us to work, Rae. I really do."

"Me, too."

It was a small confession, but it soothed some of the unease building in his chest. They were both smart, capable adults. They both wanted the same thing—each other. Between them, they'd find a way for that to happen.

They had to, because the alternative was simply unacceptable.

Chapter 27

Meeting Rachel's fathers was just as bad as he'd imagined it might be.

Maybe worse, considering all he could think about was how many times he'd had their daughter naked over the past two weeks. Some of those times right here in their own house. On their front stairs.

It didn't matter she was twenty-eight, not eighteen. He still felt like a fraud and debaucher as he smiled and shook their hands and sat at their dinner table Friday night.

Because they knew.

At least, Dellin did. It was there in the quick, assessing gaze. The unhappy tuck of his mouth as he watched the casual touches and affectionate glances Rachel was giving him as they chatted and passed the food around.

Karl seemed more oblivious. Or so he'd thought until he caught the glitter of ice-blue eyes watching from under lowered lashes when Rachel ladled gravy onto his potatoes instead of handing him it to do himself.

Oh yeah. Karl definitely knew.

And yet, it didn't bother him as much as it maybe should have. He enjoyed being fussed over by her. And if she was comfortable enough to do it in front of her silently disapproving fathers, all the better. Because it sent a message, whether she'd meant it to or not.

She was claiming him.

It didn't mean they wouldn't hate the hell out of him anyway. But maybe, just maybe, in their eyes it would make him more than merely the guy defiling their little girl.

As if he knew the exact thought going through Theo's mind, as Dellin passed the bowl of peas he gave him a look which had probably once scared criminals into confessing everything they'd ever done all the way back to kindergarten. "So, what is it you do for a living when you're not rescuing women on ski slopes, Theo?"

"Pop, I already told you..." Rachel gave an exaggerated sigh when the look turned her way. "Fine." With a pained look of apology in Theo's direction, she applied herself to her pot roast.

He managed a polite smile that gave no hint his balls were trying to crawl up into his body in cowardly retreat. "I work at my family's investment firm with my older brother and father."

Dellin's dark gaze never wavered. "That's understating things, don't you think? A Fortune 500 company is a little more than just a family firm. It's an empire." He didn't make it sound like a compliment.

Which made no sense. "Most fathers would be happy to hear their daughter was dating someone financially stable."

"Is that what you're doing? Dating?" This from Karl at the other end of the table.

"Yes, sir. We are." He reached under the table and squeezed Rachel's hand as he smiled at her. Here, at least, he was on solid ground. They'd agreed ahead of time on how they'd define their current relationship to her parents when it came up. Because there was no way it wouldn't come up.

He was just surprised it had taken this long.

He'd thought the interrogation would begin the minute he hit the front door. What he hadn't expected was that they'd have done some background on him ahead of time and come prepared.

But he should have. Rule one before any important meeting was to gather as much intel as you could about the other party. Hell, he and Richard had done the same to every one of Lillian's boyfriends since college.

Karl looked from Theo to Rachel, then grunted and went back to eating.

Not waiting for the next question, he took the opportunity to gain control of the conversation. "Mr. Long, Rachel tells me you're a retired police officer. My little brother, Peter, is in the BPD. He's studying for the detective's exam, in fact."

"Is that right?" Dellin forked up some meat and chewed as he continued to keep eye contact with him. It was damned unnerving. Which was probably the intent. "I'm surprised he didn't take the easy road and join the family business like you and your other brother did."

It was tough, but he let the insinuation slide without rising to the bait.

"Everyone has to follow the path that's true to their heart. Peter's led him to law enforcement. The way my sister's path led to her art instead of the office down the hall. She could have done the job, she was perfectly qualified, but she would have been miserable working there. Loving what you do is as important as being good at it. I'm ashamed to say it took me a while to understand that."

Beside him, Rachel made a small noise, but when he glanced over she was studiously applying herself to her food.

Chewing another bite of roast, Dellin's gaze grew sharper before turning to something shrewd and almost thoughtful. "Hmm."

Rachel jumped into the conversation with an almost frenetic enthusiasm.

"Lillian's very talented. Theo has one of her paintings in his living room. It's gorgeous, and very nuanced. The way she did the sunset on the mountains is stunning. I notice some new detail every time I see it."

He swallowed a groan. With that last statement, she'd reminded her fathers the two of them had been spending a lot of time together while they were gone.

Sure enough, Dellin and Karl exchanged a quick look across the length of the table, and the interrogation resumed, this time with Karl taking the lead.

"So, Theo, what does a young, wealthy bachelor like yourself do for fun? Besides skiing, which you obviously do since that's how you met our Rachel." There was a slight emphasis on the 'our' as if to remind him they had prior claim to her. "What other wild and crazy things do you get up to? Lots of parties? Drugs?"

"Oh, my God." Rachel groaned, putting her face in her hand. "Dad, you promised."

The line of questioning continued to confuse him. How the hell did being rich somehow become a mark against him with these two?

"I guess it depends on your definition of wild and crazy. While I go to some parties, I'm well past the age of getting drunk and stupid every night." His conscience twinged about the night not too long ago when he'd done precisely that. "And I guess you could say my drug of choice is adrenaline, with my habit being sports. Mostly rock climbing."

"Rock climbing? That's a little dangerous, isn't it?"

"More dangerous than hurtling down a mountain at eighty miles an hour?"

They stared at each other, neither flinching, until finally Karl gave a grudging nod before going back to his food. "Point taken."

Rachel made big eyes at him, as though shocked he'd seemed to win that round. Theo gave her a wink and patted her leg under the table. He should have remembered Karl was only one half of the gauntlet he needed to navigate.

"Still seems more reckless than fun to me." Dellin's tone wasn't disapproving so much as honestly concerned.

"Not if you know what you're doing and take the proper precautions. I'm not saying it doesn't have inherent risks. Most sports do, to one degree or another. But as long as you follow the rules, it can be an exhilarating experience."

"Theo's even climbed El Capitan." Pride shone in Rachel's eyes. "He said it was one of the best days of his life."

The usual shaft of pain and guilt when he thought of Gavin was still there, sharp and hot. But it hurt a little less this time as he remembered the good instead of the bad.

He cleared his throat. "It was. There's nothing quite like standing at the top of a seven-thousand-foot summit and knowing you just conquered that bi—uh, beast with pretty much your bare hands."

Dellin gave him a considering look. "I guess it's one of those things you can't really understand the full impact of unless you're there. Kind of like going to space. The pictures they send back are impressive, but nowhere near the actual experience."

"Yeah, that's a fair analogy."

"Okay. How about you take me out and show me, then?"

"Show you?" A nervous laugh burbled up. Or maybe it was terror. "Sir, no disrespect, but you don't take a novice out and just 'show' him how to climb. That would be the definition of reckless."

Not to mention currently impossible.

Rachel might have made a breakthrough on her mental block. But his visits to North Table Mountain the past two Saturdays while she worked had proven he was no closer to conquering his own.

"Okay, then how would this *novice* get started?"

"Are you kidding?"

He hadn't meant to sound condescending. But no matter how fit Dellin Long looked, he was still somewhere close to the six-decade mark. While not exactly *old*, it was perhaps not the best age to be starting such a physically demanding sport.

Rachel stared at her father like he'd grown a second head. "Pop, you can't be serious!"

"Why not? I have lots of time on my hands. I'll have even more once you and your dad start training again. Seems like the perfect time to pick up a new hobby." He shot a long look filled with some deep meaning down the length of the table at Karl, who met it without comment before he went back to eating.

Clearly there was a whole different issue going on tonight besides his suitability being weighed and measured. He just wasn't sure what it was.

Realizing Dellin was waiting for an answer, he scrambled to come up with one. "Um, I guess I'd suggest starting in a rock-climbing club. There's several here in Boulder to pick from. They all have indoor practice walls to learn on and safety equipment to keep you from getting hurt when you fall. Because you will at first. A lot."

He didn't know how to make it any clearer without being rude.

Again.

"Do you belong to one of them?"

"Yeah, I do. Would you like me to give you the address?"

"Actually, why don't you take me there one of these days and get me started?"

Feeling Rachel's gaze boring into him from the side, he mustered a halfway convincing smile for her father. "Sure, if you really want to." Which he was hoping he really didn't. Hoped this was merely a threat, a chess move in whatever game was going on between Rachel's dads, and that he wasn't about to get caught in the middle of it.

"How about Sunday?"

So much for hope. "This Sunday?"

"Why not? Karl will be putting Rachel through her paces at Copper. That leaves the both of us at loose ends for most of the day until they're done."

The fact he didn't even ask if Theo might have other plans was a good indication the suggestion was more a command than an option. Funny, but the thought of spending a day one-on-one with Rachel's imposing father didn't scare him half as much as the thought of *where* they'd spend it.

"Sure, why not," he echoed.

The click of silverware against plate was exceptionally loud from Karl's end of the table as he attacked his food with increasing aggression. "You're going to hurt your damn shoulder again," he muttered without looking up.

Theo glanced at Dellin for his reaction, but he continued to eat without comment. A quick look at Rachel showed she was as confused by the undercurrents in the room as he was.

"It wouldn't be smart to try climbing with an injury, sir, not even on an indoor wall. We should wait until it's healed."

"It's an old injury. My shoulder's fine. Good enough for this, anyway."

"Well, if you're sure..."

"I am." Dellin's gaze flicked down the table. "I'm tired of waiting."

Karl's shoulders hunched, but he didn't meet Dellin's gaze. "Do what you want, then."

"Oh, if only," Dellin said with a derisive snort.

Silence descended over the table, but it wasn't the comfortable kind Theo was used to with Rachel. This silence was like a living, breathing mass of badness just waiting to explode over all of them.

Trying to avoid that, he sought a new topic.

"The meal is delicious, sir."

"Thank you."

"Rachel told me you took some professional cooking classes. That must have been interesting."

One shoulder shrugged. "Just another hobby."

"Oh, please, you loved those classes," Karl snapped. "You love cooking."

"I love cooking for you."

As the two men held another silent communication across the table, Theo glanced at Rachel with a questioning look. She quickly tossed her napkin on the table and pushed her chair back to stand.

"I think I'll go get the dessert. Theo, why don't you help me?"

Grateful for any excuse to get out of the line of fire, he picked up his plate and followed her to the kitchen. "What was that all about?" he asked as soon as he was sure they were out of earshot.

"I have no idea. They've been acting a little weird ever since they got home this morning. I thought maybe it was jetlag or something, but..."

She shook her head as she looked in the direction they'd just retreated from, then focused back on him. "I'm sorry about tonight. If they're in the middle of arguing about something, I don't know why they would have insisted you come for dinner."

He knew exactly why.

The invitation—which was more of a summons—had come right after Rachel informed Karl they wouldn't be able to start training the next day as he wanted, since she was going to the charity brunch with Theo.

It was probably the first time she'd ever put her foot down and refused to follow her coach's schedule. That it was for a man she'd known less than a month and they'd never met just made it exponentially worse.

Such an out-of-character divergence would have no doubt raised a lot of red flags for both men. Thus creating an immediate need to meet Theo and assess for themselves who he was and what kind of threat he might pose to their daughter. That would have eclipsed any private issues they were having between themselves.

Nothing pulled parents into a united front faster than protecting their child.

It was just his bad luck he was the thing they were protecting her from.

Chapter 28

By the time they returned to the dining room a few minutes later with the cake and plates, things seemed to have deteriorated even further. Karl was gone, and given the hard set of Dellin's mouth, whatever had precipitated his exit hadn't been pretty.

The thought of sitting through another half hour of small talk in the tension-thick room held no appeal, but he gamely took his seat, willing to endure it for Rachel's sake.

Thankfully, Dellin had other ideas.

"I'm sorry to cut the evening short, kids, but I think the jetlag is finally catching up with me." He pushed back his chair and stood, waving them both down when they followed suit. "No, no, stay and enjoy your dessert."

Not about to take the more submissive position, even if the other man hadn't meant it that way, Theo remained standing. "Thank you for dinner, sir. It was a pleasure to meet you. Both of you." He held out his hand, and there was a long moment when he thought Dellin might not take it.

Then he gave a grudging nod and clasped Theo's hand in a firm, not-quite crushing grip. "You, too." He hung on for an extra second when Theo would have let go. "Sunday, right? You and me?"

Giving in to the inevitable, he nodded. "Looking forward to it, sir."

With a flicker of expression that might have been a smile under other circumstances, Dellin gave his shoulder a firm pat and released him. "I doubt that."

Walking around Theo, he leaned down and kissed Rachel on the cheek. "Put the food away when you're done, please. I'll take care of the dishes in the morning."

"Sure, Pop." She caught his hand as he turned. "Is everything okay?"

He looked down at her with such naked affection in his eyes, Theo knew in that instant he needed this man on his side in order to keep his place in Rachel's life. There was zero doubt if Dellin Long thought he wasn't good enough for his daughter, for any reason, he'd make Theo's life a living hell doing anything in his power to get rid of him.

"Everything's fine, baby girl." He gave her hand a squeeze. "Don't you worry."

But she did look worried.

They went through the familiar motions of cleaning up the remains of the meal, packing away leftovers in the fridge and stacking the dishwasher despite Dellin's instructions. Theo sensed her unease in her agitated movements and the way she was gnawing on her lower lip like she was drilling for oil.

Not able to take it any longer, he grabbed the damp dishrag she was using to wipe down the counters and tossed it aside, capturing both her hands in his. "Are you okay?"

"Yes. Fine." She sighed when he gave her a chiding look. "Okay, no, not really. I just hate it when they fight. Or...whatever that was."

Leaning his butt against the counter, he drew her between his legs and wrapped his hands loosely around her waist, clasping them in the small of her back. Not a sexual embrace, but one offering comfort. "Do they fight a lot?"

"No more than other couples, I guess." She looped her hands over his shoulders, but didn't relax into him the way she normally did. Another indication of her stress level. "I've always hated any sort of disagreement. 'Keep the house happy. Don't make trouble.'"

"That sounded like a quote of some kind, but I'm not familiar with it. Emily Post?"

"Ivy." She gave a quicksilver grin at his confusion. "She was one of the kids at the foster home I was in. She'd been in the system long enough to come up with her own set of rules on how to keep your foster family from kicking you out."

He startled. "That can happen?"

"Sure. If they think you're disruptive or causing trouble, they just call up Social Services and poof, you're off to the next foster home with your garbage bag of stuff to start all over again."

It probably wasn't as simple as that, but he supposed to a kid it could feel that way. Children in general had little control over their lives. How much worse was it for kids with nothing permanent to anchor themselves to? No family or home they knew was theirs, no matter what they said or did?

"Did that happen to you?"

"No, I was lucky. I only got moved once, from where they sent me right after my mom died. It was an emergency placement where I stayed while they tried to find any relatives who could take me. When they didn't, I got sent to a more long-term foster family."

"How old were you?"

"Six."

"Jesus." The thought of Rachel as a scared little girl nearly broke his heart. "You didn't have any family at all?"

"Not that they could find."

"What about your dad?"

"I never knew him. Mom never talked about him, so I guess he just didn't want us." She shrugged like it didn't matter, but her eyes told a different story.

Theo kissed her forehead. "Then he was an idiot."

A little of the sadness left her expression.

"Anyway, when they moved me to the second family is when I met Ivy, and she warned me right off about how to behave if I wanted to stay where I was. And I did, because she was there. She was like a big sister to the younger kids. Zeke and Queenie were okay, too, I guess. My fosters," she said when he tipped his head in question. "It was a decent place, overall, just really crowded. Two bunk beds in each bedroom, eight kids, two adults, and only two bathrooms." She made a small moue of distaste at the memory that hinted it was worse than she was making it sound.

"Sounds a little overwhelming." The comment she'd once made about being thrilled to have a bedroom all to herself when she'd come to live here made more sense now.

"It felt like it sometimes. But it was still a lot better place than some stories I heard from the other kids who'd been around the system longer, so I did whatever I had to do to stay."

"Ivy's rules?"

"Yup. They were pretty simple, really. Common sense kind of stuff that, as a kid, you're not always smart enough to think about on your own. Don't talk back. Don't be ungrateful. Always keep your ears open and your mouth shut. Never tell anyone—" She bit her lip and looked away.

His gut clenched.

"Never tell anyone what?"

Her throat worked as she swallowed. "Your secrets."

"Hey." He waited until she looked at him again. "You know your secrets are safe with me, right?"

She studied him as though trying to see through his skull straight into his brain.

Or maybe his soul.

Finally, with another hard swallow, she gave the tiniest of nods. "I trust you."

Those three words meant more to him than he would have thought possible. They changed something, irrevocably, somewhere deep inside, close to his heart.

It wasn't love. Not yet.

But it tremored so close to the edge of it that it would only take one last nudge to send him crashing headlong into something he doubted he'd ever recover from.

Suddenly unnerved by his own thoughts, he shifted the tension which had sprung up between them back to the kind neither of them ever had any trouble handling. He kissed her as though trying to climb inside her mouth, and she responded with equal desperation.

Pressing her body tight to his, she licked and nipped at his lips while he slipped one hand beneath the waistband of her jeans. He cupped her firm ass while he ground his quickly emerging erection against the vee of her legs.

He needed more. More skin, more touch, more everything.

More Rachel.

But as he popped the button open on her jeans to the accompaniment of her groan of approval, sanity returned in a cold splash. He tore his mouth from hers with a harsh gasp. "Can't. Not alone."

"Oh, my God." She rested her head against his shoulder, hiding her face. "I can't believe I almost...with my dads right upstairs. What's wrong with me?"

"Come home with me." It was as much a plea as a demand, but he already knew her answer before she shook her head.

"I can't. Not their first night home. Besides, if I leave now, they'd know..."

"That it was so you could have your wicked way with me?"

His teasing got the desired effect when she raised her head and smacked him lightly on the chest. At least he'd made her smile.

"Tomorrow, then. Promise me you'll stay the night with me tomorrow. This way we'll have the whole day together, and we can talk about, well, everything." It wouldn't help his lonely bed tonight, but at least he'd have something to look forward to.

It was a lot to ask of her. He knew that.

They hadn't actually discussed what would happen to their sleeping arrangements after her fathers were home again. But he didn't want to go back to saying goodnight on her doorstep every night. "Promise," he whispered against her ear before he flicked the shell of it with his tongue.

She shuddered. "Okay, yes. I promise."

Triumphant, he kissed her, careful this time to keep tight control so it didn't get out of hand. Even so, it was nearly impossible to walk out the front door and leave her there, knowing she belonged at his side. In his bed.

Tomorrow couldn't come soon enough.

Chapter 29

THE CHARITY BRUNCH AND fashion show was a much bigger deal than she'd expected.

Walking into the crowded ballroom on Theo's arm, the first thing she noticed was the noise level, which seemed disproportionate to the amount of people in the room. The second thing she noticed was the reason for it.

Kids.

Dozens of them, from about kindergarten size ranging up to young teens. Some lined up to shoot a hockey puck into a net set up in the corner. The rest stood around in small groups, talking to very large men in slacks and polo shirts. Most with the kind of enthusiasm she'd often seen in fans waiting at the sidelines of a race, hoping for a moment's attention from their favorite skier.

It wasn't too big a leap to deduce the men listening so attentively to the star-struck kids were the members of the Avalanche hockey team.

"I knew this was to raise funds for kids' sports programs, but I didn't realize that meant the kids were actually going to be a part of it."

She bit back a chuckle at the sight of one of the massive players practically lying on the floor in order to make himself eye-level with the delicate little girl talking a mile a minute at him. Slightly behind her watching were her parents, judging by the happy, indulgent smiles on their faces. And no wonder.

It was adorable as hell.

"Oh, yeah. The day's as much for them to have fun as it is to raise money. They get to spend the morning hanging with the players, then they hit the runway with them after we eat. They have a blast."

She looked at him in surprise. "The kids do the fashion show?"

"Yeah, they're great. Some of them are born hams. You'll see."

Rachel digested that bit of news as they strolled through the room, greeting people here and there. Everyone was dressed well but casually, making her glad she'd gone with the simple red wool dress and flats she'd dug out of her closet. Even Theo had toned down his usual designer look with a pair of dark slacks and a royal blue dress shirt, sans tie.

Not that it made him any less yummy to look at.

She hadn't been sure what to expect from the event. But clearly, this wasn't going to be the stuffy, snooty kind of affair she'd suffered through when Stefan insisted they attend fashion week in Milan. No one here was rocking couture or dripping diamonds. Or looking down their cultured noses at those who weren't.

Something inside her relaxed.

Maybe today wouldn't be too horrible after all.

"Theo, dear. I'm so glad to see you. And on time, no less."

Turning at the warm tone, she knew immediately this had to be Theo's mother. The resemblance was strong, right down to the teasing twinkle in her rich brown eyes. Eyes that took a good, long look in her direction before focusing back on Theo, who leaned down and bussed her cheek.

"I'm never late for one of your parties, Mom. You must be thinking of one of your other sons. You know, the inconsiderate ones."

"None of my sons are inconsiderate," she replied with a sniff. "Simply prone to losing track of time when it suits them to." Her gaze went back to Rachel expectantly.

"Mom, this is Rachel Long, my date. Rachel, this is my mother, Patricia, the maestro of this whole shindig and the reason it's such a success."

"Hardly that," Patricia said with a negligent wave of her manicured hand. "The players and the Avalanche organization make it a success. The Everbrite Foundation simply handles logistics." She smiled at Rachel. "It's nice to meet you, dear. So, how long have you and my son known each other?"

"Mom." He gave her a warning look, to which his mother gave him a blandly innocent one in return.

"What? It was a simple question."

Feeling Theo take a breath to respond, Rachel hugged his arm tighter to her body and answered first. "About three weeks, depending."

"On what?"

"If you go by the first time we met, or the first time we went on a date. We can't seem to agree which to count."

"I thought what we couldn't agree on was which was the first date, lunch or dinner?" Theo gave her a wink when she rolled her eyes at him.

"That, too."

Patricia watched the exchange with keen interest. "Only three weeks?" she murmured. "Interesting. So, tell me, Rachel—may I call you Rachel, dear?"

"Of course."

"Lovely. So, Rachel, what is it you do?"

"I'm a professional skier."

"An athlete. Of course." She looked like she'd just had an epiphany. "Do tell me you're a local and not here visiting one of the resorts."

"Mom, don't you have other guests to bother?"

Rachel gave him a nudge. "Theo, that's rude."

"No, rude is giving you the third degree."

"Oh, please, you had worse from my dads last night." She smiled in apology at Patricia. "I've lived in Boulder most of my life. I do travel a lot for training and competitions, but this will always be home."

"Really? How nice." The words were drawn out enough to carry much more weight than they should have.

Theo seemed to think so, too. He stiffened and put his hand on her elbow. "We're going to mingle some more, Mom, since that's what you wanted me here for. Right?"

She looked like she might have protested, then made a small *hmph* noise and shooed him away. "Fine, yes, go. Mingle. And find your younger brother. He's lurking somewhere in the room. Avoiding me, I suppose." The affection in her voice took out the sting of the words.

Rachel gave his mother another smile, not sure why they were retreating but willing to follow Theo's lead. "It was very nice to meet you, Mrs. Beaumont." The smile she got in return was hard to interpret, wide and full of teeth. It almost felt like a shark eyeing a tasty meal that had blundered unknowingly into its path.

"Oh please, dear. Call me Patricia."

As Theo led her away, she asked quietly, "Why do I feel like I said something wrong back there?"

"Not wrong, exactly."

"Then what?"

"You mentioned that I'd met your parents."

She thought back over her words. "Barely."

"For my mother, barely is good enough."

"Good enough for what?"

"To think about sticking her nose into our business."

He brought them to a halt near the end of the runway set up for the fashion show. There were fewer people at this end of the ballroom, giving them an illusion of privacy. "My mother seems to think none of her children can navigate their own love lives without her steering the boat for them. It's getting to be a real problem."

"I thought two of your siblings were already in committed relationships?"

"They are. Which is why it's becoming a problem. Now she's got more time to concentrate her meddling on the two of us who are left."

She laughed. "Come on, it can't be that bad. Your mother seems like a perfectly sweet woman."

"Patricia is the absolute sweetest, and don't let this ungrateful jackanapes try to tell you any different."

Starting at the unexpected interruption, she turned to see a surprisingly familiar face.

"Des!"

The man approaching looked just as shocked. His dark Mediterranean features arranged themselves into an almost comic jaw-drop before he snapped his mouth shut and hurried forward to throw his arms around her.

"Rachel! What a lovely surprise to see you here. And on the arm of one of those divinely made Beaumont boys, no less." He pulled back and gave Theo a lascivious wink.

She held her breath, worried how Theo might react to the blatant flirtation from another man. To her amazement, he gave Des an indulgent grin.

"Better not let Michael hear you say that."

"Please." Des gave a dramatic roll of his dark eyes. "He knows I flirt like I breathe. And while you're a treat for the eyes, dear Theo, I know what team you play for, and alas, it isn't mine. More's the pity." He made a disappointed moue that was over-the-top enough to make it obvious he wasn't serious.

Looking back and forth between the two men, she asked, "How do you know each other?"

"Des is good friends with my sister." He turned a curious gaze on her. "What about you?"

"Michael is a friend of my dads."

"What a small, small world. And me, right in the center of it." Des threw out his hands in a *voilà* gesture, making her laugh.

"Just the way you like it," she teased.

"But of course!" His theatrical expression calmed to something more serious. "Actually, it's quite serendipitous I ran into you two. I could desperately use a few more hands backstage to help wrangle the players and kiddies when the time comes for them to hit the catwalk later. Do you think I could press the both of you into service, pretty please, darlings?" He batted his lashes like a practiced coquette.

Theo laughed and looked to Rachel. "I'm game if you are."

Hiding her surprise, she nodded. "Sure, happy to help."

"Lovely! My sanity thanks you. Come find me as soon as you've eaten, and I'll show you what needs to be done." He looked like he was going to say something else, then simply smiled and walked off.

"That man is exhausting." Theo watched Des melt into the crowd before turning back to her. "Are you sure you don't mind? I know you weren't expecting to be put to work when you agreed to come."

"No, it's fine. I love kids." Obnoxious tween birthday parties excluded, of course. "But I'm kind of surprised you'd rather help backstage than be out here in all of...this." She waved a hand toward the crowded ballroom filled with a large chunk of Boulder's high society milling around, making small talk, seeing and being seen.

"This"—he mimicked her hand gesture—"isn't why I'm here." He nodded to a group of kids swarming around two of the players who were signing hockey pucks and handing them out like candy.

"They are. Making today a success for them is the only thing that matters."

She bit her lip against the shimmer of warmth his words caused in her chest. "You're a good man, Theo Beaumont." She leaned up and gave him a quick kiss on the cheek.

Arm in arm, they strolled back into the throng. After they'd stopped to chat with some of the children and their parents, Rachel realized a lot of them were actually from foster and group homes.

She recognized the slightly jaded glint in the eyes of the older ones who hung a little more at the fringes of everything, wary and standoffish. Like they didn't quite trust this much goodwill came without a price.

Sadly, many of them probably had good reason to be so distrustful.

Those were the ones she made an extra effort to engage with, trying to draw them into the conversations. With limited success. But the few who relaxed their guard a bit, to talk and even smile once or twice, made it feel like she'd accomplished something even more satisfying than any race she'd ever won.

When the brunch buffet line opened a while later, she was surprised once again. Not professional waitstaff, but the hockey players lined up behind the tables of chafing dishes, ready to serve their guests. The big men should have looked silly wearing bib aprons with the event's logo stitched in the signature Avalanche blue, black, and burgundy.

Instead, they were delightfully charming.

After making their way down the food line, Theo led them to a round table with four other people already sitting at it, eating. A weary-looking couple dressed in neat but slightly threadbare clothes smiled in welcome when Theo asked, "Mind if we join you?"

"Not at all." The man stood and offered his hand. "I'm Harry Wick. My wife, Felicity, and that's our boy, Harry Junior."

"Nice to meet you all. I'm Theo, and this is Rachel. And that," he added as he held Rachel's chair, nodding across the table to the large man in animated conversation with the Wicks' son, "is my little brother, Peter."

Yet one more surprise.

From his powerful build, she'd assumed the man to be one of the hockey players. But looking at him now as he grinned over at her with a wave, she could see the family resemblance to Theo and their mother.

"Nice to meet everyone." To Theo she said, "*Little* brother?" Theo topped six feet by an inch or two and was sleekly muscled, but the other man had the biceps of a bull with a body to match.

Peter's grin widened. "In age only." He flexed one of his arms, making the muscle bulge under the sleeve of what had to be a custom-fitted white dress shirt.

Good God, the man could probably bench press a school bus.

Next to him, Harry Jr. let out a boyish giggle. "He eats his Wheaties."

"And my vegetables, too." Peter sent a wink to the boy's parents, who hid grins as their son shoveled a forkful of what looked like a previously untouched spinach omelet into his mouth.

Rachel took a bite of her own omelet, practically groaning as the fresh flavors of cheese and crisp, seasoned ham burst over her tongue. It might have been a buffet, but this was five-star food being served.

"Is there room for three more?"

The booming voice of Matt DiBenedetto had Rachel letting out a loud, internal groan as the food nearly stuck going down.

Why me?

Chapter 30

Not waiting for a reply, Matt pulled out a chair for his wife, the question a mere formality. Of course, he'd never assume he might not be welcome anywhere. Money opened doors. And he had lots of it.

Plus, if Rachel was honest, he wasn't an unpleasant guy, aside from the blind spot he had for his daughter. She wouldn't have minded him and Maureen joining them.

It was the third DiBenedetto who slid into a seat directly across the round table from her that made her want to snarl out a curse or two.

Which was why she was careful not to let her smile slip when she greeted them all.

As she listened to the introductions between the DiBenedettos and the Wicks, though, she realized that, unlike Matt, Theo hadn't mentioned his surname to the family. Or to any of the other people they'd stopped and talked to today, for that matter.

An oversight, or deliberate omission?

The Beaumont name was closely associated with the Everbrite Foundation. She knew because she'd checked it out online after Theo had sandbagged her into attending today's event with him.

The list of things the foundation raised money for was enormous. Most of them having to do with underprivileged kids and underserved communities in the greater Boulder area.

She'd been honestly impressed. Theo's family didn't merely give lip-service to doing good works. They delivered.

So why hide who he was from the very people he was helping?

Then she remembered his answer when she asked why he'd rather help backstage than mingle and schmooze as one of the big-money patrons. He was there for the kids, not the glory or accolades.

Something warm fizzed inside her. Theo really *was* a good man.

Later, she'd show him exactly how much she appreciated that about him. Right now, though, she had to do the one thing she least wanted to do in the world.

"Vicky, congratulations on the race. You skied really well." There. That had sounded sincere, and she hadn't choked on a single word. They weren't friends, but she could still be civil when she had to be.

Even when she didn't want to be.

"Yeah, congratulations," Theo added.

Matt and Maureen beamed with pride, but Vicky was too busy darting confused glances between Theo and Rachel to respond. Her eyebrows pinched as she seemed to reach the correct conclusion.

That's right. He's mine.

A swell of pure feminine satisfaction filled her.

"Thank you," Matt said when Vicky didn't. He gave Rachel a look of gratitude. "Karl was a godsend. Thanks for talking him into it."

She squirmed in her seat. "I didn't." But she had, kind of.

A mistake she wouldn't be repeating. Ever.

"Then maybe you can 'not' talk him into accepting my offer."

Unease prickled down her spine. "Your offer?"

"To coach Victoria full time next season." He beamed a look of pride at his daughter. "He said he thinks she has what it takes to go to the top. I want him to make that happen."

The unease turned to a jolt of betrayal.

"I'm sorry to disappoint you, Matt," she said through stiff lips, "but my dad's going to be coaching me next season. Just like he always has."

His smile dimmed. "I know that's what he said, but I thought...well." He forced the smile back into place. "I'm glad to hear you're going to be racing again. But if anything changes, you tell Karl to come see me first."

"Sure."

When hell freezes over.

Theo placed his napkin beside his mostly empty plate and stood. "Sorry, but we need to get backstage to help Des."

Grateful for the lifeline, she nodded and let him pull her chair back. "Right. Nice to see you all. And it was nice to meet you," she added to the Wicks and Peter, who had all been watching the back-and-forth conversation in quiet fascination. Especially Peter.

As they made a swift retreat, she heard Felicity Wick ask in an awed tone, "Were you at the Olympics?"

"No, but you can bet she'll be at the next one," came Matt's exuberant reply. "Our Vicky is a rising star."

"Not using *my* dad, she isn't," Rachel muttered. She stiffened as Theo put an arm around her as they walked, then relaxed into his sheltering embrace. "Thanks for the quick escape, by the way."

"No problem. It seemed like you were a little shaken by what Matt said."

"You could say that." She let out an unhappy laugh. "God. I knew he'd try to poach my dad if he could, but still. That was pretty ballsy, even for him."

"Was that what bothered you, or what your father said about Vicky?"

Damn the man for being so perceptive.

"Both. I guess that makes me kind of petty, huh?"

He hugged her closer. "No, it makes you kind of human."

As they made their way past the black curtains set up to block the backstage area from the rest of the ballroom, she found herself caught up in the whirlwind that was Des in his element. She was quickly introduced to Theo's remaining two siblings and their significant others, who it seemed had all been dragooned into service, before they were all put to work by Des in full martinet mode.

Two hours later, the last of the kids had strutted down the catwalk alongside their favorite team members and been returned to their proud parents with the brand-new set of clothes they'd worn and got to keep. Rachel gratefully accepted the flute of champagne from the tray Lillian Beaumont's fiancé, Rafe, passed around.

"Thank you all for your help." Des lifted his glass to the weary crew who'd kept things running despite several moments of stage-fright and one major meltdown by a precocious six-year-old who didn't want to leave the runway once she got out there. "We couldn't have done it without you."

"Or you," Lillian said, tipping her glass in his direction. He acknowledged the praise with a grin and a humble nod. It was the most low-key Rachel had ever seen him. Which probably had a lot to do with his partner, who was at his side.

A long-time friend of her dads, Michael had always struck her as someone who could be calm in the face of an oncoming train. Which was a useful trait in his profession as an emergency room doctor.

As Des leaned into Michael and whispered something that made them both smile, there was a small pinch in the vicinity of her heart. She wanted that. The quiet intimacy, the unspoken support, the simple being half of a happy whole.

The warm press of Theo's body against her side reminded her the only thing keeping her from having those things was her own stubborn refusal to believe she could.

Was she just making excuses because she was afraid of trying and failing?

Her father had pointed out he and Karl had both had careers with insane schedules, and they'd made it work. No doubt Des and Michael were equally busy, and they seemed to be doing just fine, too.

So why was she fighting so hard against something she wanted almost more than that stupid gold medal?

The question plagued her all the way back to Theo's. She was glad he'd declined the invitation from his older brother to join them for dinner. Richard seemed pleasant enough, but he was a little too intense for her taste. The five minutes of conversation they'd had felt more like a job interview than a friendly nice-to-meet-you chat.

Besides, she agreed with Theo's reasoning. She hadn't wanted to share their time together with his family any more than he did.

This might be the last time they got to spend a whole evening alone for a while. At least until she figured out what her training schedule would look like. It could be weeks before they had a weekend when their schedules lined up again.

And wasn't that a depressing thought.

"Do I want to know what's put that look on your face?"

Breaking her gaze from the gorgeous view of the mountains in the distance, she looked up at Theo and took the glass of fruit-infused water he held out. "I was thinking about how much I'm going to miss spending all this time with you. I guess I've kind of gotten spoiled over the last few weeks."

"Me, too." He dropped onto the padded patio swing beside her, sending it into a gentle rocking motion. The large propane heater purred away nearby, keeping them toasty warm in the chilly late afternoon air. "But I also know how important it is to you to be ready to race again in time for the start of the season."

Something in his voice made her pause in raising the glass to her lips. "But?"

He hesitated, then shook his head. "Nothing."

She shifted so she could see his face better. "It's not nothing. Tell me."

With a sigh, he studied the contents of his glass rather than look at her. "If you were to, I don't know, say...have some doubts or second thoughts about it, about racing, you know you could talk to me about it, right?"

It was a good thing he wasn't looking at her, because she was pretty sure he would have seen full-blown shock on her face.

"What? Why would you..." A horrible thought struck. The ice in her glass rattled as she stuck her foot down to stop the swing's motion. "You were awake."

He confirmed the quiet accusation with a grimace. "Barely, but yeah. I heard what you said."

I'm not sure I want to race anymore.

Everything inside her tensed into a rigid ball of nerves. Foolish to think saying those words out loud wouldn't come back to bite her in the ass. She could practically hear Ivy groaning.

"I was just tired. I didn't mean it."

Wow, that didn't sound defensive at all.

He gave a small nod. "Okay."

"I mean it."

"So do I. It's okay. Whatever you want to do is okay. I just want to be sure whatever that is, it's what you really want, not what you think you *should* want."

"Then why bring it up at all?"

"Because I wanted you to know you can talk to me about it if you need to."

"I don't need to talk about it. To anyone. And neither can you."

"I would never do that."

Heart pounding triple-time in her chest, she had a hard time working up the spit to swallow. "You promise?" Because if he said anything, *anything*, to her parents, she wasn't sure she could handle the world-shattering fallout.

"I swear. I would never betray your confidence that way. As of right now, consider what you said stricken from memory."

If only it were that easy.

His words still chased around her head as she lay tucked against his side later that night, sleep a distant promise that wouldn't come. Last night, she'd trusted this man with her secrets about her parents and the foster home. Now he held one more.

One that could blow her carefully controlled world apart.

Although, to be fair, he'd already known this secret. For weeks. And hadn't let so much as a hint color his conversation with her fathers last night despite the tag-team interrogation they'd thrown at him.

Never tell anyone your secrets.

Ivy's rules had been the bedrock she'd built her entire life on. They'd kept her safe in the uncertain world of foster care. They'd been her yardstick for fitting in with her adoptive family. But maybe, just maybe, it was time to let go of the child's insecurities of the past and free the woman to embrace the possibilities of the future.

Chapter 31

Rachel's dad turned out to be a ringer.

From where he held the belay rope that would keep Dellin from falling should he lose his grip, Theo watched in considerable awe as the older man attacked the beginner's line of holds with the confidence and single-mindedness of a pro. He didn't just nail his ascent to the top of the wall.

He crushed it.

It wasn't until Dellin was bouncing back down to earth with the ease of a seasoned rappeler that Theo began to wonder if he'd been had. After Dellin unhooked the rope from his harness with a shit-eating grin, he was sure of it.

"I take it this wasn't your first climb," he said dryly.

"Son, I grew up in Boulder. What do you think?"

That I'm an idiot who walked right into a setup.

"Sir, please don't take this the wrong way, but why the hell did you let me spend all that time going over the equipment and demonstrating climbing technique like you were a novice if you already knew it all?"

"Maybe I wanted to see if you were the real deal, and not some bullshit artist making up stories about summiting El Capitan to impress people who don't know any better."

"Why the hell would you think that?"

"You nearly puked when I suggested going for a climb. What was I supposed to think?"

"That I wasn't crazy enough to take a novice"—he ground his teeth—"someone I *thought* was a novice on a live climb their first time out."

Dellin studied him with the same intensity he had over the dinner table. "Maybe. But..." He shook his head. "There's something else."

Fuck.

Just his luck the man was a human lie detector.

Needing to move off the subject, he glanced around the busy club. "We should probably make way for other people to climb. Unless you wanted another go? Maybe try the intermediate route?"

He swept a hand at the more advanced arrangement of holds, each tagged with a number signifying the degree of difficulty for each one. He might be completely grounded outside, but he could still handle an indoor 5.10 route without breaking a sweat.

After looking like he was considering it, Dellin rubbed his left shoulder with a grimace and shook his head. "Better not."

The unconscious gesture reminded him of the mention of an old injury. "What happened? If you don't mind me asking," he added when Dellin gave him a startled look.

The look turned cunning. "I'll tell you mine, if you tell me yours."

Not fucking likely.

Before he could form a more polite version of that sentiment, Dellin was already ushering him toward the locker room. "Come on. We'll grab a burger and talk."

"Oh, well..." He glanced at his watch.

"Don't worry, we've got plenty of time. They won't be done for hours yet." The slightest hint of bitterness laced his words.

"I wasn't..." But he was.

Counting the minutes until he saw her again. When he'd only left her a few hours ago. After glutting himself on her all night long.

Was he pathetic or what?

A sudden thought hit which literally stopped him in his tracks.

"Rachel had to know you were a climber." And she hadn't said a word to him about it. The sense of betrayal stung.

"Actually, she probably doesn't even remember I did. I gave it up when she was pretty young, after she...well, that's not a story for a locker room." He turned away and started pulling on his street clothes.

He fought it for all of thirty seconds.

But Dellin had baited his hook much too well. With a grunt of disgust, he changed out of his climbing clothes, knowing he'd be having lunch with Rachel's ex-detective dad, no matter how bad an idea it was.

The diner Dellin directed him to was a sorely run-down greasy spoon on the outskirts of town, complete with duct tape-patched red vinyl booths and worn-out waitresses. They sat themselves. Dellin chose a spot away from both the windows and the other customers. The table with the peeling laminate wobbled a little as Theo slid in across from him.

He almost suggested they change booths, then bit his tongue. Given the shots Dellin had taken at him during dinner about his money, it was a safe bet he was testing him. He'd probably picked the worst place he knew, just to see if Theo would balk.

Then the waitress came over and blew that theory out of the water.

"Detective! Haven't seen you in a dog's age. How've ya been?"

Dellin grinned. "Been good, Wanda, thanks. How about you? How's that son of yours doing at college?"

She made a face. "Cries about how hard it is to go to school and hold a job at the same time, but so far he's sticking with both and keeping his nose nice and clean."

"That's good. You tell him I'll come around for a talk if he needs it." It sounded more like a threat than a social call, but Wanda just cackled.

"I'll do that." Her gaze shifted across the booth to Theo, washed-out blue eyes narrowing. "And who's this handsome young thing?"

It wasn't what she said, but how she said it that clued Theo in she wasn't sure she liked him yet. The smart rule of thumb was to stay on the good side of the people who touched your food, so he gave her one of his best smiles.

"Nice to meet you, Wanda. I'm Theo. I'm dating Dellin's daughter, Rachel."

Her expression cleared, and she gave him a genuine smile. "Well, isn't that nice." She pulled out her pad. "Should I give you two a minute to look at the menu, or do you know what you want?"

Dellin never touched the grease-spotted menu on the table. "Deluxe bacon cheeseburger platter, please. Medium rare."

Wanda made a squiggle on her order pad before looking at Theo. "And you?"

"That sounds artery-clogging, but delicious. Make it two."

"Good deal. Be back in a few." She shoved her pad into her apron pocket, grabbed the menus, and headed toward the counter, bellowing, "Burt, give me two number nines, medium rare."

Theo pressed his lips together to keep from laughing. Regardless of how the food was, he'd have to bring Richard here for lunch one day, just to see his reaction. Especially to the yelling.

The stickler in the family for decorum, he'd likely have an aneurysm.

He dared a sip of water from the large plastic glass Wanda had brought, and caught Dellin watching him with an inscrutable expression. "What?"

"You do realize she was wondering if I was stepping out on my husband. With you."

"Ah...no, I didn't catch that." But the hostility made a little more sense now.

"And that doesn't bother you, even a little?"

"Well, I don't like someone thinking I'd cheat with a married person. But I don't know her, so no." He shrugged.

"Not even a married, older, black man?"

Ah. Now he understood.

Leaning forward on the table that tilted his way, he steepled his fingers and gave Dellin a direct stare. "Have I ever given any indication I'm at all bothered by you being either black or gay?"

Dellin held the stare a long time. Neither of them flinched. Finally, he conceded with a sigh, his large frame relaxing the slightest degree. "No."

"So why all the picking, looking for something to get pissed over?"

"The truth? Because you seemed a little too good to be true. Rich, good looking, athletic, well-mannered—"

"You're right, that sounds awful."

Dellin didn't miss a beat. "You're also part of the crème of Boulder society, with your fancy car, your fancy house...your fancy women."

A sour knot formed in his gut. He kept most of his romantic entanglements out of the society pages despite the terrier-like tenacity of some paparazzi. But the events he attended for work or the foundation often ended up in the news, so pictures of him with various dates were out there for anyone who really wanted to find them.

"Dating a lot of women isn't a crime."

"No, but dating and dumping them in quick succession is a pretty predictable pattern."

Theo bristled. Only the fact the man was looking out for Rachel's best interests kept him civil. "I've never mistreated a woman, or misrepresented exactly what our relationship was or wasn't. Have I dated a lot? Yes. Have I been an asshole about it? Never."

"And what happens when you get tired of Rachel and move on to the next woman?"

Just the thought made his stomach cramp.

"Then that would be between me and her."

"So, you *can* see yourself getting tired of her."

He took a long breath. Strangling her father would probably upset Rachel, so he wrapped his hands around his water glass instead. "Rachel is an amazing woman. I can't see myself getting tired of her any time soon." Or ever, for that matter.

"But it'll happen eventually." Dellin gave a scoffing snort. "It's not like you love her or anything."

"Who says I don't?"

Chapter 32

THE WORDS WERE OUT before he had a chance to think them through.

He froze.

Wait.

Did he love Rachel?

He'd known he was close, so close. But when had he slid over that edge, and how hadn't he noticed? It seemed like he should have been aware of something so momentous when it happened.

But there it was. In the pain from thinking about leaving her. In the certainty he'd never tire of having her in his life.

He *loved* her.

The impact of it made him slump back in astonished wonder.

Across the booth, Dellin gave a low chuckle. When Theo looked at him, the man wore a look of satisfaction that probably should have bothered him, since it made him realize he'd just been manipulated by a master.

"You must have been formidable in the interrogation room," he said with grudging respect. "But if you don't mind me asking, why was is so important to get me to admit it now? Rachel and I have only been dating a few weeks."

"I thought the other night you might have already taken the fall. I wanted to be sure before I talked to you about this. Otherwise, I wouldn't waste my breath."

Wanda arrived with their food, two large platters overflowing with burgers the size of small saucers and enough fries to choke a horse. Theo waited with barely restrained impatience as she set everything down and asked if they needed anything else before she finally sauntered off.

Then he waited again while Dellin took a huge bite of his burger.

Frustrated and hungry, he picked up his burger and tore off a bite, only to groan in satisfaction as the flavors exploded over his taste buds.

"Now I get why you come here. Damn, that's good."

"Can't always judge a book by its cover," Dellin said, pointing a fry in his direction before snapping it in half with his teeth.

"I could say the same."

Dellin gave a nod, conceding the point. "You're nothing like those rich assholes from the ski circuit who've come sniffing around Rae in the past. I apologize." He finished the fry and picked up another, loading it with a swipe of ketchup. "How much has she told you about her adoption?"

Finally.

Although he did make a mental bookmark to come back to the first comment. There was no way he could let that slide without an explanation, if there was some rich asshole who needed to be straightened out on how you treated a woman.

Especially *his* woman.

"She told me her mom died when she was six and she ended up in foster care for a couple of years. That you and Karl adopted her when she was eight."

"Not exactly. Same-sex marriage wasn't legal here yet, so even though Karl and I had been together for years, we couldn't both adopt her. I had the more stable career at the time, since Karl was still on the pro ski circuit, so we decided I should be the one to do the legal adoption. Which is why she has my last name."

"But Karl took your name, too."

Dellin nodded, looking pleased he knew that. "When we got married, right after Colorado made it legal. His reputation was in his name, though, so he hyphenated it to Miller-Long."

"Is that when he legally adopted Rachel, too?"

"He didn't have to wait that long." Dellin's grin grew. "The day she turned eighteen, when it was still up in the air if the courts would rule in our favor or not, she went down to the courthouse, got the paperwork for an adult adoption, and brought them home all filled out and ready to go. All Karl had to do was sign. The look on his face when he realized what she was handing him. Well."

Dellin looked down, his eyes turning a little moist. "She gave us a present that day, instead of the other way around."

"That sounds like Rachel." Bold. Assertive. Take-charge.

Yeah, totally her.

"Rachel now, maybe, but not then. Back when she first came to us, she was a lot more timid, and careful not to ask for much. Which was to be expected after being in foster care for so long. Plus, she'd grown up before that without a dad, and suddenly she had two of them. We figured it would take a little time and understanding to get her to come out of her shell."

"She said one thing all the kids worried about was having their potential adoptive parents change their minds and send them back." He took another quick bite of his juicy burger as Dellin nodded. Damn, it was good.

"Yeah. The child psychologist we worked with for the adoption told us abandonment issues were a common problem with adoptees. We did everything we could think to make her feel as safe and secure as possible. But it still took a while for her to stop worrying about it all the time. That's why I gave up climbing. I already had a dangerous job. No need for a dangerous hobby, too."

"Well, you both did a great job raising her, sir. Thanks to you, she turned out confident and self-assured." He frowned when he saw Dellin roll his lips, like he wanted to say something. "You don't think so?"

"I love Rachel with all my heart," Dellin said slowly, as though picking his words with care. "But her early experiences and concerns turned her into something of a people pleaser. When she was younger, she rarely expressed a strong opinion about anything. It was always, 'I don't care' and 'whatever you want is fine with me.' It got so bad we finally had to force her to make her own decisions. You're right, she has grown into a confident young woman. But in some ways, she's still that scared, uncertain child seeking to keep everyone around her happy at all costs."

"And, what? You think she's only going out with me to make me happy?"

Despite Theo's angry tone, Dellin grinned. "No, not at all. In fact, I think you're the first thing in a long time she's done entirely for herself." The grin slid away. "I'm just hoping she doesn't fall back into old habits and do something she'll end up regretting."

"In what way?" He flinched under the exasperated look he got.

"Do you really need me to spell it out for you?"

Warning bells began to clang.

"I think maybe I do."

Because if he was hinting at what Theo thought he was, they were entering dangerous waters filled with secrets he was honor-bound to keep to himself.

"From the day Rachel decided she wanted to ski competitively, I was one hundred percent onboard, even though a part of me always worried she'd chosen that path to please Karl, since he couldn't legally be her parent. Like she needed to make sure he liked her enough to stick around. But she honestly seemed to enjoy it. And she was *good*." Despite everything, pride shone from his eyes.

"I saw all the awards on the wall. She's better than good."

"That wall." Something close to a sneer curled his lip. "I probably shouldn't be saying this to you, but I fucking hate that wall. Always have, even when it was Karl's. Know why?"

Careful.

"The blank spot in the middle?"

"I knew there was more to you than just a pretty face. Yes, that damn spot. The holy grail." He shook his head. "Instead of savoring all the awards they've already won, they're both obsessed with the one damn medal they don't have yet. Nothing else matters."

There was no ignoring the deep bitterness in those words.

Dropping the fry he'd been holding onto the plate, Dellin shoved the whole thing away and leaned back. "Then she crashed on that mountain fifteen months ago, and I thought I'd lost my baby girl for good."

The echo of Rachel's screams turned Theo's mouth dry.

"You were at that race?"

Dellin nodded. "It was a nightmare. But then it turned into a blessing in disguise."

"Oh?"

"I know. How could anything that horrible be in any way good, right? But because of it, everything changed. Life didn't revolve around training and travel anymore. It sounds awful, but despite the surgeries and everything that came with them, this past year has been the most normal we've had as a family in a long time."

He grimaced. "Let me rephrase that. It's the longest we've all been in the same city at the same time together in a long time. And it might be selfish as hell of me, but I've enjoyed having my husband home with me all the time. It's been a little like being newlyweds all over again. And I don't want to go back to the way things were, both of us always heading in different directions, having to practically schedule time to be together, being in different time zones more often than we weren't."

Ah.

The sniping battle at the dinner table the other night finally made some sense.

"After seeing you and Rae together, I thought maybe she didn't want to go back to that, either." Dellin huffed out a laugh at himself. "But they're at Copper, and we're here, so I guess it was wishful thinking on my part."

Not entirely.

But he couldn't say that, not without breaking Rachel's confidence. He chewed a bite of burger to give himself time to think.

"If you're hoping I'll try and get her to change her mind about racing, forget it. It's her decision. I won't try to influence her." Even if thinking about her on that course left a knot of worry in his gut he couldn't seem to dislodge.

"You might feel differently once she's hardly in town anymore, and you're lucky to see her a few nights out of the month."

"No, I won't." He wouldn't do that to her.

No matter how much her being gone would suck.

Dellin gave him the cold cop stare again before shaking his head in disgust. "Damn it. Not only looks, money, and brains, but morals, too. Just my luck."

"Why doesn't that sound like a compliment?"

Dragging his plate back in front of him instead of answering, Dellin picked up what was left of his burger. "So, I told you mine. Your turn."

"Ah..." Talk about being blindsided. The usual denials rose up, but when he opened his mouth, what came out was something else entirely. "I haven't been able to climb a foot off the ground anywhere but the clubs for the past five months."

"Did you take a fall?"

Cold clenched his gut. "Not me."

"Ah." Dellin chewed a fry. "Five months. That would be about the time that climber died down at North Table Mountain."

He gave a curt nod and applied himself to his food despite his appetite suddenly vanishing.

"A friend of yours?"

Another nod.

"Were you there when it happened?"

"No. But I should have been." He meant to leave it at that. But then the words started pouring out.

The party the night before. The early morning phone call. His brusque refusal. Gavin's decision to climb alone and take risks he knew better than to take. The fear the accident wasn't entirely accidental. His inability to carry out his friend's last wishes to spread his ashes from the top of the cliff. The pattern of increasingly dangerous exploits that had his family wondering about his mental and emotional well-being.

Once the words petered out, Theo sat back, drained.

And embarrassed.

More and more so as Dellin sat in silence, staring at his food as he poked a fry into the last of the ketchup and ate it. Finally, Dellin wiped his hands on his napkin and sat back in the booth, and started talking.

"When I was a street cop, Karl would always worry that every day would be the day I didn't come home. It drove him crazy. He never asked me to quit, because he understood being a cop was who I am, but I know he was relieved when I made detective. Even more so when we adopted Rachel a few years after that."

He was confused where Dellin was going with this story after he'd essentially spread his guts across the table, but he nodded.

"I get it. Boulder's a pretty safe place, but my mother still worries herself sick over my brother." Especially after the nightmare Lillian's fiancé, Rafe, went through being injured on the job while trying to apprehend a suspect.

"For twenty-eight years, I did my job with barely a scratch, and I was damn good at it. Then, when I was only two years from having my thirty in and retiring, I caught a burglary case. Nothing I hadn't handled a hundred times before. I had a newly minted gold shield as my partner. Frank was a good cop, but a little too eager to prove himself."

"Tough to be the new guy."

"Very. It was your typical apartment burglary. Someone broke the window from the fire escape and cleaned out what little there was worth stealing while the victims were at work. The next step after processing the scene was to canvas the neighbors, to see if anyone saw or heard anything. There were seven other apartments on the floor, so we split up and started knocking on doors, him on one side of the hall, me the other."

Theo got a bad feeling about where this was heading, but held his tongue and listened.

"I was talking to this old lady in her apartment at the other end of the hall—God, I still remember the smell of mothballs and cat piss—when there was a gunshot. By the time I got into the hall, Frank was slumped against the wall, blood everywhere, and the guy who shot him was standing over him, getting ready to put another bullet in his head." He took a sip of water, his large hand shaking ever-so slightly.

"You stopped him."

Dellin nodded. "I shot him before he could finish Frank off, but he got off a shot at me from the ground before I could end it." His hand went to his left shoulder and rubbed.

"Turned out, the guy was wanted for a string of carjackings in Denver, and he'd been holing up with a friend who just happened to live down the hall from the apartment that was robbed. He had nothing to do with it. But when he heard Frank announce himself as BPD when he knocked, he panicked and started shooting as soon as he opened the door."

"Jesus." Bad enough to risk the normal dangers of the job. But to be blindsided by sheer coincidence? "That's horrible. But at least you and your partner made it." The flash of pain across the older man's face had Theo cursing under his breath. "I'm sorry."

"So am I. Frank was a good cop. A good man. He left behind a wife and kid, and I had no explanation to give them at his funeral why they were burying him when I walked away with nothing worse than a bum shoulder."

"It was pure chance. It could have been either of you who knocked on that door."

"But it wasn't. I told him to take the apartments on that side of the hall. I sent him to his execution."

"It wasn't your fault."

"No. But it felt like it was. For a very long time, I told myself it should have been me. I should have been the one to go to that apartment. I should have been the one to face that lunatic. Maybe I would have reacted faster than he did, or said something different which wouldn't set him off, or, fuck, if we hadn't split up in the first place, maybe I could have pulled him out of the way in time. Something. Anything."

Theo froze. It was like he was listening to himself about Gavin.

I should have been there. I could have saved him. Things would have gone differently. It should have been me.

He licked suddenly dry lips and asked, "Do you ever stop blaming yourself?"

"Eventually. But sometimes you need a little help to get there before you rip yourself up too badly." He pulled out his wallet and fished out a business card, which he slid across the table. "Survivor's guilt isn't something to dick around with, son. Especially when you start doing dangerous stunts like you have, thumbing your nose at fate. Lyle's a good listener. You should give him a call."

Rubbing his thumb over the edge of the therapist's card, his mind spun.

Part of him rebelled at the thought of going to a shrink. But another part, the one that had already decided days ago he needed help before he did irreparable harm to either himself or his relationship with Rachel, made him nod and tuck the card into his pocket.

"Thanks."

"Don't take this the wrong way, because your business is your business, but while you're with Rae, it's also *my* business. I'll be keeping an eye on you. Understood?"

He held the direct stare without flinching.

"Understood."

When Dellin plucked the check from where Wanda had left it tucked between the salt and pepper shakers, he didn't bother fighting him for it. Instead, he dropped a ten-dollar bill on the table for the tip and followed him to the cash register near the front door. Wanda sauntered up to take Dellin's money.

"How was everything?"

"Never had a better burger." It was the truth.

"Maybe I'll see you back here sometime, then." She handed Dellin his change. "Say hi to Rachel and Karl for me."

"You bet. And tell Frankie I'll be stopping by next weekend to see how he's doing. Maybe give him some pointers on his jump shot."

"Lord, does he need it!" Wanda patted his arm with a smile and walked off to one of the tables where a customer was waving their menu in the air, bellowing, "I'm coming already. I only have two legs."

Frankie. Frank.

The proverbial lightbulb went off over Theo's head, where all sorts of things suddenly lined up and made sense. "She's your partner's wife."

"Widow."

"So, what? You come here to torture yourself?"

Dellin cast a wistful look in the waitress's direction before pushing out the door. "Like I said, eventually you get past it, but you never forget."

Chapter 33

"How did today go? Did you play nice with Theo, or did you spend the day grilling him on his net worth and political leanings?"

After kissing her father hello in the kitchen, Rachel asked the question with a grin to soften it, because she wasn't entirely joking. He wasn't the type to pass up a golden opportunity to interrogate Theo the second he got him alone.

Adding some blueberries to the protein smoothie he was building in the blender, he gave her a wounded look. "Would I do that?"

"In a heartbeat." She had to wait while the blender screamed before speaking again. "So? Did everything go okay?"

He took his time pouring two large glasses of the purplish drink, then pushed one toward her on the dark granite island. "We had a very nice talk."

Which told her exactly nothing. "About?"

"You. Him. Things."

A chill skated up her spine, but she suppressed it as she took a long swallow of the fruity-sweet drink. Theo had sworn he'd never say a word about what she'd told him. She had to trust he'd keep his word. She'd told him she did.

And yet the paranoia remained, lurking right below the surface.

"How was the climbing?"

He gave a wry grin. "It reminded me I was too old to learn new tricks."

"Oh, Pop, you're not old." To her, both of her parents were forever timeless. But she knew hitting the big six-oh was a milestone her father hadn't enjoyed.

"Enough about me. How did your day go?"

"It went well enough," Karl answered for her as he entered the kitchen and joined her on one of the wooden stools at the island.

That he didn't make the effort to kiss Dellin hello first told her things were still on bumpy ground between them. She did her best to ignore the tension suddenly snapping through the room.

"It went *really* well, actually. I ran the course four times in a row without a single fall, and I bettered my time on each run." She'd been both relieved and excited she could replicate her previous success with her dad watching. It meant whatever breakthrough she'd made was permanent.

She really was back.

So why wasn't she more excited?

"Bettered," Karl repeated, tone repressive. "But still awful. You've got a long road ahead before you're ready to race." He grabbed the second smoothie and swallowed half of it down in several large gulps.

Usually, his bluntness didn't bother her. When he was in coach-mode, he focused on one thing only: being the best. And to be the best, you sometimes had to face hard truths about yourself, no matter how much they hurt. She accepted that.

Today, though, she found herself wearing thinner skin than normal, because his words stung. A lot.

"Two weeks ago, I couldn't even make it to the bottom in one shot. Don't I at least get credit for that accomplishment?"

She took another drink, only realizing in the ensuing silence both her fathers were looking at her. Karl in shock. Dellin with what could only be described as sharp intensity tinged with anticipation. She'd seen the same look on his face during dinner when he'd been about to pounce on something Theo said.

Uh-oh.

"Of course you do, sweetheart," Dellin said. But it wasn't her he was looking at as he said it. Then he shifted his focus to her and smiled. "That's a wonderful accomplishment. Why don't we celebrate? I'll make your favorite meal."

"Thanks, Pop, but I'm actually having dinner with Theo." She glanced at the clock and the anticipation that had been simmering all day came to a full boil. It was pathetic, but she'd missed him.

And if she felt like this after only a couple of hours, what was it going to be like when she was gone for weeks or months at a time?

Karl's attention snapped to her with a scowl. "We still have to go over the video of today's runs and work out your training schedule going forward."

Damn, she forgot. "We can do it tomorrow."

"We always spend the evening after training going over what needs to be improved, while it's still fresh." He sounded scandalized she'd even suggest changing something that was as routine to them as breathing.

Just like it was routine for her to buckle under and go along with whatever he wanted her to do when it came to any clash of wills between them.

Only this time, giving in felt a little too much like giving up.

And what she'd be giving up was Theo.

If she caved now, it would set the tone for the entire year to come about where her time with him would rank in the grand scheme of her training schedule. And in her life in general. At the very bottom, squished beneath the weight of her dad's expectations.

But hadn't that been the plan all along? Hadn't she gone into their relationship knowing it would probably disintegrate the moment she was back on the slopes? So...why was she getting upset about cancelling one stupid dinner?

I just want to be sure it's what you really want, not what you think you should want.

Theo's heartfelt words gave her the answer.

It was because somewhere along the line, her priorities had shifted. Obliterating all of her earlier plans like a sudden storm covering a well-worn trail through the snow, leaving her to cut a fresh path. Maybe parallel to the old one, but still her own.

Because somewhere, somehow, she'd gone and fallen in love.

Warmth bloomed in her chest even as her gut tightened.

How did I not realize it before?

She focused back on Karl, and her gut tightened even more.

"I know it's what we usually do, Dad, but—"

"So, call and tell him you can't come."

"I can't do that. He's expecting me."

Karl waved a negligent hand. "He knows what you are. If he truly cares about you, he'll understand and won't get in your way."

His words froze her. "What I am?"

"Yes. A competitor. A winner." He said the words with pride, but each one made her flinch inside. "You've worked too hard to give up now just for a...a fling."

"It's not a fling!"

He blinked at the vehemence of her declaration. "But..."

"Look, I'm sorry if this is a surprise, but I'm still figuring it all out for myself, too. I like Theo. A lot. I might even—"

"Don't say it!"

"—love him." She tried not to be hurt by her dad's groan as he slipped off the stool beside her and stalked to the end of the kitchen, hands covering his face. "It doesn't mean my training has to suffer."

"Of course it will." He dropped his hands and glared at her. "No. This isn't love. You haven't been with anyone since Misha. You've been lonely. That's natural. But don't mistake companionship for something more."

Her hackles went up. "I'm not stupid, Dad. I know what I feel."

"And you're willing to throw away everything you've worked for? For a *feeling*?"

"Would you rather she was alone the rest of her life, just to win that damn medal?" Dellin's voice was rich with some emotion that had Karl shooting daggers at him.

She looked back and forth between them. It seemed at least some of the tension she was feeling between them had to do with her. Her stomach cramped as old anxieties churned to the surface, but she pushed on.

"I'm not planning on being alone, and I'm not throwing anything away. We'll have to make some adjustments, that's all." She swallowed past the nausea. "I would have wanted to do that, anyway."

There. She'd said it.

"Adjustments?" Her dad gave an incredulous laugh. "I don't believe this. I go away for two weeks and come home to a quitter." He ignored her sharp gasp and went for the jugular. "Do you know how I know? Because I just spent ten days coaching a winner. *She* wants it. *She's* willing to do whatever it takes to get it."

Every word was like acid being poured over her body.

"Then maybe you should be coaching her." It came out as barely a whisper but he heard, because his eyes flashed electric blue.

"Maybe I should."

"Karl, that's enough!" But even as Dellin barked at him, he spun and stalked out of the room, thundering up the stairs with heavy footfalls. They both stared at the empty doorway, but she was the only one who flinched when the bedroom door slammed above them.

What the hell just happened?

Rachel hugged herself as she tried to sort through what was probably only the second real argument she'd ever had with her dad.

And both of them had been about Theo.

Was he right? Was she really throwing away her chance to win gold by dividing her focus? And was she willing to lose his respect and affection for a man she'd known less than a month?

Dellin's strong arms came around her in a comforting hug. "Don't worry, baby girl. He didn't mean it."

She swallowed back the tears threatening to choke her. "I think he did."

"You know his bark is always worse than his bite, especially when it comes to something interfering with his plans. He's just..."

"Disappointed in me."

"Stubborn and set in his ways." He kissed the top of her head. "You get changed and go have a nice dinner with your young man like you planned. I'll talk to your dad." That last was said with a grim determination which didn't bode well for the conversation.

Biting her lip to hold in a sob, she made a quick escape to her room. The first tear broke loose as she closed the door. Dashing it away with an unsteady hand, she stood for a minute, feeling lost and confused. She'd finally thrown Ivy's rules in the garbage and stood up for herself with her dad, and what had it gotten her?

Pain, disappointment, and possibly a fracture in their relationship which might never fully mend.

God, what had she been thinking?

That she loved Theo.

That she wanted more with him than a few evenings here and there whenever her schedule had a convenient gap in it.

That she could have more than one thing which was important to her, just like her father and Ari kept telling her.

Yeah, and that worked out real great, didn't it?

By the time she'd changed into jeans and a long-sleeved tee, and bathed her face with cool water at the bathroom sink, her rioting emotions were almost back under control.

And she knew what she had to do.

As much as she hated confrontation with her dads, as raw as her feelings were right then, she needed to straighten this out. Now. Before it had time to fester and grow into something even worse than it already was.

If she was going to prove she was serious about her feelings for Theo, then she had to show a little backbone and fight for what she wanted.

Screwing on her game face, she marched down the hallway to her fathers' bedroom at the opposite end. She lifted her hand to knock, but raised voices made her hesitate. She bit her lip again as the argument raging on the other side of the door drifted through.

"...totally shitty thing to say to her. How could you?"

"You wouldn't understand. You never have."

"What, being cruel?"

"Motivation! Every athlete needs to be constantly driven. Especially when they start to falter."

"She didn't falter. She nearly died! That can change the trajectory of anyone's life."

Rachel found herself nodding at Dellin's words. Nothing had been the same since waking up in that hospital bed. Not even her.

"Nothing changed until she met that...*person*." The word came out like it tasted sour.

"Then you're blind as well as stubborn. This isn't about him. This is about Rachel, and what she wants out of life."

"And she wants to be a winner!"

"My God, listen to yourself. She wants, or you want?"

"How could you even accuse me of that? Everything I've done—we've done—has always been for her."

Feeling like an eavesdropper, she started to back away, but Dellin's next words rocked her, freezing her in place.

"What about what Theo said?"

Theo? What did he have to...

No. No, he couldn't have. He wouldn't.

"What the hell do I care what he says? I know my daughter. She wants this as much as I do. More. You didn't see her out on that mountain today. I did. *This* is what she was made for. *This* is what she loves. She's no quitter. It doesn't matter what that Beaumont bastard says about anything."

Dellin made some response, but the buzzing in her ears was too loud to hear it.

He'd told.

After all his promises, after all his assurances she could trust him, he'd gone and told her father her secret the very first chance he got.

Never trust anyone but yourself unless you want to get screwed.

Ivy's cynical words whispered through her brain like a great big "I told you so."

Numb, she started back toward her room, but when she got to the stairs, her feet sent her down them instead. At the bottom, she stood for a minute, trying to figure out what she should do. Stay and talk to her fathers? Confront Theo with his betrayal? Get in the car and just keep driving?

Choosing the easiest option, she grabbed her purse and keys and got into her Jeep, determined to put as many miles as she could between her and the nightmare nipping at her heels.

Chapter 34

Rachel had the radio blasting as she drove. Hard rock. Head banging music she could scream her lungs out to. But nothing could drown out the memory of her father's words.

What about what Theo said?

Why? Why would he break his word like that?

Did a promise mean so little to him? And if that was the case, then how could she trust *anything* he'd told her? Maybe he'd been lying to her about everything since the first day they met. Including how he felt.

Something inside her rebelled at the thought, but she crushed it. She had to stop making excuses. All her life she'd lived by Ivy's rules, and she'd been safe. The second she started breaking them, everything went to shit.

Because of him.

From her purse on the other seat, her phone dinged with a text alert. She ignored it. There was absolutely no one she wanted to talk to right now. Scream, yell, and rage at, yes. Talk, no. It would be a while before she could handle doing that.

So instead, she drove.

The text alert went off again. And again. Finally, the phone rang with Theo's ringtone. She tightened her fingers around the steering wheel and pressed a little harder on the gas, even though she was already going a little too fast for the curving road.

The hurt little girl in her wanted to pull over and answer. To rage and scream. To ask why.

But the cowardly part of her, the part that followed Ivy's rules like they were gems from the mouth of a prophet instead of an angry teenager, was afraid she'd cave as soon as she heard his voice. Ready to forgive and forget all. To pacify, even at her own expense, so things could go back to being calm and peaceful.

She drove faster.

But like the music she cranked even higher, speed was only a temporary solution that solved nothing. No matter how far or how fast she traveled, the problem would still be waiting for her when she got home. She needed to stop being such a chickenshit and deal with it—with him—whether she wanted to or not.

She glanced at the clock on the dash and winced. She'd been driving aimlessly for over two hours. Time to suck it up and head home.

Which would be easier if she knew where the heck she was. In all her angry driving, she'd stopped paying attention to where she was going. But before she could pull over to get her phone and check the map app, flashing lights lit up her rearview mirror.

"You've got to be kidding me." One look at her speedometer and she groaned. "Perfect. Freaking perfect. Exactly what the day needed."

Resigned, she pulled to the shoulder of the road. She put the Jeep in park, rolled down her window, and grabbed her license from her purse. Hands back on the steering wheel as her father had taught her, she breathed in long, calming breaths of the crisp evening air and waited as the tall uniformed officer approached from the police car parked behind her.

All she could see in her side-view mirror was an intimidatingly muscular body wrapped in a black uniform, gun at his hip, his face all but hidden beneath sunglasses and a baseball hat. She swallowed as he paused to glance in her rear seat before leaning down beside her open window.

"Miss Long."

Surprise that he knew her name was followed by shock as he removed the mirrored sunglasses, leaving her staring into brown eyes so familiar it was painful.

"Peter! I mean, um, Officer Beaumont."

He gave a small grin, lending his stern features a hint of boyishness. "Peter's fine." The grin vanished. "Is everything all right, ma'am?"

Relief that she'd been pulled over by someone she knew was met by an equal amount of embarrassment for the same reason.

"I'm so sorry. I didn't realize how fast I was going. It was stupid, I know. I swear, it won't happen again." She held out her license.

He stared at it for a second, a funny look on his face, but didn't take it. "Do you know why I pulled you over?"

"Um...I was speeding?"

Heaving a deep sigh, he looked up as though seeking divine intervention, before fixing her with his version of cop-stare. It was a pretty good one. But her father's was way better, so it didn't have the effect he probably thought it would.

"Can you possibly be that oblivious?"

She blinked. "I'm sorry?"

"You should be. You've got a lot of people worried about you. Enough to call in a bunch of favors to get a BOLO put out on you and your car."

A be-on-the-lookout order? Like a common criminal?

Outrage sucked away every drop of embarrassment. "My father has the police looking for me? For God's sake, why?"

"You didn't show up where you were supposed to be going and didn't answer any texts or calls from people trying to make sure you were okay. They were afraid you might have had an accident somewhere, been hurt, abducted, or worse. That's why."

A tiny shred of guilt tried to worm its way through her anger. She squashed it.

"I'm sorry I worried anyone, and I'm sorry the police had to get involved." Sorrier than he could know. Talk about humiliating. "But as you can see, I'm perfectly fine. Thank you for doing your job, Officer. You can report back that the irresponsible problem child has been found and call off the manhunt."

Peter had the decency to wince. "Just...call them, okay? Your father and Theo are both going a little crazy, and that won't change until they know you're safe." He started to turn away, then stopped. "Rachel, whatever's going on, be careful, okay? My brother doesn't always show it, but he feels things pretty deeply. Especially now. He's...vulnerable. Please don't break his heart."

"What about mine?" she whispered to his retreating form in the mirror.

The urge to scream was a seething, squirming need clawing at her. She held it back, waiting for him to leave so she could let it loose. But as a minute turned into two, she realized he wasn't going anywhere until she did.

"Damn it!" Throwing the Jeep into drive, she made a wide—and illegal—tire-screeching U-turn. "Go on, give me a ticket!" she snarled under her breath.

He didn't.

But he did stay right behind her until they reached the edge of town. Then he sped up and passed her with a honk, leaving her to fume as she navigated the streets to the only place she could think to go where she wasn't pissed at anyone.

Pulling into the parking lot behind Ari's building, she turned the Jeep off and sat listening to the engine tick in the sudden silence.

How had it come to this?

The day had started so well, then somehow turned into a shitshow of epic proportions.

And it wasn't over yet.

Deciding she was only delaying the inevitable, she took out her phone.

Twenty-three texts, seven missed calls, and three voice messages. It was harder to hold back the guilt this time. No wonder the troops had been called out on her.

She tapped out a quick text to her father, saying she was fine and spending the night at Ari's and would talk to him tomorrow. She started to do the same for Theo, then gave in to morbid curiosity and scrolled back through his unanswered texts.

Hey babe, your dinner's getting cold. On your way?

Everything okay? If you're running behind let me know so I can keep everything warm and ready. Including me.

Did training not go well today? Babe, it's okay. Come over and we'll talk about it. Or not talk about it. Whatever you want. Just let me know you're okay.

Rachel, check your phone. I left a message.

Babe, PLEASE answer me.

I just talked to your dad and he said you left the house to come here almost an hour ago. I'm starting to freak the fuck out. WHERE ARE YOU?

RACHEL!

God, you don't have any idea the things I'm imagining. Call me!!!

Answer the damn phone!

RACHEL!!!!

A riot of emotions battled inside her as she read through the increasingly angry and demanding texts. How *dare* he? Like she was obligated to answer him, whether she'd wanted to or not?

Which she obviously hadn't.

He should have accepted that and left her alone. But no. He'd gotten her father involved, who'd gotten the police involved, and she'd ended up being escorted back like a recalcitrant runaway.

Fingers shaking with the force of her anger, she called Theo's number.

He answered on the first ring. "Rachel! Thank God you're okay! I was going out of my mind. Why didn't you call me as soon as Peter told you how worried I was?"

Of course, his brother would have called him. The dirty snitch.

"I was a little too busy being angry."

"Babe, it's okay if your training didn't go as well as you expected, but that's no reason to scare me half to death by disappearing without a word like that. I didn't know where you were!"

She pulled the phone away and stared at it like he was crazy.

Because clearly he was.

"My training went just fine, thank you. Better than fine. It was excellent! Dad was happy with my progress. I was happy with it. Everyone was freaking happy!"

Silence boomed through the phone.

"Okay," he said finally. "Then would you care to tell me what you *were* so angry about that you decided to scare the hell out of me by driving off and not bothering to answer your damn phone when you knew I was expecting you to come here for dinner?"

"Oh, I'd love to tell you why," she purred, seething with the anger being fed by the exasperation in his tone. "I was angry...no, that's too mild. I was *furious* to find out that someone I thought could be trusted with something deeply personal had betrayed me by opening his big mouth and blabbing about it instead."

A sigh whispered in her ear. "So, which one of your fathers are you pissed at?"

"Not my fathers! You!"

"Me?" He had the nerve to sound shocked.

Her jaw ached from grinding her teeth. "Evidently, you had a nice little chat with my father today." She could still remember Dellin's oh-so evasive answer when she'd asked what about.

You. Him. Things.

Things. Right.

"Yeah." Caution had crept into his voice. "So? I thought that was the point. Spending time with him. Getting to know each other better?"

"Getting to know each other doesn't include spilling your guts to him about things that are none of his business!"

"Things that are…" He cursed. "I can't believe he told you."

Having her suspicions confirmed only made her blood boil hotter. "I can't believe *you* told *him*. How could you?"

"I didn't mean to. We were talking and suddenly it just came out. I'm sorry. I know it's something I should have said to you first, but, well, he would have found out eventually, so…what's the harm?"

"What's the harm? What's the *harm*? Are you kidding me right now? You tell my dad I don't want to race anymore, and you ask *what's the harm*?" Judging by the odd look she got from the woman getting into the car next to her, she was shouting.

Normally, she would have looked away in embarrassment.

Instead, she bared her teeth at the woman in a smile that made her start her car and pull away in a hurry.

The silence from the other end of the phone became oppressive. "Well?"

"You think I told your father that?"

"I know you did!"

"He said that?"

"No, I heard him talking to my dad when they were arguing over me wanting to lighten my training schedule."

Because of you.

That part she kept to herself. She was humiliated enough already. No need to make herself look even more foolish.

"He was talking about what I wanted out of life besides a medal, and he asked, 'What about what Theo said?'" The words still echoed inside her like a death knell.

Theo was silent for a long moment.

When he spoke, his voice was low, calm, and totally devoid of emotion. "So, of course you assumed that meant I'd broken your trust and told him what you'd specifically asked me not to. What I promised you I wouldn't tell anybody, for any reason."

"What else could it mean?"

More silence, then a low chuckle that sounded like it came from the bottom of a crypt. "Babe, how about when you figure that out, you give me a call and we'll see if I still care enough to explain it to you."

"What are you—" She was talking to dead air.

The bastard hung up on her!

She started to call him back, then dropped the phone to her lap. Why bother? There was nothing left to say.

Give him a call? When Hell froze over, maybe. He'd already broken her trust, and her heart. She wouldn't give him the satisfaction of taking what was left of her dignity as well.

They were done.

The finality of that thought stabbed through the anger blanketing the rest of her emotions, stripping away the comforting numbness as that reality flooded in. They were done.

Dropping her face into her hands, she wept.

Chapter 35

"Jesus, you stink."

Bleary-eyed, Theo blinked up from where he lay sprawled on the patio swing, wishing his brother would stop yelling. "I just haven't showered yet. I'm sure you're no rose garden when you wake up in the morning, either."

"Maybe not, but I don't smell like the alley behind a bar during Mardi Gras." Richard wrinkled his nose as he gestured with his fingers. "Come on. Get up, go take a shower, and I'll make you something to eat."

Stomach doing a double-dip at the thought of food, he shook his head, then grabbed it with a groan. "No food. I'll puke."

"Smells like you already did that."

Hazy bits of memory poked through the cotton in his head of heaving beneath the rhododendron next to the patio. Not his finest moment. It also explained why his throat felt like it had been polished with sandpaper.

Why the hell had he had so much to drink last night?

Hadn't he sworn to temper his booze intake after the last time, when Rachel had needed to drive them both home from the pub?

Rachel.

The whys of last night came flooding back with a painful rush. He groaned again. That was the problem with drinking to forget.

Eventually, the alcohol wore off.

"That's it. Let's go."

Richard grabbed his arm and hauled him to his unsteady feet, making his stomach pitch like a raft caught in a whirlpool at the sudden movement. He swallowed hard to keep from christening his brother's shoes.

Barely.

Concentrating on keeping his head from exploding as Richard dragged him up the stairs and to his bathroom kept him from thinking too much. But when his brother reached for his shirt, he finally found the strength to snarl in rebellion.

"I will kick your ass if you try to undress me."

Richard merely gave him a sardonic smile, because they both knew Theo wasn't capable of kicking a butterfly's ass at the moment. But he held his hands up in surrender and stepped back, anyway. "Just try not to fall and crack your head open."

Closing the door behind his brother's retreating back, Theo went about undressing with deliberate care. As he pulled his t-shirt off, he caught a whiff of himself and gagged.

Jesus, he really was ripe.

Probably should have showered and changed after he'd tried to work out his anger and frustration down in the gym last night. Instead, he had grabbed the bottle of Scotch he'd been saving since Christmas, gone out to where he and Rachel sat not too long ago contemplating the view, and proceeded to try and drink the infuriating woman right out of his head.

"Yeah, that really showed her," he muttered as he stepped under the jets.

It wasn't until the hot water hit his skin that he realized he was freezing. It was a good thing he'd turned on the patio heater last night, or he might have had a much bigger problem than a hangover and a sour stomach.

As he stood under the water, shivering as he warmed up, he concentrated on not thinking about Rachel. Which turned out to be a lot harder than it seemed. By the time he got dressed and gingerly made his way back downstairs, he'd done nothing *but* think about her and the conversation that had sent him on his self-destructive downward spiral.

And he still couldn't figure out what the hell had gone so very wrong, so very fast.

His stomach gurgled at the powerful smell of coffee as he entered the kitchen. Thankfully, Richard had only made it for himself. A glass of ginger ale and two triangles of dry toast were set on the table for him. He sat and took a resigned nibble, hoping for the best. "Thanks."

"Sure."

He waited for the lecture to start. When it didn't, he glanced up through his lashes at his brother, who looked totally out of place leaning against the kitchen counter in one of his thousand-dollar designer suits, calmly sipping coffee from a cup that proclaimed *Rock climbing isn't just a hobby, it's a zombie apocalypse life skill.*

The clock on the nearby microwave read 10:32. "Shouldn't you be at work?"

"Shouldn't you?"

Touché.

"Yeah, sorry about that. I..." He cast about for a reasonable explanation and came up empty. There was no good excuse for not showing up at the office.

Especially without calling in.

His assistant, Sabrina, had no doubt tried to get hold of him this morning. Only he hadn't heard the phone ring since he'd left it in the house last night before he started his personal pity party.

No, not pity. Anger.

He'd been so furious, he'd needed to go work it off on the heavy bag and the weight bench to keep from exploding from it. Now, the anger was banked and everything had gone numb, as though it were encased in ice. All he felt now was exhausted.

And nauseated.

He took another bite of toast. "It won't happen again."

"No. It won't."

Theo didn't like the grim sound of that pronouncement. "I don't have a problem. Last night was the first time I've had a drink in two weeks."

"If it had only been *a* drink, I might agree with you."

Grinding his teeth made his head hurt worse, so he loosened his jaw and met his brother's shuttered gaze. "Say the word intervention, and we're done here."

"You could have killed yourself last night, passing out outside like that."

"Close enough." Theo pushed his chair back with a screech as he stood.

"Sit your ass back down before I do it for you."

The quiet whip of Richard's voice stopped him cold. He contemplated his brother with a wary look.

This was no idle threat. He might have the advantage in upper body strength, but Richard had years of martial arts training and a black belt. If it came down to it, right now, with the condition he was in, he was pretty sure his brother would mop the floor with him.

Then he made an even worse threat. "Or I could just have Mom come out and talk to you instead."

Theo sat.

Richard was definitely the lesser evil.

"Fine. Talk."

"You know, I came here because I was worried about you. But if you don't want to listen to what I have to say as your brother, then you can damn well listen to me as your boss. Your choice."

It was a nominal difference in the firm's power structure. But as COO being groomed to become CEO one day, Richard technically was his boss. He didn't pull that card out often, which meant he was well and truly pissed.

"Okay, fine. Impart your brotherly wisdom on this. What do you do when someone you love thinks you told a secret they shared with you, even after you promised you never would? How do you deal with that kind of lack of faith?"

Richard opened his mouth, closed it, then tried again. "This isn't about Gavin?" He blinked. "Wait, someone you *love*?"

"I thought I did." Why else would this have hit him so damn hard?

Any other woman he'd dated, he would have simply shrugged it off and walked away. It wouldn't have been worth the bandwidth to care. But Rachel's harsh accusation had sliced him deeper than he ever thought he could feel.

Richard pulled out a chair and sat across from him. "Okay, I'm going to need a lot more context here. I assume we're talking about Rachel?" When Theo gave him an 'are you kidding me?' look, he shook his head. "I knew I should have had her checked out."

"I already know everything I need to about her past. And she still managed to blindside me." Or had she?

He *did* know about her past. About her almost obsessive adherence to those stupid rules. Most especially the one about not trusting anyone with her secrets.

Was it any wonder her default reasoning would be to doubt him?

But she hadn't even asked him if he'd done it. That was the part he had a hard time getting past. She'd assumed he had, so it had to be true. Judged, tried, and convicted without a shred of proof or a chance to defend himself.

"I know things looked pretty cozy between you two the other day at the fashion show, but isn't it a little early to be using the L word?"

"And exactly how long did it take for you to fall for Amber?"

"This isn't about me." But he let it drop, which meant Theo had won that point. "So, what happened?"

"She told me something a few weeks ago—actually, she didn't even tell me. She said it when she didn't think I would hear, because she's got this crazy thing about trusting people with secrets. Anyway, I told her Saturday night that I knew, and I promised I wouldn't tell anyone, no matter what."

His hand made an agitated swipe through his damp hair. "Then not even a day later, she accuses me of telling her father. No benefit of the doubt. No coming to talk about it like a rational adult. She just drives off and disappears for *hours*. No one knew where she was or if she was okay. And when she finally did call, instead of apologizing for scaring the fucking hell out of me, she hits me with this 'you broke your promise' crap."

"And what did you say?"

He winced. "I told her to call me when she figured out she was wrong and hung up on her."

"Mature."

"Bite me."

"I rest my case."

Shredding the remains of the second piece of toast, he held back a growl. "It was hang up or say something I would've regretted. She'd been missing for hours. She didn't answer any of my texts or calls. Or her father's. I finally had to pull in some favors with the chief of police to find her and make sure she was okay."

Richard's eyes widened. "You sicced the police on her?"

"I thought she might have been hurt or in trouble. What else was I supposed to do?"

"Oh, sure, what else? No wonder she was pissed at you."

Theo hesitated. "Actually, she thought her dad was responsible for that. And Pete let her keep thinking it."

"Peter was the one to..." Pinching the bridge of his nose, Richard let out a gusty sigh. "What else?"

"That's pretty much it." He shrugged, doing his best to ignore the feeling beginning to gnaw at him he might have been at least a little in the wrong. "After Pete told her everyone was worried about her, she called me and started yelling about how I'd spilled her secret to her father, and how could I break my promise like that?"

"Did you? Don't look at me like that. It's a legitimate question."

"No, I didn't. And it wasn't easy, either. He was fishing around on the subject—and no, I'm not telling you what it was about." He rolled his eyes at his brother, who gave a disgruntled grunt. Richard hated puzzles he didn't have the answer for. "Suffice it to say, he wants her to be happy, and he thought I might be his partner in crime, so to speak."

"And do you want her to be happy?"

"What kind of stupid question is that? Of course, I do."

"Would telling her father this secret help make that happen?"

"Yes. Maybe. I don't know." He sighed. "It doesn't matter. It's not my secret to tell, and I won't. I just wish she could see that."

"How hard did you try to convince her?"

"I didn't." He scowled at Richard's look of disbelief. "What? I shouldn't have to defend myself."

"Did you at least say 'no, I didn't do it'?"

"Ah..." He thought back over their brief phone conversation. *Well, fuck.*

"Maybe not in those exact words."

"In any words even remotely resembling those?" He rolled his eyes skyward at Theo's silence. "It's official. Our parents raised a moron."

"You know what? Fuck you. I'd been out of my mind with worry she was either lying dead in a ravine somewhere or on her way out of state in the trunk of some sex trafficker's car, and she didn't even care! I think I get a pass on forgetting to use my debate club skills."

But there it was again. That gnawing feeling he'd handled things all wrong.

Richard stared at him, his gaze narrowing the way it always did when he was working through a problem. "Son of a bitch. This *is* about Gavin."

"What the hell are you talking about?"

"This compulsive worrying you do about everyone that borders on paranoia."

The accusation would have stung more if he hadn't already recognized the same thing weeks ago.

Still, he felt the need to defend himself.

"It's not paranoia if it's true. That sound I heard in your car you swore wasn't there turned out to be something. Milo said you might have blown the engine if you hadn't brought it in for him to look at."

"True. And the mole on Amber's neck you kept telling her looked 'suspicious' until she finally had it checked out was just a mole. You were so persistent about it you had Derek scared half to death his mom had cancer and was going to die."

He winced. "I'm sorry about that. I shouldn't have brought it up in front of him. But the point is, it could have been something. It was better she had it checked out."

"No, the point is, your perceived feelings of having failed Gavin are making you hyper-focus on everyone around you to try and keep anything bad from happening to them, too."

"What's wrong with trying to keep the people I love safe?"

"Other than it turning you into a paranoid crazy person who sics the police on his girlfriend because she's late for dinner?"

Well, when he put it that way, it did sound kind of bad.

Theo brushed the crumbs from his fingers and pushed the plate of mangled toast away, thinking over what his brother said. He knew he'd been getting on everyone's nerves the past few months, butting into their business and worrying over them like a mother hen.

Hadn't he done the same thing to Rachel the very first time they'd met, after her collision with the snowboarder on the slopes?

And she'd hated it.

So much so that she'd walked away from him, ending their acquaintance before it ever really began. And that was just for trying to convince her to go see a doctor.

How much more would she have resented being tracked down, pulled over, and ordered home because he'd freaked out and started thinking of every bad thing that could have happened to her, no matter how unlikely or farfetched? She was an adult with a mind and will of her own, and he'd totally disregarded both because he'd gone into panic mode and turned into a raving asshole.

He dropped his face into his hands with a groan. "Shit. I fucked up."

"No arguments from me."

"Not. Helping."

"Okay, how about this. Call her. Apologize. Fix it."

If only it were that simple.

"Have you forgotten the part where she thinks I told her secret?"

"And you never told her she was wrong." Richard's expression turned pained. "Trust me, you don't want to let a stupid misunderstanding destroy what you could have with this woman. If you love her, if you *really* love her, then don't be an ass and let stubborn pride stand in your way. Call her."

Normally, Richard was one of the most emotionally reserved people he knew. He'd almost lost his chance with Amber because of it, but now he was the happiest bastard in the world.

Did he want to lose his chance at having that for himself all because he let his feelings get hurt?

"I'll think about it."

He was pretty sure he wouldn't be able to think about anything else.

Richard nodded. "Fair enough." He paused, his expression turning wary. "About the drinking..."

"It's not an issue," Theo snapped, then took a deep breath and let it out. "Okay, it may be an issue. But I'm going to take care of it."

"I've heard that before."

"This time I mean it." He picked up the therapist's card from the table, where he'd put it the day before so he could look at it while he was making dinner. Running his thumb along the edge, he explained Dellin's theory about survivor's guilt. When he was done, he waited while his brother digested everything with that focused, working-it-through gaze again.

Finally, Richard nodded. "Okay. Okay. That...it makes sense." His expression softened. "If you need anything, you let me know, all right? Anything at all. You're not in this alone, you know."

Where he normally felt an ember of resentment in his belly when his family stuck their noses into his business, this time he felt the comforting warmth of relief instead.

"I know. Thanks."

Long after Richard left to go back to the office, telling him to take the rest of the day to do whatever he needed to do, he sat and stared at the card in his hands. He needed to do this. He knew he did. But...

What if he didn't? What if now that he knew what was wrong with him, what had been making him act like someone else these past months, he just dealt with it on his own? That had to be better than spilling his guts to a total stranger for a couple hundred bucks an hour. Really, how hard could it be to put himself back on the right path?

His gaze landed on the almost empty scotch bottle his brother must have retrieved from the patio. It had been full when he'd started drinking last night.

He picked up the phone and dialed.

Chapter 36

"How did you sleep? Did the lavender help?"

Shuffling into the kitchen wearing the previous day's clothes, with a case of bed-head that wouldn't be tamed and a back that ached from her night on Ari's sofa, Rachel felt like the walking dead. Everything inside was numb.

"Yeah, a little. Thanks."

After listening to Rachel pour out her tale of woe in between sobs, Ari had given her a large mug of chamomile tea, rubbed lavender on her temples, and put her to bed with a lavender-soaked cotton ball tucked inside her pillowcase.

Somehow, between the lavender, the tea, and the complete exhaustion of being emotionally wrung dry, she'd finally fallen asleep. It had been troubled, but at least she hadn't spent the entire night staring at the ceiling, thinking.

Ari slid a bowl of oatmeal in front of her. "Eat."

It wasn't her favorite breakfast food, but she dug in anyway, too weary to care. The brown sugar and cinnamon burst on her tongue with the first spoonful, awakening her appetite with a vengeance. Only then did she remember she'd missed dinner the night before.

The why of that she ruthlessly ignored, at least for the moment. Instead, she attacked the food with methodical precision, until she scraped up the last mouthful and dropped her spoon in the bowl with a sated sigh.

"Better?"

"Much. Thanks." She'd put her body through a hell of a workout on the mountain the day before, then treated it poorly by not giving it the calories it needed to recover properly. No wonder she felt so shitty this morning.

Right, that's why.

Ignoring her snarky inner commentator, she brought her bowl to the sink and rinsed it out. "Thanks for breakfast, and for putting me up for the night, but I should—"

"Oh, no." Ari pointed at the chair. "Sit."

Since she wasn't really in a hurry to go deal with her dads, she did. When Ari placed a mug of reddish tea in front of her, she gave it a cautious sniff. "What is it?"

"Hawthorn with hibiscus."

Sounded harmless enough. Taking a small sip, the fruity taste pleasantly surprised her, both a little sweet and tart at the same time. "It's good."

"Of course it is."

Hiding a smile at her friend's huffy reply, she took another sip. It really was tasty. Ari had a real skill for blending teas and tisanes based on what her clients' needs were. Even those not into the woo-woo came to her for her aromatherapy and herbalist skills.

That reminder stopped the mug halfway to her mouth. Pulling it back, she eyed it with a healthy pinch of suspicion. "What's it for?"

"It helps with the fourth chakra."

Okay, she knew this. Silently, she counted them off.

Root, sacral, solar plexus...

The mug hit the table with an angry thud. "That's the heart chakra. What the hell, Ari? Not cool."

"It's not a love potion, for goddess's sake. It simply helps unblock whatever tangled up mess you've got going on in there." She narrowed her eyes at Rachel as though she could see inside her chest. "And believe me, it *is* a mess."

"Gee, thanks for the tip. I never would have known my love life just imploded like the Death Star." Pain nipped at the numbness around her heart. Without thinking, she took another sip of tea. The warmth rolled down her throat in a soothing wave.

"It's not about your love life, it's about you closing yourself off."

"Only because when I opened myself up, I got my guts ripped out for my trouble."

"I think you're making more out of this than there is."

She stared at her friend in wounded disbelief. "Seriously? He broke his promise, betrayed my trust, and had his brother track me down and drag me back to town, all because I wouldn't answer his texts. You don't think that qualifies?"

More of the numbness melted as her anger rekindled.

"To be fair, that last bit of stupidity was your da's doing, but okay, yes. He was a complete and total ass. You have every right to be pissed at him. I just think maybe it might not be a bad idea to take another look at it all with a slightly calmer head. Like those texts, for instance."

"The texts?" She pulled her phone from her pocket and brought them up. "You mean these texts, where Mr. Bossypants starts out all sweet and nice, and quickly becomes a demanding tyrant who *orders* me to call him because he wants to know where I am?" She slapped the phone to the table.

"Didn't you tell me the very first time you met him, he got up in your business about seeing a doctor because you were knocked off your feet on the slopes?"

"Yeah, so? That just shows he was a controlling jerk even then." So much so she'd walked away.

If only he hadn't come back the next day to apologize.

If only she hadn't accepted.

Then none of this would have happened, and her life wouldn't be a smoldering pile of nuclear waste.

Ari tapped her nails against her mug. "There had to be a reason you gave him a second chance. What was it?"

"He told me he'd overreacted because he was worried I'd been hurt." Because of everything that had happened with Gavin.

Not that she'd known it at the time. But after hearing his drunken confession about blaming himself for his friend's death, it had made perfect sense.

"Maybe like he overreacted last night?" Ari asked.

Her heart leapt, but she stomped it back down.

No. She refused to make excuses for him. She'd given him a second shot, and he'd stabbed her in the back with it. "It doesn't matter."

"I think it matters more than you want to admit. If it didn't, you wouldn't have spent last night crying your bloody heart out on my shoulder. Read the texts again."

She cringed inside. "I don't think so."

With an impatient scowl, Ari leaned forward. "Read them again. Not how *you* think he meant them. Read them and let the words tell you what *he* was thinking."

There was practically nothing she wanted to do less.

Steeling herself, she scrolled to the first text and read each one again, trying her best not to hear the words in her head spoken in anger, but rather in a neutral tone. She fidgeted in her seat. "Okay, maybe he wasn't exactly yelling at me, but still..."

"Did you ever listen to the voicemails he left?" Rachel shook her head. "Don't you think maybe you should?"

Maybe. But she didn't want to.

Still, she dialed and listened to the computerized voice tell her she had three messages. The first one was from Theo.

"Babe, it's me. I'm just checking to make sure everything's all right, since you never run late without calling to let me know. So, call me, okay?"

He sounded a little on edge, uncertainty coloring his tone.

The second was from Dellin.

"Rachel, where are you? I thought you went to Theo's for dinner, but he just called looking for you and said you haven't gotten there yet. You've got everyone worried now, so please call me as soon as you get this."

The final one was from Theo again.

"Rachel, I'm hoping your phone is just dead and you didn't realize it, because I'm starting to get pretty worried here. Are you okay? If something happened, I'll fix it, I swear. Sweetheart, please call and let me know you're all right. PLEASE."

She hung up, swallowing the lump clogging her throat. He hadn't sounded angry at all. He'd sounded panicked.

She read the texts again. This time the ghost of Theo's voice in her head was edged with worry, the words in all caps no longer demanding, but frantic begging.

"Oh, damn."

She looked at Ari, her perch on the high ground slipping. "Okay, he was more upset than mad. But it still doesn't make the other thing he did okay. He still broke his promise."

And my heart.

Ari just looked at her with those witchy green eyes and sipped her tea.

"What?"

"You need to talk to your das."

Glad to leave the topic of Theo behind, she sighed. "I know. I will."

"No, I mean, you *really* have to talk to them. About everything."

She started. "I don't know what—"

"Do you remember the spread we did the last time you came to the shop?"

"You mean when the cards predicted joy and happiness in my relationship with Theo?"

And there had been, for a while. Too bad the cards hadn't mentioned the quick expiration date on that outcome.

"That's what you heard." Ari passed her hands over the table as though spreading a Tarot deck. She pointed to a non-existent card and recited the spread from memory, something that never failed to creep Rachel out.

"The Hermit. Your goals can be attained, but the journey hasn't always been a smooth or easy one." *Point.* "Reversed Five of Wands. There is some discord going on, and it will take some time to work through and fix it." *Point.* "Ten of Cups. New beginnings. Happiness and long-term joy. Dreams coming true."

Rachel's heart pulsed with a hollow ache. "Some dream."

Leaning back as she cradled her mug in her hands, Ari gave her an enigmatic look. "I never said the reading had anything to do with your love life."

"Then what—" She stared at Ari and got a shiver down her spine. "How could you know?" she whispered. How could she have possibly figured out her deepest secret? The one she'd only ever shared with Theo.

Ari's answering smile was sad. "Only you can decide what your dreams are, Rae. And only you can make them come true. If you wait too long, you just might miss your chance."

Chapter 37

Rachel was still feeling a bit off-balance when she walked into her parents' house a half hour later. Ari had refused to discuss her little bombshell. Not even to say how she'd figured out what Rachel had thought was a tightly guarded secret.

She'd been so frustrated by that, she finally wondered out loud if Theo had gone and taken out an ad somewhere about it, since everyone seemed to know.

That bit of nonsense earned her a lecture on the cost of jumping to conclusions without a shred of proof. It wasn't undeserved. It also wasn't a stretch to realize Ari hadn't just been talking about her snarky comment, either.

Fair enough. She might have overreacted to what she'd thought was the tone of Theo's texts. But it didn't change the facts of what he'd done. She had heard the proof with her own two ears, and there was no misinterpreting that.

As she dropped her purse on the chair by the door, she pushed all thoughts of Theo out of her mind. She'd torture herself some more over him in private later. Right now, she needed to focus on talking to her dads.

Only you can decide what your dreams are.

Gritting her teeth, she shoved Ari's words away.

She knew what her dream was. What it had always been. She'd just gotten a little sidetracked by the lure of good sex and a handsome face. But that was over, and now she could get back to working toward the only thing that really mattered.

Winning gold.

She ignored the little voice that called her an idiot.

Following the sound of the television, she found both of her parents in the den. She stood in the doorway for a moment, looking at them. These were the men who had taken her into their home, their lives, and given her the world. How could she have even for a second thought about throwing it all back in their faces?

God, she was such a selfish bitch.

She must have made a noise, because Dellin's head jerked around. His expression melted into one of such relief, it made her start to tear up at what she'd put them through by running off yesterday.

She gave an awkward lift of her arms. "I'm home."

"Rae." Dellin met her halfway across the room and enveloped her in a bone-crushing hug until she squeaked. "We were so worried about you last night." He put her at arm's length and gave her a stern look that made her feel about two inches tall. "Don't ever do that again."

"I'm sorry I didn't return your calls. I was driving off my mad."

Karl pulled her into his arms with a sigh. "I'm sorry, Rae. I shouldn't have said what I did. Any of it. You had every right to be mad."

She gave him a hard squeeze, inhaling his familiar tang of Old Spice, before letting go. "No, *I'm* sorry. You were right. I was thinking like a quitter. I was letting Theo get in the way of our dreams."

He winced and shot a quick look at Dellin before focusing back on her with a quiet intensity he usually reserved for the starting gate. "*Your* dreams, Rae. They should be your dreams, not ours."

"They're the same dream."

"They shouldn't be." He sighed and took her hand, leading her to sit on the sofa. "Rachel, sweetheart, I love you. I've loved you from the second I saw you, and that feeling has only grown with every passing year. The day you handed me those papers to have me officially adopt you was the best day of my life, and I couldn't be any prouder of you and everything you do than I am right now."

The words, the validation that all the years she'd devoted to making him happy hadn't been for nothing, should have left her thrilled.

Instead, all she could hear was the great, big "but" coming.

"But I think somewhere along the line, I lost track of what was really important. To all of us." He shot another look at Dellin, who gave him a tentative smile in return.

She looked back and forth between the two of them. "I don't understand."

"I didn't, either. Or, at least, I told myself I didn't. But your father saw. He knew. And you were telling me, too, in so many ways I just didn't want to acknowledge."

He paused as though ordering his thoughts. "You've always pushed to give more than a hundred percent in everything you do. Any other time you've gotten hurt over the years, we had to practically tie you down to keep you from trying to get back on your skis too soon. But this time was different."

"Well, yeah. I had the surgeries, and PT. It took a long time to heal."

But it was more than that, and you know it, that annoying little voice whispered.

"It did. But I expected you to be nagging at me to get up on the course months ago, even if you weren't physically ready for it. But you never even brought it up. I accused you of goofing off, when really I should have been seeing there was a much more serious problem."

The sense she'd disappointed him cracked over her like a whip. "I'm sorry, Dad. I should have—"

"No, *I'm* sorry. I should have seen the change. Should have understood what it meant."

Confused, fearful, hopeful, she shook her head. "Understood what?"

"Sweetheart, why was it so important to you to do well at Copper yesterday?"

"Why?" She looked at him like he'd lost his mind. She jumped up, went to the wall, and gestured to the glaring empty spot in the middle. "Because...this."

"Oh, sweetheart." He got up to join her and mimicked her gesture. "This means nothing if this"—he passed his hand over her heart—"isn't the reason you want it."

"But...it's what we've always talked about. Dreamed about. I was supposed to finish what you gave up for me."

"Gave up?" Confusion turned into pain, then sorrow. "Oh, sweetheart, no. That's not what happened."

"You stopped racing before you reached your goal so you could coach me."

And she meant to repay that debt.

"No. I stopped racing because it wasn't the most important thing in my life anymore. I had you, and your father, and suddenly being away from home for weeks at a time, season after season, just wasn't as appealing as it used to be. The drive wasn't here"—he touched his chest—"for me anymore. I would have hung up my skis even if you'd never chosen to compete."

Rachel stared at him in shock. Every belief she'd built her life on was collapsing beneath her feet like sand being sucked out by the retreating tide. "But...the gold."

"I'll admit when you showed an interest in competing, I got pulled back into the whole gold fever whirlwind." He sounded chagrined by the admission. "I'm sorry if I've been pushing you all these years toward something that wasn't what you wanted."

"But I did want it!" That was no lie. She'd enjoyed her years of competing.

Right up until she hadn't.

"Did, or do?" The sad, knowing look in his eyes made her glance away. "That's what I thought."

"I don't want to let you down." The words were a pained whisper.

"Sweetheart, the only way you could do that would be to continue competing for me instead of for yourself."

"I..." She looked over at Dellin, who was doing his best to keep a neutral expression, and failing. Karl's hand cupped her cheek, drawing her attention back to him.

"It's okay. You don't have to decide anything today. It's not a now or never thing. You think about what it is you truly want, and that's what we'll do, no matter what it is. Okay? I will still love you—*we* will still love you—no matter what you decide to do."

Tears clogged her throat as he pulled her into a tight hug. What she truly wanted? She honestly had no idea what that was anymore.

When he released her, she found herself caught right back up in another embrace. Dellin rocked her gently, the way he had when she was little. "Don't cry, baby girl."

"I'm sorry." She sniffled, but the tears still leaked down her face, wetting his shirt.

"Don't be sorry. Be happy. That's all we ever wanted for you. And I've known you haven't been for a while now. I just didn't know how to get you to talk about it."

Bitterness added to the tears in her throat. "And then Theo went and did it for me."

"Theo? Did what?"

"Told you I was having doubts about wanting to race anymore."

The rocking stopped. "He knew that?"

She pulled back from the hug, anger trickling in to join the bitterness and tears. "Pop, you don't have to protect him. I already know he told you."

"No, he didn't. I'm telling you," he said when she started to protest again, "he didn't. Not even when I was trying to pump him for information yesterday."

He sounded like he was telling the truth. But...

"I heard you. You said something to Dad like, what about what Theo said?" She winced at Dellin's raised brow.

"Eavesdropping? Really, Rae?"

"It's not exactly eavesdropping if you're yelling loud enough to be heard through the closed door."

It was a weak defense, but it was the only one she had, so she was sticking to it.

"It is if you only hear part of the conversation and take its meaning out of context. We were talking about...something else. Theo never mentioned anything about racing." He huffed an annoyed breath as she shook her head in denial. "Rachel, what was the one rule we told you we had in this house when we brought you home?"

"No lies," she answered in a small voice.

"And have I ever lied to you?"

"No, sir."

But that would mean she'd made a horrible, unforgiveable mistake.

"Then what was it Theo said?"

Dellin shook his head. "That's something you'll have to ask him."

She winced. That might be a little difficult.

Babe, how about when you figure that out, you give me a call and we'll see if I still care enough to explain it to you.

Yeah, that didn't sound like a man ready and willing to forgive.

Not that she blamed him. She'd called him a liar. Attacked both his honor and his pride. Not to mention his integrity. Sure, what man wouldn't respond well to "oops, sorry, my bad, let's have a do-over" after that?

After escaping to her room saying she wanted to shower and change, she collapsed onto her bed, head whirling. How could she have been so wrong?

About *everything*?

Not just Theo, but her fathers, too? All these months she'd been agonizing over the stirrings of rebellion she felt inside, when all along the only person she'd been fighting was herself.

The question of what she was going to do about her career got put aside in favor of the more immediate, and, she admitted it, the more important problem of what she was going to do about Theo.

Because she knew she had to do *something*. What they had was too special to let him go. It was too bad she hadn't realized it until now.

Only you can decide what your dreams are.

Well, she knew what those were now, and they had nothing to do with any medals.

She wanted *him*.

But what good did that do her? She'd ruined everything. Calling him to try and apologize was going to be awkward as hell. Where did she even start?

Maybe she should wait.

That would give his temper time to cool down, and give her a chance to figure out the best way to fix the mess she'd made. She could make a list. Maybe run it by Ari and see what she thought had the best chance of success with the least potential for humiliation.

Then she remembered the rest of Ari's advice about her dreams.

Only you can make them come true. If you wait too long, you just might miss your chance.

She may not buy her friend's woo-woo, but she did trust her advice. Waiting and planning and making lists wouldn't get her what she wanted.

She needed to act, and soon. Today. Before Theo had time to realize she wasn't worth the effort to forgive. Maybe if she could figure out what would make him happy...

No.

That thought got slapped right out of her head. She was through thinking like the scared little foster kid who'd allowed Ivy's rules to shape her entire life. It was time to stop using the crutch of her past and make her future what she wanted it to be, not what she thought it needed to be to please everyone else.

It was time to grab her dream—*her* dream, *her* life, nobody else's—and never let go.

If she could figure out how before it was too late.

Chapter 38

The knock at his door wasn't totally unexpected.

But it was entirely unwelcome. He was in no mood to go through another round of psychoanalysis from his family. Especially since he'd just gotten back from having it done by a professional.

Not that Lyle did much analyzing. Mostly, he'd listened while Theo talked.

And talked.

And fuck him sideways, *talked*.

When he'd snagged the same-day appointment thanks to a cancellation, he'd expected to go in and sign some forms. Maybe get to know the guy a little. Get comfortable with him before he'd feel at ease giving up any of his tightly tangled issues and neuroses.

Instead, he'd spewed words like his mouth had sprung a fucking leak.

And damn it, he did feel better.

Just a little. Only so much could be accomplished in an hour. But at least the boulder of guilt and self-loathing sitting on his chest wasn't crushing him under its weight anymore. Had shifted just enough so he could draw a breath without feeling he was suffocating.

That it wasn't going to destroy him.

The knock came again.

He took mental odds on who it would be this time. No one had asked to be buzzed through the gate, so the possibilities were limited.

Richard had already had his turn, and he doubted Peter would feel inclined to stop by and check on him. He was still pretty raw about Theo using his friendship with the chief of police for a personal favor. His brother was constantly fighting the image of entitled-rich-boy with his fellow officers. Theo's actions had probably made things worse for him.

He still wasn't sure how he could fix that one.

Since his father was the last person he'd expect to show up to talk feelings, that left either his mother or his sister. Neither was going to be a pleasant conversation, but as he walked to the mudroom door, he kind of hoped it was Lillian. At least with her, he wouldn't have to deal with the patented mom-guilt card their mother played so well.

His phone rang. Slipping it out of his pocket, he answered "Yeah?" at the same time he opened the door.

Phone to her ear as she stood on the other side of it, Rachel blinked in surprise. "Um..." She lowered her phone. "I thought maybe you weren't home from work yet, so I was calling to check."

Several emotions flooded him at the sight of her. Anger. Frustration. Sadness.

Hope.

He grabbed onto the first two and ignored the rest.

"Why are you here?" Her slight flinch at his harsh words made him feel like an ass, but he didn't let it soften him. He had a right to be pissed at the woman who'd fractured his heart with her lack of trust. Whether she knew she had or not.

"I was wrong."

The quiet admission made that poor, damaged heart thud hard in his chest, but he remained silent. It was a start, but it wasn't nearly enough.

When he didn't respond, she said, "I want to—no, I *need* to apologize. And explain." Her eyes tightened at the corners. "Please."

It was the pain he saw deep in her eyes that made him move aside and let her in the house. Regardless of what she'd done, she was hurting as much as he was over it. That gave the hope he'd been trying to squash a fresh gasp of life.

As he prowled behind her into the living room, he inhaled the faint hint of vanilla left in her wake. He struggled to maintain his outward calm, caught between the ecstasy and agony of what the next few minutes might decide for them.

Rachel stopped to face him in front of the fireplace, hands knotted together in a nervous tangle. "I know you didn't tell my father my secret, and I'm so sorry I believed for even a second that you would."

"But you did believe it." Again, she flinched. Again, he held on to his resolve. "You didn't *just* believe it, though. You *assumed* it based on whatever it was you thought you heard, which tells me you never really trusted me in the first place."

"That's not true! I trusted you."

"For all of a day."

She looked like she wanted to argue, but they both knew she couldn't.

"You're right. I should have trusted you more. I shouldn't have assumed. I should have asked you about it. Or my dads. Or...something, anything, other than jumping to conclusions and believing the worst."

"Yeah. You should have."

"God, Theo." She took half a step in his direction, then seemed to catch herself and stopped, nervous hands fisting. "I am *so* sorry. I know saying it doesn't make everything better, but I want you to know I really, really am. I hate that I let my old insecurities lead me down such a horrible path. But more than anything, I hate that I hurt you. You've been the best thing that's ever happened to me, and I almost threw it all away just because I was scared and hurt that the man I loved would break his word to me. Something I should have known you'd never do. I don't have the right to ask for another chance, but I'm asking anyway. Please. Give me—give us—another chance."

It took a few seconds for the words to process. "What did you say?"

A disbelieving little huff escaped her. "You're going to make me say it again?"

"Just the part about where you...love me?"

Her expression softened to an almost-smile. "Yeah. I do."

His heart lifted.

Then plummeted.

"This is because your father told you what we really talked about, didn't he? That's the only reason you're saying it." Because Dellin had told her of his own confession about being in love with her.

Damn it! Talk about secrets that shouldn't be shared.

"I'm saying it because it's true. It's been true for a while now, I think. I just wasn't ready to accept it until I thought I'd lost you. Besides," she added in a disgruntled tone, "Pop wouldn't tell me what you talked about. He said I had to ask you if I wanted to know." She looked at him expectantly.

You don't want to let a stupid misunderstanding destroy what you could have with this woman.

His brother's advice echoed in his head, but he wasn't about to come clean about his feelings. Not just yet. Not until he was sure they had everything else straightened out between them first.

"We'll circle back to that in a minute." Maybe. "Let me ask you this first. Do they both know?"

The pained look on her face said she knew exactly what he was asking about. Her indecision about racing again. "Yes."

"And?"

"They're okay with it." She sounded a little lost by that.

"And what about you?"

"I'm not sure how I feel. About any of it."

Disappointment deflated his growing bubble of hope.

"Okay. You need time to think about what you want to do, I get that."

"No, that's not—"

"But let me say this, even if you're not ready to hear it. If you're still going to compete because it's for you, then that's fine. I'd be behind you a thousand percent."

"I'm not—"

"But if you're only going to do it for your father's sake, I don't think I can stand back and watch you do that to yourself for the next three years. And what happens if you don't win the gold at the next Olympics? Will you keep pushing yourself until the next one? And the next? Where does it stop?"

"I want to get a dog," she blurted out.

He stared at her. "What?"

"A dog. You know, furry, four legs, one tail, lots of responsibility?"

"I know what...oh." Right. When they'd discussed why neither of them had pets, they'd both agreed their lifestyles weren't conducive to taking care of one. That neither was home enough, so it wouldn't be fair to have one.

But if she wanted one now, that meant...

"What are you saying? Because I want everything we say to each other to be very clear from here on out. No more misunderstandings, no more confusion. One hundred percent straight up talk." His battered heart couldn't take anything less.

She stood taller and looked him in the eye.

"I'm straight up telling you I plan to be around. A lot. Maybe more than you'll want me to be, but that's okay. I screwed this up between us. I'm willing to put in whatever effort it takes to make it work this time. If you'll let there *be* a this time."

"You're sure you want to give up competing?"

She started to nod, then bit her lip. "I may want to go back for just one race, so I can retire on a better ending than being airlifted off the mountain. But that's it. After that, I'm done."

"Are you sure? Maybe you should give yourself a little time to think about it before you decide." He wanted to kick his own ass for even saying it.

But this needed to be a decision she could live with. Not a knee-jerk reaction she'd come to regret somewhere down the line.

"I've done nothing *but* think about it all afternoon. I know what I want, what's really important to me. And it isn't a gold medal."

It was the look of desperate longing on her face, not her words, that broke through the last of his reserve.

With a curse, he swept her up in his arms, taking her mouth in a kiss that held all the pain, the hurt, the sadness of the past twenty-four hours and expelled them like the poison they were. Her lips met his with the same voracity, filling him back up with need and anticipation until he felt ready to burst.

They stumbled up the stairs to his bedroom, leaving behind a tangle of clothing in their haste to get skin-to-skin. Falling naked onto the bed with Rachel under him, he pressed a frantic line of kisses from her neck to her breasts, worshipping at each to the accompaniment of her groans and whimpers.

As much as he wanted to continue the journey down her belly and between her legs, he didn't think he had it in him to hold out that long. Thankfully, she seemed to be as impatient as he was.

She reached down and grabbed his head with both hands, urging him back up to her mouth, where she nibbled and licked and stoked their passion even higher. While she did, one of those nimble hands snaked down to stroke his erection in a rhythm that left no doubt what she wanted.

Before he hit the point of no return, he tore himself away and grabbed a condom, then drove himself into her welcoming body with a sense of homecoming that almost ended things before they really got started. Stilling, he breathed through the sparks that raced up his spine, willing back the orgasm hovering right at the edge of his self-control.

When he was certain he wouldn't come, he opened his eyes and found himself staring into Rachel's arousal-darkened gaze. What he saw there told him more than any apology or explanation how she truly felt about him.

And it wasn't the sex, although it was undeniably amazing between them. It was the connection. The feeling that this was the person who was their other half. Their perfect interlocking piece.

Speaking of those...

Never taking his eyes from hers, he moved his hips, pulling back from her body's tight grasp and driving in again with a steadily increasing tempo. He watched as the ecstasy took hold of her, washing over her expression, bowing her spine as the orgasm seemed to go on forever.

The pulsing of her body around him shredded the last of his control. Letting go, he threw his head back as his body's pleasure spilled out into hers with every stroke.

A million years later, he roused from the lethargy that held him in its embrace and pressed a kiss to her shoulder, still dewy with the sweat of their exertions.

"It's my turn to apologize. I'm sorry I overreacted to you being late and not answering a few texts. And for embarrassing you. Asking the police chief to put out a BOLO to find you was over the top, I know, but—

Rachel's mouth dropped open. "Wait, that was you? I thought it was my father!"

He winced. "Yeah, sorry."

Turning more fully to face him, she pinned him with an incredulous look. "Why would you do that?"

"Because I was scared to death you were hurt or in trouble. And I know that's crazy. That I'm crazy. It's something I need to work on. And I am." He hesitated. "Which is why I went to see a therapist today."

"You did?"

"Your dad recommended him, actually. After our talk yesterday, he told me he thought part of what's been going on with me is survivor's guilt. The hypervigilance, the worry, the sense of failure. And the doc agrees. Classic signs. That doesn't excuse the way I freaked out about you going radio silence for a couple of hours, but maybe you can cut me a little slack over it, all things considered."

He ended on a hopeful note, but wasn't exactly encouraged by the serious expression she was wearing. Which was why her next words surprised him.

"You weren't the only one who overreacted. I read your texts like you were mad, not worried, and I assumed..." She shook her head. "God, that word again. I hate it. Let's promise never to use it again."

"Agreed." Leaning forward, he pressed his lips to hers to seal the vow. "So, am I forgiven?"

"Of course. Am I?"

"Yes." He linked his hand with hers and brought it to his mouth, kissing the back of it gently. A shiver wracked her body.

"So, um, that's what you and my father talked about? What happened with..."

"Gavin. It's okay, you can say his name." It still hurt, but he wouldn't hide from it anymore. Denial had only let the whole thing fester. "That was part of it." He kissed her hand again. "Among other things."

Another shiver. "What kind of things?"

He loved how he could make her body react with such a small touch.

"Oh, you know, the usual things men talk to the father of the woman they love about." The next kiss was to her wrist, where her pulse beat a rapid tempo beneath the delicate skin.

Distracted by the intimate touch, it took a second before she reacted to his words. Her eyes opened wide. "You love me?"

"I do." He started kissing his way up her arm. "I really"—*kiss*—"really"—*kiss*—"do." The last kiss hovered over her mouth like a promise. "I love you, Rachel Long. And I'm telling you right now, I'm going to screw up and make mistakes, because that's all I seem to do with you. But as long as you're willing to put up with me, I'm never letting you go."

"Then that's a damn good thing, Theo Beaumont, because I don't want you to. I'm going to screw up and make mistakes, too, you know. But please, don't ever give up on me."

"Never. You're mine." A promise he sealed with more than a kiss.

Chapter 39

THE OCTOBER AFTERNOON SUN beat down, warming the rock face as Theo reached for the next foothold and lifted himself closer to the summit. This wasn't the first climb he'd made since breaking the stranglehold his guilt had placed on him that kept him grounded for so many months. But it was the first one at Pretty Ugly.

And by far the most important.

Clipping his rope into the carabiner on the quickdraw he'd attached to the anchor nut, he reached up, knowing exactly where the next handhold would be. Then the next foothold. And the next.

His body's muscle memory relaxed into the familiar motions, warming and stretching, his blood pumping in a steady, unhurried rhythm through his veins. It was like slipping on a pair of comfy, well-worn jeans.

Not that there weren't small twinges of unease.

Like when he set and checked his anchors. The urge to recheck and re-recheck each one nipped at him, to obsess over whether or not it would hold. But he could push past the need and trust in himself and his equipment to move on. Lyle was a great therapist, but he hadn't been able to work Theo through all of his issues yet. Not entirely.

But today's climb would mark the culmination of all those months of talk and introspection, and prove—hopefully—he'd finally gotten himself over the last stumbling block that held him knotted to the past.

The things I do for you, buddy.

The last few yards seemed to stretch out for miles, the top edge an unattainable goal. Ignoring the doubt that gnawed at his confidence, he pushed on. Reaching. Stepping. Pulling. Until finally, his fingers curled around the rough, gritty rock of the upper shelf.

The electric thrill of success kept him moving. Heaving himself up over the edge and onto the small flat area that crowned the cliff, he collapsed onto his back, staring up at the blue, blue sky.

The climb was only about two hundred feet, but he felt like he'd just summited El Capitan all over again. And in a way, he had. Making this climb hadn't been about the size of the cliff, but the size of the obstacles he'd put in his own way.

Obstacles he'd bested every one of to get where he was right this second.

Thank you, Doc.

He basked in the glow of triumph for a few long moments while he caught his breath, then got back to his true purpose. This climb wasn't only for him.

"Off belay," he called down, unclipping from the rope and getting to his feet. The vista of the land spread out around him. From this vantage point, he could have been the only person for miles, or even in the world.

In the past, the adrenaline of the climb would have been what he needed to soothe his restless, searching soul. But now, that soul had met its mate, and she was waiting down below for him to finish.

Probably chewing her pretty lip raw with worry.

Lucky for her and her nerves, climbing, like the rest of his high-octane adventures, had slipped from necessity back to occasional entertainment. All he needed to find his sense of contentment these days was Rachel by his side.

Slipping off his backpack, he removed the silver urn that had been there since the lawyer who'd handled Gavin's will had put it in his reluctant hands almost a year ago. He'd tried to give it to Gav's mother and sister more than once.

They'd refused.

Despite the great big hate they had on for Theo, they still wanted Gavin's last wishes to be followed.

Holding the urn, the metal warmed at his touch.

He gave a shuddery sigh.

"Well, Gav, I finally made it. Sorry it took me so long. But the truth? That's partly on you, bud. I don't know why you did what you did, if it was carelessness or something else. That's your secret to keep. But I really wish you'd talked to me first. Or to anyone. Nothing is worth giving all this up for, no matter how bad it seems at the time."

He paused, fighting down the lump making his voice raspy. It took a few attempts to clear his throat.

"But today isn't about blame, or what-ifs, or how you died. This is about celebrating the life you lived. Every crazy, wild minute of it. And I'm thankful I got to be a part of it. That you were my friend. You made the world a better place, and I miss you like hell."

As he unscrewed the lid, he looked out over the park again, taking in the grandeur. A sad smile touched his lips. "A year ago, we lost you here. Now, I'm finally ready to let you go. Rest in peace, my friend."

Carefully, he tilted the urn and let the powdery contents drift out onto the breeze. Some fell to the ground at his feet. But most was lifted and buoyed away on the air currents, spreading it far and wide over the rocky landscape, until there was nothing left.

Disappearing along with the ashes was the rest of the guilt, which slipped from his shoulders like a weighted coat, leaving him feeling lighter than he had in a very long time.

It was done. He'd honored his friend's request and his life. Now he could finally move forward without the burdens of the past to drag him down.

He was free.

Heart sad but at peace, he made the climb back to the ground with growing anticipation. The moment he unhooked from the rope, Rachel was there, wrapping her arms around him, holding him, grounding him. Loving him.

It was all he could have ever wanted. All he needed.

"Are you okay?"

"Yeah. I think I am." He pulled back enough to place a gentle kiss on her mouth. "Thank you for coming with me." He knew she'd had reservations about how well she'd handle watching him climb for the first time. But she'd put aside her own fears and been there for him the entire way. "I'm not sure I could have done it without you."

"Of course you could have." Her hand patted his chest. "That doesn't mean I wanted you to do it alone. Nobody did."

Theo glanced around at the small group of people who'd made the trek out with them today. Mostly fellow climbers who wanted to come offer not only their support, but also their own kind of memorial to their lost friend.

Even now, several of them were gearing up to scale to the top and say their own goodbyes. But everyone had agreed the first climb would be Theo's alone.

Stepping out of his harness, he glanced around. "They didn't come, after all."

"No. But then, you didn't really expect them to, did you?"

"I guess not."

But he'd kind of hoped they might. It would have been nice to get the same closure with Gavin's family as he had with his friend's ghost. But he supposed he'd have to settle for the fact they no longer actively blamed him for his death.

Hopefully, the grief counseling he'd steered them towards—through a third-party, of course, or they'd have refused to go out of spite—had helped their road to healing.

"Some of your friends were talking about going to Shanahan's afterward to talk about Gavin. Kind of like an Irish wake, I guess. Did you want to go?"

Shanahan's had been Gavin's favorite pub. Lifting a can of that pale ale crap in his honor while his friends swapped increasingly embarrassing stories about him was the perfect way to send him off. But he shook his head.

"I already said my goodbyes up there. I'd rather go home and finish unpacking your stuff." There was no keeping the satisfaction from his voice. After months of asking, she'd finally agreed to move in with him.

The faster he got her settled in and putting down roots, the better.

Her main reason for holding out had been worry about how her fathers would react. More specifically, what they might do to Theo.

No amount of reassurance had persuaded her until he took the bull by the horns and went to see them and explain how things were going to go. They'd been surprisingly okay with the idea. And while he'd done it for Rachel's peace of mind, it had served his own purposes as well.

He'd taken the opportunity to ask for their blessings to marry her.

They'd been surprisingly okay with that idea, as well.

Not that she knew about it. It would have ruined the surprise.

He'd considered proposing before she moved in, but decided to hold off until after everything else they had going on was settled. His next thought had been the anniversary of their first date. But that would have been impossible, and not just because they still couldn't agree on when, exactly, that was.

No way was he waiting another five months to make her his.

In the end, he decided to just have the ring ready for whenever the time and the moment felt right and go from there. Spontaneity seemed to have worked for them so far. Why mess with success?

The drive home was made in contented quiet, which was shattered the moment they walked through the mudroom door. Two wild, wriggling bodies greeted them as though they'd been gone for years instead of hours, happy moans and barks interspersed with a few sloppy kisses before they both obeyed Theo's command of "sit!" and plopped their furry bottoms down in unison.

"Good dogs," he praised, giving them each a treat they ran off with to gnaw on.

When he accompanied Rachel to the shelter to "just look," she'd immediately adopted Miss Bliss, so christened because of the way the hound-mix always seemed to be smiling. Theo would have teased her mercilessly about her lack of willpower.

If he'd come home empty-handed himself.

But he hadn't been able to resist the silver-colored pittie who'd watched him with such quiet intensity from its cage, intelligent blue eyes following his every move.

Rachel had called him as big a soft touch as her. Which, it turned out, was true. But he'd also wanted to prove she wasn't the only one ready to settle down and stay home more.

Preferably with her.

"I think my dads miss having Bliss around the house. They've been talking about going out to the shelter," she said as they climbed the stairs to his bedroom.

Their bedroom, now.

That thought could still put a satisfied smile on his face.

"They should. There are too many dogs in need of a good home." And since Karl had declined Matt's offer to coach Vicky in favor of sharing Dellin's retirement—much to his husband's delight—they'd have plenty of time and love to lavish on whatever lucky mutt they chose.

Stripping off his climbing clothes, he felt Rachel's appreciative gaze on his naked body as he walked to the bathroom and turned on the shower. Stepping under the multiple jets, he let the hot water slough away the remnants of the day from both his body and his mind.

He was rinsing the last of the suds off when Rachel joined him. Seeing her gloriously naked form stepping under the water had the expected effect, his body hardening in a rush that left him slightly lightheaded.

A feeling which only increased when she went to her knees and took him in her mouth. She played, teased, and drove him slowly, madly wild. When he felt himself approaching the danger zone, he tried to pull away, wanting to return the favor. Make her just as crazy as she was making him.

But she refused to relinquish her prize.

There was nothing he could do but close his eyes and absorb the sensations she created. Using her tongue and teeth to ratchet his arousal to increasing heights, until finally he sailed over the edge with a groan that seemed to come from the very depths of his soul.

His hips stuttered in jerky pulses as she continued to lick and suck until he was so spent he could barely stand.

Only when he sagged back against the tiled wall did she release him, giving a smug grin as she stood. "You needed that."

He managed a half-laugh, still catching his breath. "And now I owe you one."

The grin turned hungry. "And I look forward to collecting."

Since it was either turn off the water and go get dressed, or take her right then and there in the shower—something they'd already learned the hard way wasn't nearly as sexy or easy as it sounded—Theo grabbed two towels from the heating rack and handed her one.

After drying off, he walked naked into the bedroom, where he pulled fresh socks and underwear from the new dresser delivered last week with the rest of the bedroom suite. Once she agreed to move in, he'd encouraged Rachel to redecorate the house however she liked.

The bedroom was the only room she'd wanted to redo.

Everything had been switched out, from the furniture and expensive linens right down to the paint and pictures on the walls. The thoroughness had surprised him until his sister had finally opened his eyes after family brunch the week before.

No woman, she told him, wanted to sleep where hundreds of other women had been before her. The 'hundreds' had been Lil's usual sense of the dramatic, but he'd gotten her point. And Rachel's. They were starting this new phase of their lives with no ghosts of the past to haunt them.

Especially not the ghosts of conquests past.

Which was why he'd come clean about his previous one-nighter with Vicky. Not a fun conversation, but a necessary one. He likened it to setting off a smaller, controlled avalanche to prevent a much worse one from burying you when you least expected it.

Rachel had taken the news better than he'd hoped, considering how she felt about Vicky. But once he'd sworn all of the women he'd been with, Vicky included, were erased from his mind the second she'd come into his life, she'd seemed at peace with it.

Dragging on jeans, he watched as she shimmied into a pair of panties. Who needed memories of the past when this was his future?

He was calculating how long it would take him to strip off the clothes they'd both just put on and lay her out on the bed when she said, "Oh, I almost forgot. Your mother is coming by in a little while to go over some last-minute tweaks for the masked ball."

He held back a sigh. So much for a little orgasmic payback.

"How's everything going with that? Mom's not making you too crazy, is she?"

She smiled. "Your mom's fine, stop worrying. I enjoy helping out."

"Helping out" was Rachel-speak for becoming Patricia's right-hand woman for the signature event.

It had started innocently enough when his mother asked Rachel if she'd like to work on one of the summer programs the Everbrite Foundation ran for at-risk kids. Of course, she said yes. And had kept saying yes every time after that, her responsibilities growing with every event.

"She's going to keep asking you to do more and more if you don't start putting limits on what you agree to."

She shrugged, not seeming bothered.

"I enjoy working with the foundation. In fact, I'm looking forward to taking on some more responsibilities once I get the race out of the way."

The reminder sent a slight chill through him, but he didn't let his trepidation show. She'd chosen for her farewell appearance the same race on the same course that had almost done her in two years before.

The thought of watching her sail down that treacherous slope still scared the ever-loving crap out of him. But he understood all about conquering demons and the mountains they lived on, so he'd given her his full support and would be there cheering her on the whole way.

But he'd be damn glad when it was over.

Wrapping his arms around her from behind, he hugged her back to his front and nuzzled her neck. "You do realize Mom's grooming you to eventually take over as head of the foundation, right? She's determined to get Dad to retire one of these days, no matter how hard he fights it."

"I know."

"And you're okay with that?"

"I think I am. I never put a lot of thought into what I'd do after I stopped racing. I was too focused on winning a gold to even consider what came next. But working with the foundation...it feels right."

She snuggled deeper into his embrace. "I know how a lot of those kids feel, lost and scared in a system that doesn't always work in their favor. Having the chance to do good things for them is better than any medal I could ever win."

Just when he thought he couldn't love her any more, she went and proved him wrong.

"Well, I think you'll do an amazing job."

"Thanks." She chuckled. "You know, Ari did a Taro reading for me right after we met that said there were going to be new beginnings that led to long-term happiness. That my dreams would come true. I don't like to encourage her woo-woo, but I have to say, she kind of nailed this one."

"Does that mean you're happy with the way everything's turned out?"

"I don't think things could be any better."

Theo grinned.

How could he possibly pass up an opportunity like that?

With a quick squeeze, he released her and walked toward the new dresser, and the black velvet box hidden in the top drawer. "Oh, I think maybe they can."

And they were.

A Note From the Author

I hope you've enjoyed Theo and Rachel's story. Now we're down to one last Beaumont brother who has yet to meet his match. And boy, is this one a doozy! Remember the whole kerfuffle between Lillian's and Rafe's siblings in Can't Help Loving You? Well, guess who gets caught in a web of unwanted attraction during the wedding festivities? You got it! Peter and Bella will have a whole lot of personal *and* family issues to dig through.

All I Need Is You will be out late summer/early fall 2024. Scan the QR code below to visit my website to read more and grab your copy from your favorite retailer.

While there, be sure to sign up for my newsletter and claim your **FREE** book, available exclusively to my subscribers. Or stay up-to-date on all future releases by following my author page on any of the major book sites.

And finally, if you loved this book, please take a moment to leave a review at your favorite retailer. They're what feeds an author's creative soul. Thank you!

Also By Nika Rhone

<u>Boulder Bodyguards series</u>
What the Lady Wants
Finding Forever
Can't Help Loving You

<u>Boulder Beaumonts series</u>
Worth Any Price
Never Let Me Go
All I Need Is You (coming soon)

About the Author

Nika Rhone spent her childhood wearing out library cards as she read her way through the extraordinary worlds far beyond her small hometown on Long Island, NY. By her teens, her imagination was taking her places all on its own, forcing her to learn how to type (badly) so she could get all the stories down on paper. After a long love affair with science fiction and fantasy, she finally discovered romance, fell head-over-heels, and now spends her days crafting happily-ever-afters for the characters who still tell their stories faster (and better) than she can type them.

You can keep up with all the latest book news, events, and giveaways by visiting her website www.nikarhone.com and joining her newsletter.

www.ingramcontent.com/pod-product-compliance
Lightning Source LLC
Chambersburg PA
CBHW030119010826

48973CB00002B/332